D0454452

THE SHOWDOWN AT YELLOWSTONE

THE
SHOWDOWN AT
YELLOWSTONE

By Larry Richardson & Tom Richardson

The Showdown at Yellowstone
by
Larry Richarson & Tom Richardson   Copyright © 2017
Putnam & Smith Publishing Company

Cover Design by: David Pascal
Book Design by: Connie Jacobs

Distributed by:
> Putnam & Smith Publishing Company
> 15915 Ventura Boulevard, Suite 101
> Encino, California 91436
> www.putnamandsmithpublishing.com

Library of Congress Control Number: 2017946611

ISBN: 978-1-939986-17-7

Printed in the United States of America

FORWARD

By Actor, Director and Western Aficionado, Perry King

I often read several books at once, and the other night I had finally completed enough work to justify the best part of the day; an hour or two of reading.

I was immersed in a Louis L'Amour western, which for me is like eating chocolate, but I had also begun to read Larry and Tom Richardson's prequel to *"The Big Horn"*, called *"The Showdown at Yellowstone"*. I found myself reaching for *Showdown,* purely because it was more fun, more intriguing. I had just made an instinctive judgment and sat there for a moment as that sank in. I wanted to read Showdown more than continue on with Louis L'Amour. There is no greater compliment I could give to Larry and Tom than to tell them that they have written a western novel that is to me even more compelling, more sheer fun to read, than a Louis L'Amour yarn.

It seems to me that Larry and Tom have upped their game tenfold over *The Big Horn*, which is a very good story and stands on its own merits. *Showdown* combines all the traits we western readers love so much: great, colorful characters, a lovely sense of time and place that is so richly THEN and not NOW, and a plot that twists and turns so deliciously that only exhaustion and eyes that refuse to stay open will let you put it down at night. If you liked *Big Horn,* you will absolutely love *The Showdown at Yellowstone.*

I sure can't wait for the next one!

--Perry King, Actor, Director, Western Aficionado

The Showdown at Yellowstone

ACKNOWLEDGEMENTS

Special thanks go to Perry King, actor, director, producer, and western enthusiast, for his generous forward to this book. We also owe thanks to Brian Hoffman for his insights into the finer points of elk hunting and skinning, and to Shane Walsh for his expertise in explosives. Finally, we are grateful to Don Davenport for his thoughtful critiques of both narrative and dialogue during the preparation of this manuscript.

SAN JUAN HEIGHTS

From the edge of the tropical forest to the 150-foot summit of San Juan Hill and nearby Kettle Hill, five hundred yards of open savanna separated the American soldiers from the entrenched Spanish stronghold. Corporal Thorn Hickum squatted behind an oak tree to catch his breath and dodge the hail of bullets coming down from the ridge. He removed his slouch hat and wiped the dripping sweat off his face. Not that it did much good; his entire uniform was drenched in sweat. In July the infernal humidity of Cuba made any outdoor exertion insufferable. The sweltering heat and dehydration could drop a man as sure as bullet and the Spaniards knew it. They hunkered down in their earthworks along the ridges and dared the Americans to assault.

The U.S. Army had landed a 17,000 troop expeditionary force on the Island of Cuba on June 22, 1898, with the plan of sweeping over the San Juan hills and capturing the city of Santiago along with the Spanish fleet anchored there. Among that force was the 1st U.S. Volunteer Cavalry, a regiment of nearly 600, named Rough Riders, led by the charismatic Colonel Theodore Roosevelt.

Now, on the morning of July 1st, the Americans wavered. To reach this point, they had already suffered heavy losses in open battle and relentless ambushes. Ebullient confidence gave way to hesitation as they considered their next move; an open-field frontal assault against an elevated fixed position. Every instinct held that this would be suicide. This had been born out 35 years earlier with the horrific failure of Pickett's Charge up Seminary Ridge at the battle of Gettysburg. Over

12,500 Confederates attempted an open-field frontal assault on the Union line, suffering over fifty percent in casualties before they were forced to retreat.

Corporal Hickum scanned the soldiers that were milling about to see who was in charge. No one dared to issue orders or rally the troops. He sensed the rumblings of retreat. Suddenly, Colonel Theodore Roosevelt galloped into the thicket on horseback with a blue bandana fastened around his hat to make himself easier to spot. Though his Rough Riders were horseless, Roosevelt chose to stay mounted to make it easier to see and be seen by his men.

"On your feet," he shouted. "We're moving forward. We're going to take that hill." A captain objected.

"My orders are to keep my men right here. I don't have the authority to charge that hill." Bullets from the ridge whizzed by, gouging the bark off a nearby tree. Suddenly, one prone soldier took a bullet through the top of his head that passed through his entire body and exited through his boot. Soldiers began to panic and retreated further back into the forest.

"Damn you, Captain," Roosevelt bellowed. "Where's your commanding officer?"

"I don't know."

"Then I'm the ranking officer here and I give the order to charge."

"I don't care what your rank is," the captain blustered. "You're not taking my men anywhere. We're staying put." Roosevelt nearly exploded.

"Let me give you a piece of military advice, Captain," he shouted for all to hear. "Orders or no orders, the best thing you can do is the right thing, the next best thing is the wrong thing, and the worst thing you can do is nothing." The captain had no reply.

Roosevelt urged his horse to the edge of the clearing and repeated, "Everyone get on your feet. Let's move. If we're in range, they're in range." Thorn looked around and saw only four or five men jump to their feet. Roosevelt shouted to the rest.

"What are you afraid of, getting shot on your bellies while I'm on horseback?" He angled his horse through the mass of hunkered troops. "You think you're safe here? Anything you do can get you shot, including nothing."

That was enough for Thorn. He grabbed his rifle and joined the others. He made up his mind that he would rather die in an inspired attempt than to cower in gutless caution. Roosevelt turned to the Captain.

"If you're not going to join us, then get out of the way so my Rough Riders can get through." Then turning to his men, he called out, "Rough Riders follow me. We are taking this hill!"

With his pistol drawn, he galloped into the clearing. At first only a handful of men joined him. But as more Rough Riders poured through the lines, the regulars could do no less than join in. They jumped up and came along, their officers and troops mingling with the Rough Riders. Spreading out like a fan, row after row of men slipped and scrambled through the smooth grass, trudging uphill as if they were wading through water.

Rifle fire from the nearby ridge began pouring down on them. Those struck by bullets pitched forward and disappeared into the high grass as the others waded on. Suddenly, three American Gatling guns began spraying the top of the ridge from artillery troops dug in at the edge of a clump of trees. Each gun poured 700 rounds a minute along the crest of the hill, wreaking terrible carnage. The withering cover fire helped keep the Spaniards at bay, allowing the Americans a chance to ascend the summit. To those troops watching from below it appeared like a thin blue ribbon creeping higher and higher up the hill, unstoppable as the rising tide. Onlookers later described it as a triumph of bulldog courage as they watched in breathless wonder.

Roosevelt rode up and down the hill, and side to side, with total disregard for his own safety, shouting encouragement for his troops to continue the assault. "We are almost there, keep moving."

One bullet nicked him in the elbow, another grazed his horse and a man running alongside him was shot and killed. Other soldiers fell to the ground, overcome from sheer heat exhaustion.

Thorn eyed Roosevelt's charge with awe. He knew a commander should inspire his troops by example, but this bravado bordered on utter recklessness. He acted as standard bearer and rallying point for the assault, a job usually assigned to 3-4 low level recruits due to the suicidal nature of this gallant gesture. But Thorn felt his heart quicken at the sight of Roosevelt's courage, despite his dread for how the assault might crumble should Roosevelt fall.

"Rally on the Colonel!" Thorn shouted to the men around him, pointing to their intrepid leader. Fifteen to twenty troops closed ranks around Roosevelt as they all neared the summit.

When the Americans approached the Spanish line at the crest, the Gatling guns ceased fire to avoid hitting their own men. That allowed the Spanish troops one final chance to repel the assault. They raised their rifles over the parapets and began pouring down bullets to the approaching troops. The Rough Riders returned fire, at almost point blank range. Spaniards dropped by the scores.

Thorn set his eyes on the Spanish flag on the ridge and trudged straight towards it, stopping to fire on any Spaniard target.

Roosevelt reached the trenches on the ridge, where he quickly killed one of the enemy with his pistol, allowing his men to continue the assault. Near the peak the broken fragments in the American line closed ranks. With a sudden burst they reached the top. The Spaniards appeared for a moment to hold the line, but not for long. The first wave of Rough Riders delivered a vicious volley of rifle fire, and the Spanish resolve melted. They turned and fled. The Rough Riders, along with remnants of the 9th, 6th, 3rd, and 10th Cavalry, and the 6th and 16th Infantry dropped to their knees and opened fire on the retreating enemy.

Roosevelt dismounted and joined his men in clearing out the blockhouse at the summit. Thorn spotted him.

"Look at the Colonel!" Thorn shouted at the trooper beside him. "He's gonna get himself killed."

"He ain't gonna die," the trooper glibly replied. "That's our job." Then he cocked both pistols in his hands and busted down the next door in search of Spanish snipers. Thorn frowned.

"He may be a lot of things, but he ain't bullet-proof," he muttered. Thorn felt the sudden need to protect the Colonel. Holstering his side arm, he ran to the door where a clutch of troopers stood behind Roosevelt, ready to bust in.

Roosevelt turned his head behind him, pistol raised.

"All right, on my count," he glared at the nine troopers, each man ready to follow his leader to the doors of Perdition. Roosevelt cocked his pistol and turned back to face the heavy oak door. The sound of gunfire around them faded from attention.

"Three, two, one," he called out, his gaze riveted on the door, as if summoning vision to peer into the room to know the danger inside. Nine pistols behind him cocked, some pointed to the side. Others aimed toward the sky, arms resting on the back of the man in front of him. Roosevelt's knee raised to his chest, spring loaded to explode with full force.

"Go!" Roosevelt shouted, and his boot smashed the door wide open.

In that instant, Roosevelt suddenly flew through the air, to the side of the shattered door. The troops behind him craned their necks to watch him land hard, face down in the dust. Just then a furious volley of Spanish pistol fire sprayed death to the would-be attackers at the door. Three troopers dropped. The remaining six spun back into action, emptying their pistols into the gaping doorway. Then silence. The smoke lifted. Every Spanish defender lay dead on the floor.

Thorn had made a flying shoulder tackle, knocking Roosevelt to the side. As they sprawled to the ground, the point-blank gun exchange ensued and the room was cleared of all treachery.

Roosevelt sat up and looked at the three dead soldiers, then gawked at Thorn, like he'd just met his guardian angel.

"You just plowed through me like Aunt Sally's mule," Roosevelt said. Thorn offered a salute in apology.

"Sorry, sir." Roosevelt delicately touched his side.

"I always wondered what a football tackle would feel

like. I think you broke a rib."

As the two leaned against the wall, the remainder of the blockhouse was cleared out. The battle was over. This hill was theirs. The silk flags of the cavalry and the Stars and Stripes were planted on the crest, and the victorious troops waved their hats and cheered. Thorn got up and walked over to the edge of the hill he just ascended. His fallen comrades lie scattered from the base to the summit. Down along the clearing below, he could see those soldiers who stayed behind now waving their hats and answering the cheer from the crest with their own shout of exultation in reply.

Thorn returned to the wall of the blockhouse to catch his breath and drink some water from his canteen. He watched the Spaniards fleeing in the distance, pursued by the Americans. Roosevelt removed his glasses, covered with sweat and dust. He wiped them clean and put them back on, then turned to Thorn.

"Corporal, I could sure use a gulp." Thorn immediately offered up his canteen and Roosevelt took a few swigs. He wiped his mouth on his sleeve and handed it back with a hearty sigh, "Dee-lightful. What's your name, Soldier?"

"Corporal Thorn Hickum," Thorn replied. He studied Roosevelt's countenance as the Colonel took that name and tucked it into a special place in his brain.

"I swear, you're something else, Colonel," Thorn shook his head. "How the hell did you make it up that hill alive?" Roosevelt smiled.

"It's an amazing thing, corporal, how so few bullets seem to hit the men they are aimed at." He gave Thorn a wink, and mounted his horse.

Larry Richardson & Tom Richardson

The Showdown at Yellowstone

CHAPTER 1

Thorn Hickum was no stranger to dodging bullets. In his time, he had wrung up so many near collisions with ruination as a deputy sheriff that he often quipped that he joined the army just to improve his chances of staying alive. But through his many near-misses with death, he had to admit that Lady Luck had a soft spot for him.

Thorn stood just over 6 feet tall, not as tall as some but a shade taller than most. Somewhat rakish, his ruddy complexion came from years of cowboying that kept him lean, trim and solidly built. At 180 pounds, his stature intimidated most would-be tough guys.

Basically a shy man who didn't talk much, to some he appeared aloof, which belied an easy-going manner. He loved a good joke and enjoyed playing pranks now and then. With sandy brown hair and pale blue eyes, he was considered good-looking if not handsome. Those men and women with whom he became friends found him welcome company.

Thorn put you in one of only two groups; friends and everybody else and most belonged in the latter. His friends he counted on one hand and the one man he trusted with his life was C.J. Mason, Sheriff for the City of Coulson, Montana. They first met in their early 20s in the fall of 1890, in Billings at a cowboy contest. Both were accomplished wranglers and fierce competitors, besting each other back and forth in various events. Thorn saw something in Mason that impressed him; a fierce commitment to fair play and decency that was rare even among cowboys, a code of honor that set him apart.

It was at that competition that Mason was bucked off a vicious horse and got his boot wedged in the stirrup. As others desperately tried to lasso the wild bronco, Mason fought to free himself or die. Thorn leaped on an idle strawberry roan and chased down the thrashing beast. He sprang on its back and took it to the ground, saving Mason and amazing every buckaroo in the arena.

The two became fast friends, sharing meals and drinks, celebrating each other's rodeo triumphs. When it ended, Mason returned to Coulson, where he served as a young deputy. Thorn chose to stay in Billings as a wrangler for a large cattle ranch, but the pay was meager and the work brutal. Branding cattle, mending fences, and chasing steers for a living began to lose its charm. He didn't want to end his days old, stove-up and nothing to show for it and no tales of glory to tell his grandchildren. His thoughts strayed to Coulson.

One day the door to the Coulson sheriff's office swung open. Mason was busy sweeping out an empty cell. He looked up to see Thorn covered in trail dust.

"What the hell brings you to paradise?" he asked with a smile.

"Just wondered where a fella can get a drink around here," Thorn said.

"Well, that depends," Mason smiled, leaning against his broom. "What do you favor?"

"I'll take a beer if it's cold, but if I got a choice then make it a whiskey," Thorn said.

"I know just the place," Mason said.

They walked over to the Crystal Palace Saloon on Minnesota Avenue. It was a sizable drinking establishment whose doors never closed and where Jake was not only the bartender, he was part owner, and took great pride in stocking the widest selection of spirits west of Bismarck.

"Jake," said Mason, "I want you to meet Thorn Hickum." Jake gave him a strong hand shake and a welcome nod. Mason continued with the introductions. "He's that fella I told you about what jumped on that hellcat bronco and saved my neck." Jake eyed Thorn with a new respect.

"Well, we're rather fond of young Mason here, so your

first drink is on the house," Jake declared. "What'll it be?" Thorn scanned the liquor shelf behind the bar.

"You carry Old Bushmills whiskey?" Thorn asked. Jake wagged his finger at Thorn and gave him a devilish grin, then turned to Mason.

"This lad's got expensive taste." Then he slapped the bar counter with his open hand so loud it startled the patrons nearby. "I like your style, boy," Jake laughed. "I promised you the first drink was free, and I'm a man of my word."

Mason and Thorn made their way over to an empty table and settled in.

"OK," said Mason, "So, what really brings you here?"

"I just wanted to see how glamorous your job was," Thorn replied. "You look pretty handy with a broom."

"Oh, that. The sheriff's out making rounds and it's the maid's day off." Thorn paused for a moment then spoke his mind.

"Truth is I'm looking for work," Thorn confessed. "I drew my pay, packed my saddlebag, and lit out. Wondered if you needed an extra hand?"

"Deputy-type work?" Mason asked. Thorn just nodded as he took a sip of his Old Bushmills whiskey.

They finished their drinks and wandered back over to the sheriff's office.

"I can't speak for the sheriff," Mason explained, "but I know he's turned down other fellers." Thorn's eyes wandered over to the bulletin board full of wanted posters.

"It looks like you could sure use some kinda help," Thorn said, pointing to the wanted posters. "Bringing in desperados might be a fulltime job."

"You don't need to be a lawman to do that," Mason said. "Ever thought about bounty hunting? It pays pretty good if you don't get your head blown off,"

"Are you serious?" Thorn asked.

Mason walked over to the posters. "There's $2,000 to bring in Kid Curry, $4,000 for Butch Cassidy, and $15,000 for the Dalton Gang – dead or alive." Thorn had never considered a career in bounty hunting, but the reward dollars were pretty enticing.

"Got anything more in my wheelhouse?" Thorn asked.

"I think we've got a $10 reward out for anyone who'll bring in Walt Jenkins to pay his fine for spitting in church," Mason offered. They both laughed. Mason went over to his desk and sifted through some papers.

"OK, here's a job you can handle," Mason said, handing the complaint notice to Thorn. "Horace Blunt is wanted for bustin' up the 15th Street Tavern three weeks ago and never payin' for the damages."

"How much does he owe?" Thorn asked. Mason checked the complaint notice.

"He threw a chair through the window, smashed up the liquor counter, and ruined a portrait hanging behind the bar." Mason said. "The total came to $95 but he refuses to pay. It's either that or jail time. Anyway, somebody's gotta bring him in."

"What's the story?" Thorn asked.

"Well, there's some blame to go around for that little fracas. That particular watering hole brews some pretty deadly drinks," Mason began.

"Oh, yeah? Like what?" asked Thorn.

"They got this thing called a Tanglefoot. It's made out of raw alcohol, burnt sugar, and turpentine," explained Mason. "It's supposed to be some kind of whiskey, but it's just pure coffin varnish."

"What happens if you drink it?" Thorn asked.

"It affects everyone a little different. I've told Harry, the owner, that he's gonna get somebody soused on that stuff and he's gonna be sorry."

"So, what happened?" asked Thorn.

"Well, Horace came in a few weeks ago and drank about three shots of that rotgut, and everything started goin' fuzzy. He was trying to clear his eyes when he fixed his gaze on the portrait of a naked lady lying on a bunch of pillows hanging behind the bar," Mason said.

"Was something wrong with it?" asked Thorn.

"Not to me, but in his condition, old Horace swore that naked lady's face looked just like his sister, and he was morally outraged. He demanded they take the picture down," said Mason. "They tried to explain to him that they bought that painting in St. Louis, and it was NOT his sister."

"I take it he was not satisfied?" Thorn concluded.

"He got pretty worked up...said if they didn't take it down, he would. By the time it was all over, the painting was torn to shreds, the liquor counter was all busted up, and a chair went through the front window. Harry demanded payment for the damages, but Horace drew his gun and backed out the door. No one's seen him since," said Mason.

"How do you wanna play it?" Thorn asked.

"Sheriff Webb had a talk with Harry – told him as long as he served that red lightning he could just figure property damage as part of the cost of doin' business. But for the sake of good will we need to bring Horace in to pay half."

"What's the bounty on him?" Thorn asked.

"The sheriff posted a $25 reward," said Mason.

"$25?" Thorn frowned.

"He ain't exactly Black Jack Ketchum," Mason replied. "Just go get him. He's got a little spread west of town."

Thorn rode out to the Blunt ranch, such as it was. The main gate was assembled from assorted fallen tree branches. A weed-lined dirt road led to the house, a modest single story clapboard structure with a front porch, stone chimney, water trough and hitching post. A small barn nearby was in need of attention, and the corral was sad and empty. A dozen cattle grazed in the field behind the house. Thorn approached the house slowly, not sure what kind of reception he might receive.

A loud voice bellowed through the window, "That's far enough!" Thorn reined his horse in and waited for Horace to make the next move.

"Who are you and what do you want?" Horace hollered.

"Thorn Hickum. I come to collect a debt, that's all."

"You the law?" Horace called out.

"No, sir. Everybody just figured it'd be a lot less hostile if an outside third party could work out a settlement," Thorn said.

"I don't owe anybody anything," Horace hollered from inside.

"Look, I'm going to get off my horse and tie it off and get out of the sun. Why don't you come out on the front porch and let's figure out what's fair," Thorn offered. "I'm going to drop my gun right here." He waited for a reply. Hearing none, he unbuckled his gun belt and dropped it on the ground. Then he slowly dismounted and walked his horse up to the hitching post and tied it off, then slowly sat down on the front porch step, with his back to the door.

He waited. And he waited. And he waited. Thirty minutes later the front door slowly opened and Horace walked out. He was in his 30s, unshaved, hair mussed up, wearing overalls and heavy boots. He said nothing – just stood behind Thorn.

"You got a nice little ranch here," Thorn said. "You got the makin's of something special – a place to call your own and a town full of folks to share your life with. That's more than I got."

Still no words from Horace. Thorn pointed to the corral. "I could imagine some horses in that corral, hay stored in the barn, some cattle in the field. I used to work on a ranch. I always thought I'd like to start my own place, kinda like this."

"It ain't that easy," Horace muttered.

"Course not," Thorn answered. "Nothing worth anything is. But it ain't out of reach. You've made a good start. You gonna throw it all away now?"

"No," Horace snorted.

"That's what you're fixin' to do. You busted up somebody else's business – his dream. You gotta make it right."

"I ain't got the money," Horace said.

"You bring in one of your steers. It'll fetch $50. That'll settle you up." Horace let that idea play around in his mind.

Thorn went on to sweeten the deal. "I'm gettin' paid $25 to bring you in. You do this thing and I'll split the $25 with you and I'll come out here next week and help you get your corral back on its feet."

"Why would you do that?" Horace asked.

"I don't know. You and I may be neighbors one day, and I might just need a favor from you. I help you now and one day you help me. That's how it works. Whaddaya say?"

The two rode into town with a steer in tow. As they rode past the sheriff's office, Simon Webb and Deputy Mason stepped out onto the boardwalk to witness this creative resolution. Thorn glanced over and tipped his hat, a Stetson with a classic Montana crease in the crown. Webb raised his coffee mug in reply.

"You keep that up and I may have to find a use for you. Come on back here when you're done," Webb called out.

The Showdown at Yellowstone

CHAPTER 2

That's exactly what Simon Webb did – he put Thorn to work. He needed someone trustworthy to hand deliver legal documents and escort prisoners from jail to trial and back again. Occasionally he helped provide extra protection for important dignitaries traveling to and from Coulson. On one such assignment he was away from Coulson when fate dealt a heavy blow to the town.

The Crystal Palace Saloon was the center for drinking, gambling and dancing in Coulson. One of the three men who owned the saloon was Jake Bass, a Texan who moved to Coulson near the end of the buffalo annihilation in 1884, and built up a thriving business. He welcomed one and all but ran a tight ship, tolerating no card sharps or grifters, and no gunplay or fighting whatsoever.

On Sunday evening in February of 1891, Jake was tending bar. The saloon was packed with patrons that night, and at the corner table a game of monte was in full swing. The dealer was enjoying a run of luck that cleaned out the pockets of two cowboys with two week's wages to burn. With a crowd of onlookers growing, these fleeced cowhands started grumbling about cheating and demanded their money back.

The dealer, an experienced card player, spoke calmly, assuring them that nothing crooked occurred. Unsatisfied, the tall cowpoke pulled out his gun and began waving it around in a reckless manner. The crowd suddenly pulled back and turned silent, leaving the gunman and the dealer front and center. The piano player stopped and the room hushed. The dealer set the deck of cards down and slowly placed both his hands on the table, staring straight ahead. Jake saw the confrontation and called for someone to get the sheriff. Then he drew a shotgun from behind the bar and moved to a position beside a support column close to the card table.

"Son, put the gun down," Jake called out, his shotgun pointed straight at the cowboy. "You ain't done nothing you can't walk away from yet, so take a breath and think about what you're doin.'" The cowboy gave Jake a look and saw the double barrel 12 gauge pointed at him. His partner backed his buddy's play by drawing on Jake, showing more loyalty than brains. The showdown suddenly escalated from explosive to deadly, but Jake held his ground. The crowd continued to ease back and away from the line of fire.

"Boys, there's no way this ends well for anyone here if you start shootin,'" Jake said.

"Oh, nobody's gonna start shootin,'" the tall one laughed nervously, "'cause this card thief's gonna hand us back our money and we're gonna walk outta here." Jake did not want to cave in to a couple of rowdies, but he didn't want his bar shot up neither. Bad for business.

"Dillon," Jake called out to the dealer, "how much did you win from these gents?"

"Fifty dollars," Dillon replied slowly. Jake thought for a moment.

"Tell you what, you refund $25 and the house will pony up the other $25. How's that sound?" Dillon turned and stared down the barrel of the pistol pointed at him, giving serious thought to testing the accuracy of these two cowpunchers. Jake saw that Dillon needed to save face as well.

"And you two tadpoles slither out of here and never show your faces again, or I'll shoot you myself," Jake pronounced loud enough for everyone to hear. The insult stung the pride of these two buckaroos, but getting their money back was a tempting offer. The tense grip on his gun softened as the cowpoke looked to his partner and nodded.

Suddenly, Sheriff Simon Webb and Deputy C.J. Mason

stormed into the saloon, guns drawn. With the shout of a growling bulldog, Webb hollered, "Drop your guns!" His style with cowpokes was to overwhelm them with shock and awe, which usually rattled them enough to acquiesce. But not tonight.

The startled cowpoke whipped his pistol around and fired at Webb. The bullet hit Webb in the chest and spun him around. Jake immediately emptied his shotgun on the cowpoke, who flew back a good ten feet from the impact. He was dead before he hit the ground. The second cowpoke fired back at Jake, but missed as the bullet tore a chunk out of the support beam that Jake hid behind. Mason drew on the remaining cowpoke and dropped him with a single shot.

"Oh, my God!" he gasped as he went down. He died on the floor. The crowd remained frozen for a few seconds to be sure the fighting was over. Jake inspected the fallen cowboys and nodded to Mason, who turned to see his boss lying on the saloon floor in a pool of blood. He dropped to his knee and held Webb in his arms, as the life slowly left his eyes. Without a word, Webb slowly exhaled and his eyes turned vacant.

After a brief investigation, Ed Randolph, the county marshal, pronounced Jake and Mason innocent of any wrongful death – strictly a case of self-defense. Mason sat at the undertaker's office to oversee the preparation of Simon Webb for his burial, and to commiserate with Samuel Stokes, the undertaker. Sam and Mason had cultivated a solid friendship over the years. Sam was about 15 years older than Mason, and seemed to Mason almost a father figure. Sam had studied medicine for several years but never got his degree. But that didn't stop local folks from seeking his medical care for their aches and pains and broken bones. He relished the role of doctor. It gave him the satisfaction of filling a vital need in the community, and afforded his wife Elinor endless bragging rights with the society ladies that she was married to a doctor.

However, as Coulson continued to grow, two young legitimate doctors hung out their shingle and basically put Sam out of the doctoring business. He settled on a career of tending to those past all medical help – the dead – and he inherited the job of "undertaker" when the previous mortician passed away. He kind of liked a job where your customers never complain. It was sort of a peaceful line of work.

And he could use the peace. His wife deeply resented his new chosen profession, and never forgave him for leaving medical school. Their marriage descended into a relentless squabble-fest over the most inconsequential matters. At first, he accepted her criticisms as part of the bargain in the "for better or worse" clause of their wedding vows. But the proverbial "last straw" that broke his back occurred the day she excoriated him for pouring gravy into the gravy boat the wrong way – as if there was a right way. At that moment something inside his heart died. He knew he would never leave her, but his home just became God's great waiting room for the two of them.

Sam enjoyed Mason's easy going ways and willingness to learn. They would sit in his office of an afternoon while Sam shared his pearls of wisdom, gleaned from his vast personal library. He basically became Mason's mentor, and Mason loved it. It was education by individual instruction, like a father to a son.

One theme he repeatedly stressed with Mason was to "trust your instincts."

"Never base your decisions strictly on what others say you should do," he lectured. "If you look inside yourself you'll find the truth." Sam never tired of reminding Mason that a camel was a horse that was built by a committee.

The mayor and the city council were sick of the lawless behavior in Coulson. They knew Sheriff Webb did his best to maintain order, but they felt he was not aggressive enough to root out gangs and bullies who gravitated to this community. Coulson was never going to become an inviting place for families to call home as long as ruffians could ride rough shod with no consequence.

In a closed session, the city fathers agreed to offer Mason the job of sheriff at the young age of 25. Mason immediately went to Sam Stokes for advice.

"Take the job," Sam advised. "Webb would have approved."

"But I'm only 25. You think I'm ready?"

"Horse shit. Morgan Earp was Deputy Marshal for Wichita when he was only 24. You're plenty ready," said Sam.

Mason met with the city fathers for his marching orders. "We are deeply troubled by the wanton killing of Sheriff Webb," the mayor began. "But unfortunately, Coulson seems to have a reputation as a safe haven for outlaws, murderers and criminals. We want that reputation extinguished, squashed without hesitation. Do you get my meaning?"

"I believe I do," Mason said. "But just to be clear, are you giving me a free hand to dispense justice as I see fit without the formality of a trial?"

"We want you to put the fear of God into anyone who poses a menace to Coulson," explained the mayor. "As far as I'm concerned, you can shoot first, then ask permission."

Mason did not reply. He just sat and thought about it to see if the concept would take root.

"Listen, Mason, we want any scoundrel thinking of making mischief to ride wide of Coulson. Are we clear?"

"I'll need a deputy," Mason said.

"Agreed."

"Then you got yourself a sheriff," Mason concluded.

The funeral for Simon Webb was attended by most everyone in the city. The cemetery was full to overflowing. Sheriff Webb had served Coulson for over 25 years and was respected by all. He had stepped in harm's way countess times to maintain law and order at great personal risk, and his death was a loss sorely felt.

At the edge of the cemetery Thorn stood, hat in hand, waiting for the service to end. As the mourners filed out, Mason, wearing his shiny new sheriff badge, spotted Thorn and took him aside.

"There's an opening for a deputy, if you're interested."

"I'll take it," Thorn said.

The Showdown at Yellowstone

CHAPTER 3

"All right. If you're going to wear the badge, I gotta know you ain't gonna get yourself killed – or worse, get me killed," Mason told Thorn. Pointing to Thorn's sidearm, he continued. "You know how to use that hog leg?" Thorn pulled his Colt .45 from its holster and showed it to Mason.

"Bout as good as the next fella," he shrugged.

"You ever killed a man?" Mason probed.

"Well, no."

"No shame in that. But this job calls for killin', so you gotta get your head right and shoot straight," Mason said.

"I been wrangling most of my days, so I ain't had the need for man killin'," Thorn confessed.

"We'll talk about that later. How fast are you?"

"I ain't no quick draw," Thorn admitted.

"You don't need to be," Mason assured. Mason took the revolver from Thorn and inspected it. Two chambers were empty and he could see carbon deposits in the barrel. He shook his head and handed it back to Thorn.

"When was the last time you fired this?" Mason asked. Thorn thought for a second.

"Dunno, maybe a couple of weeks ago, scaring off a coyote."

"Clean your piece tonight and meet me outside the sheriff's office tomorrow morning at 6:00. We're gonna find out what else you don't know."

The sun was just inching above the horizon when Thorn met up with Mason and Sam Stokes.

"I want you to meet Samuel Stokes," Mason began.

"Howdy," Thorn said as they shook hands.

"You might as well get to know him," Mason explained. "Sam's the Coulson undertaker. That means depending on how well we do our job, we're either gonna send him business, or we're going to end up being one of his customers one day."

The early morning air was still chilly as the three rode out to an open meadow five miles north of town, where Mason spent many hours practicing with his pistol and rifle. Sam brought along dozens of empty bottles for targets and boxes of cartridges. Thorn noted the empty bottles.

"These bottles all from your personal stock, Sam?"

"No, found 'em all out back of Mason's place," Sam replied with a grin. Mason turned in his saddle to see if Thorn was buying what Sam was spilling. Thorn and Sam grinned back at Mason, waiting for his response.

"Sometimes Sam gets his drinking whisky confused with his embalming fluid," Mason said, "so you never know for sure which one he downs and which one he pumps into someone else."

"As a matter of fact, they are probably interchangeable," Sam chuckled. "I've handled a few customers that looked like they already pickled themselves before they got to me." Mason smiled looking at them both.

"When you meet Sam's wife you're gonna understand why he drinks and why he dumps all his bottles in my backyard."

They reined up at the meadow Mason favored. "This'll do," he said as he dismounted. Thorn followed suit. Mason surveyed the sky. Looked like it was gonna be a nice day. He took in a deep breath of clean fresh air, then exhaled slowly through his nose. He turned to Thorn.

"Do you like people, in general?"

The question puzzled Thorn. "I guess so. Don't know that I have a lot of friends, never needed many I spose." Mason glanced at the ground for a long thoughtful moment. The death of Simon Webb was still fresh in his mind, and it weighed heavy on his heart.

"Just hear me out for a minute," Mason began. "I ain't

a preacher, but I got a few things to say." Thorn shifted his weight a bit to get comfortable for whatever Mason was about to say.

"You're expected to do two things in this job. First, and most important – stay alive."

"What's the other?" Thorn asked.

"Enforce the law," Mason said in all dead earnest.

"You ain't the executioner. You ain't the judge. You apprehend law-breakers and bring them to justice. There's a difference, and don't you ever forget it." Then he pulled out his pistol.

"And these are the tools of your trade." He turned the gun in his hand to display every angle of its shiny surface. Then he holstered it again.

"This job requires more than some ability with firearms," Mason began. "Ya gotta know how to read and handle men, and I don't mean the clear-thinking, rational type. In this job you don't come into contact with many of them. I'm talking about handling the filthy, most godforsaken drunken tramps ever to get up on their hind legs and scratch. You have to size them up and decide in a split second if they're gonna come peaceably or if you're gonna have to bend a branding iron over their head. At any rate, a drunken man stubbornly committed foursquare to causing mischief is the most unpredictable wretch you'll ever lay eyes on. He'll look harmless enough, then kill you in a split second if the notion takes hold. You have to be ready to kill him if you can't contain him. Talk him down when you can, whack him over the head if he talks back, kill him if he draws. Because he'll kill you just to see if he can."

Thorn stared at Mason for a while, letting his words wash around in his head. He swallowed hard and readjusted his gun belt.

"Okay", Thorn replied, "let's get to work."

Sam paced off 15 feet and began setting up bottle targets. Since this was Mason's regular practice spot, there was already a 2 x 6 plank lying next to a cottonwood tree. It looked pretty chewed up from previous sessions, but still good enough to use. He straddled the plank atop a couple of old stumps and lined the bottles up. Thorn paced off about 50 feet, turned and faced the bottle targets. His revolver was in its holster, his right hand hanging loose at his side, ready to shatter the bottles at Mason's go. Mason stood only about 15 feet from the targets. He waved his arms at Thorn.

"Whoa, whoa! You're too far back," Mason called out.

Surprised, Thorn answered "I can't show you how well I shoot if I'm standing too close." Mason waved him over.

"Come over here." Thorn walked back to where Mason was standing.

"Most of your work is going to be in town, usually in a saloon," Mason began. "That means the distance between you and any troublemaker is gonna be about 5 to 10 feet. You're gonna run across them in a card room or dram house. You're not gonna pick 'em off at 30 yards away while they step out of an outhouse. You'll be up close. Remember I said you don't have to have the fastest draw in the west? Not for this work and the short distance between you and the other fella. You point your gun like you'd point your finger. He sees that hog leg pointed at his belly, and that stone cold look on your face, most times he won't want to fight.

"I'm not sure I got a stone cold look," Thorn said. "What does it look like?'

"Like you just whacked your own thumb with a hammer."

"OK," Thorn nodded.

"The situation doesn't usually get that far anyway, they almost always back down when they see you mean business."

"OK," Thorn nodded again.

"But before you step into that situation, you have to make up your mind to kill that son-of-a-bitch if you have to. And don't talk to 'em too much. Tell 'em what you want and if their response isn't immediately docile, you whack 'em over the head with your gun. If he goes for a knife or pistol, you shoot him. You do it because you have to and you do it to make it clear to anyone watching who thinks they might want to test you later. If you aren't prepared to do that," Mason smiled, "go find another line of work, 'cause you're just gonna get yourself killed."

Mason then turned and faced the bottle targets, drew

his six shooter, slowly and with deliberation, raised it up to eye level, and calmly thumbed back the hammer and fired efficiently, shattering six bottles one by one.

Sam leaned back in the shade of a cottonwood tree, his hands folded behind his head, puffing on his pipe, the picture of relaxation. Thorn stood watching, letting it all sink in.

The Showdown at Yellowstone

.

CHAPTER 4

Thorn dug down deep and gave the job his best. By 1894 he grew into his job and made a formidable team with Mason. The two worked together, ate together, socialized together, thought alike, and learned to anticipate each other's moves. In a saloon brawl, for instance, the two acted with the precision of dance partners. Without speaking, Mason chose to confront the troublemaker face-to-face, while Thorn circled around behind the culprit to watch Mason's back. Yes, sir, the town of Coulson was getting used to the fact that with the one you got the other, like a rock and a hard place.

With a population of about 4,000, Coulson was growing fast, and prospering. But with prosperity came temptation from thievin' scoundrels trying to take what was not theirs. Mason and Thorn squashed lawlessness like a blacksmith pounding metal smooth. Always eager to learn, Thorn often asked perplexing philosophical questions about the law, justice, and the rights of citizens to defend themselves. At dinner one evening at the Huntley Diner, Mason and Thorn tackled the subject with Sam Stokes, who was more than happy to share his sage insights.

"Hear me out, boys," Sam began. "Here's how it is. For freedom in this country to survive, we have to collectively agree on the laws we'll be governed by, then voluntarily comply with those laws. 'Cause there just aren't enough policemen around to force everybody to behave." Mason nodded in agreement as he finished his bite of steak.

"I'll give you a for instance," Mason added. "There's a

cattle ranch west of town that covers over 75,000 square miles. Nobody can keep an eye on that much land to stop thieves who don't care about the law."

"That's what I'm trying to say," Sam nodded. He paused to take a sip of wine and wiped his mouth. Mason went on.

"And listen to this. I got a visit from the Cattlemen Association a few days ago. Well, it wasn't so much a friendly visit as a friendly warning. They're sick and tired of all the cattle thieving, and they've voted to enforce the law themselves."

"Just bypass you altogether?" Sam listened.

"Well, here's what they say they're gonna do. They're hiring enforcers to protect their herd – they're calling them cattle detectives or stock inspectors. Nothing wrong with that. But if they find any cattle with their brand in anyone else's corral, they're threatening retribution with no trial, and that could start off a range war like the Johnson County war down in Wyoming last year."

"God help us," muttered Sam. "You boys just be careful. It ain't worth getting yourself killed over someone else's damn cattle."

After dinner, as Mason and Thorn walked back to the sheriff's office, Thorn offered a confession.

"I have to come clean with you," Thorn began. "I wasn't completely honest about my reasons for leaving the ranch I was working for, when I came looking to you for a job."

"Is that so?" Mason said.

"I said I was just tired of the long hours and back-breaking work, but that wasn't the whole story," Thorn continued.

"Go on," Mason said.

"The fact is my boss wanted me to start shootin' rustlers on sight, make a few examples and discourage others. I told him I didn't sign on to do no killing. He gave me a choice – either do what I'm told or draw my pay."

"I give you credit for standing up to him," Mason said.

"Yeah, well, I thought I could get away from it by comin' down here, but now I'm right back in the middle of it."

"I just need to know one thing," Mason said. "Whose

side are you on?"

"I'm on your side, pard," Thorn said.

———

In 1896 the two biggest Montana spreads – the Lazy D and the Bar W – joined forces to wipe out outlaws and small ranchers suspected of rustling. To make clear their intent, they hired the reputed gunfighter Jim Whitley, with the title 'Stock Detective' and a salary of $250 a month plus bounties for obtaining convictions for horse thieves or cattle rustlers. That was easily over three times the typical pay rate of a deputy U.S. marshal. His job was clear – to make the penalty for stealing so severe that it would lose its attraction altogether. He was definitely the man for the job.

Whitley was a fearless, angular cowpoke out of New Mexico, and stood over six feet tall. He proved himself as a roving gunman for the Pinkerton Detective Agency for five years, and was thought to put away over 20 victims. He was interviewed once by a Wyoming reporter, and was quoted as saying, "Killing men is my specialty. I treat it like a business, and I'm pretty good at it."

His handiwork soon drew attention. After tracking down two suspected horse thieves, Whitley cornered them in a cabin. He counted 25 horses in the corral with well-known brands, and ordered them to come out with their hands up. They denied stealing any horses, except from Indians, but their guilt was plain enough for Whitley. When they refused to surrender, he set fire to the cabin, smoking them out into the open as nearby ranchers looked on, then gunned them down and hanged their bodies on a nearby tree.

Another Montana stockman swore that small ranchers and homesteaders were pilfering his land and cattle to claim their own piece of the range, snitching calves from the big operator's cattle to start their own herd. Whitley moved in and found one small rancher who claimed his cows had twin calves, and sometimes triplets. Whitley put a gun to the rancher's head and promised, "I'll put a bullet through your skull if your cows give birth to one more set of twins."

Some small ranchers finding strays out on the open range with a well-known brand, took those cows to their ranch and devised a new brand to overlay on the original brand to create the look of a new brand. So, for instance, a brand with the letter "E" would be converted to a "B", an "S" could be changed to an "8", and a "T" might be converted into a "Double Cross" ($\neq$) brand. Most of these counterfeits were easy enough to spot, with deadly consequences for the offender.

Word spread that Whitley was killing not only rustlers but land squatters as well, which enraged the small ranchers in the region. As the dead bodies mounted, tensions boiled over. Both small ranchers and large cattle owners demanded protection and justice from the law, putting Mason and Thorn right in the middle. Mason sought the help of Ed Randolph, the County Marshal, who personally met with both parties and demanded a 30-day cooling-off period.

But Jim Whitley could not leave well enough alone. In the fall of 1896 he came across two Swedish immigrant homesteaders who dared to settle on a small tract of disputed land claimed by a wealthy cattle baron. The husband and wife argued the land was theirs, to no avail. Whitley and his men took the couple out of the cabin and hanged them from the same tree, side by side. The lynching caused a furious outcry from citizens in the area. Mason and Thorn rode out to the site of the lynching. The bodies had already been buried out of compassion, but the nooses still hung from the tree. They paused under the tree and scanned the area.

"What the hell, Mase," Thorn uttered in exasperation. "This is gonna reap the whirlwind for sure."

"Let's get busy and do our job," Mason muttered in a low voice. They began a complete investigation of the claims by the cattle baron and found that the land in question did not belong to the cattleman, but had been used by him for several years to graze his immense herd. The homesteaders were merely enterprising Swedes who owned no cattle at all, but were simply an innocent couple wantonly killed.

A warrant was put out for Jim Whitley's arrest, and the cattleman was fined $10,000 to be paid to the couple's next of kin. For the next month the telegraph wires sizzled with rumors of Whitley's whereabouts. He was supposedly sighted in Bozeman, Whitehall, and as far away as Missoula.

"Don't worry," Marshal Randolph assured Mason. "He'll turn up sooner or later. His kind always does. And when that happens, we are gonna bring him down hard."

As luck would have it, that moment came sooner rather than later.

The Showdown at Yellowstone

CHAPTER 5

In the summer of 1897 Marshall Ed Randolph tied off his horse and paid Mason a visit. He usually stopped by the Coulson office once a month for a report on the progress of various cases, and the overall state of law enforcement in the City. This visit was unscheduled and rather urgent. When Mason and Thorn were seated, Marshal Randolph got down to business.

"Boys, Jim Whitley just surfaced. Him and some of the Wild Bunch gang just robbed the Union Pacific outside of Three Forks and were last seen headed east." Mason didn't like the sound of that. Three Forks was about 150 miles west of Coulson. It got its name from Lewis and Clark back in 1805. A town grew from that storied past, due largely from the Union Pacific Railroad, whose tracks ran right through the town.

"We got a lot on our plate here in Coulson," Mason said. He was not trying to dodge Randolph's request for help, but knew that any extended absences from Coulson would rankle the city fathers.

"Lonnie Jones was with the gang when they robbed that train," Randolph added. Jones was one of the most sought after criminals in the territory. He was wanted for bank robberies, cattle rustling, train hold-ups, murder, and horse stealing in several states. Putting his crime spree to an end would be a feather in any lawman's hat.

"Jones is back here in Montana?" asked Mason. I thought he was still down in Texas or New Mexico."

"He's made a serious mistake comin' back to Montana,"

Randolph said. "We're going to run him and Whitley to ground."

Mason knew what "running to ground" meant – tracking Jones and Whitley relentlessly, endlessly until he was finally cornered. But that could take weeks, months, even longer. Most outlaws counted on wearing down their pursuers by staying one step ahead until the posse simply became discouraged and disbanded. Running a crook to ground was a last resort that often ended in a shoot-out with no guarantee of success. Earlier that year, Lonnie Jones and Will Carver were recognized in St. Johns, Arizona when Lonnie made some large purchases with money suspected of being from the Wilcox Robbery. Local Sheriff Edward Beeler and deputies Andrew Gibbons and Frank LeSeuer chased them down and finally cornered them. But the outlaws refused to be taken. In the ensuing shoot-out both deputies were killed and Lonnie escaped.

"Here's what we're gonna do," Randolph explained as he rolled out a map of the region and spread it on Mason's desk. "The Three Forks lawmen and the Union Pacific posse are chasing Whitley and Jones east. They wired me today that they intend to push them right into our hands." He pointed to the map. "We get our asses moving, we'll head 'em off around Springdale." They all checked the map to see that Springdale was about halfway between Three Forks and Coulson.

"I'm bringing along some extra help. Captain Ethan Thomas, retired Civil War vet, wagon train scout. He's an explosives expert and knows every rock and creek bed between here and Missoula."

"I like the sound of that," Mason said.

"Any questions?" Randolph concluded. Mason and Thorn looked at each other, then back at Randolph.

"How long you figure we'll be gone?" Thorn asked.

"As long as it takes," Randolph replied.

"When do we leave?" Mason asked.

"Get your gear together and meet back here in an hour. We're taking the train to Big Timber to get a jump on closing the gap. We'll load our horses on the cattle car."

Once on the train, Mason and Thorn got better acquainted with Capt. Thomas. He was lean of build with a full beard and wisps of wavy grey hair. He was 55 years old and hard as a whetstone. They sat across from each other in the passenger car.

"Randolph says you served in the Civil War," Mason said.

"That's right. I fought with Hancock's 2nd Corp in the Battle of the Wilderness. Nasty bit of fighting. Twenty-five thousand killed or wounded on both sides after three days, and the goddamn battle ends in a draw. What a waste."

"What have you been doing since?" Thorn asked.

"I did some Indian fighting for a bit, but got sick of all the double dealin'. Lately I've been scouting for wagon trains headin' west. Easy work. A lot of sleeping under the stars."

The train ride to Big Timber took about two hours, which saved them 15 hours on horseback. The four men gathered their riding horses and pack horse, and met by the side of the depot. Randolph laid out the plan.

"All right, men. We got the advantage of surprise and we've covered a lot of ground fast. Capt. Thomas, you jump in here anytime, but we figure that the posse has been pushing Whitley and Jones east on horseback for three days. That means they should be closing in on Springdale pretty soon," explained Randolph.

"That's assuming they didn't turn north or south," added Capt. Thomas.

"Their tracks have been nothing but due east," countered Randolph. "We'd a known if they veered off in a new direction." Capt. Thomas nodded.

"I know those Three Forks lawmen. I trust what they say. And them boys with the Union Pacific could track bees in a blizzard," he added. Randolph continued.

"Now, they think all their trouble is behind 'em, and all they gotta do is stay ahead long enough to wear a posse down. They got no idea the reception they're about to get."

"What happens when they hit the Yellowstone River at Livingston? They could turn south then," Mason asked. Capt. Thomas shook his head no.

"They really got no choice. They gotta keep coming east. They can't go south. There's nothing south but Yellowstone Park, and there's too many troops there. They can't take that chance."

"OK, then," Randolph said. "We go to Springdale and hunker down. When they pass through, we jump 'em. You all know 'em on sight?"

"Oh, yeah, I seen Jim Whitley enough," said Mason. Randolph passed out wanted posters of both Whitley and Jones.

"Just the same, here's photos of each. They should be riding through tomorrow. They'll be low on supplies, so I doubt they'll skirt the town."

They rode 14 miles to get to Springdale, which sits on the south bank of the Yellowstone River. About a half mile east of town a foot bridge crossed the river, about 100 feet long and 20 feet wide - just wide enough for two wagons to pass each other abreast This bridge was the only way travelers could get north of the river for several miles. At the foot bridge Capt. Thomas got an idea.

"You know, at the Battle of the Wilderness, we trapped a whole regiment of Johnny rebs by blowing a bridge over a river too deep to cross," he recalled. "What do you say we blow this bridge tonight. We'll have 'em trapped between the town and the river." Randolph thought it over.

"I'm sure the townsfolk would not appreciate it. But I say what the hell. The reward money on Whitley alone can pay to rebuild the bridge." He looked at Capt Thomas. "Do it." Thomas unloaded several sticks of dynamite from the pack horse, and attached them underneath the bridge at both ends, then covered the fuses with brush.

"We'll come back and set 'em off after sundown," he said.

The four strangers slowly rode into the quiet town of Springdale late in the day, loaded for bear with sidearms, rifles, leg irons, and a pack horse full of dynamite. They didn't look like hunters, but no one dared to ask their business.

"I'll find out who the law is here, and let 'em know who we are," Randolph said. "Thorn, you take the first watch at the west end of town. The rest of you find a boarding house and settle in. Thorn, you see 'em, you let 'em pass through. Just come back and let us know. We'll take 'em east of town by the bridge." Thorn nodded and rode on through town to the last building, a trading supply store. He dismounted and tied off his horse and pulled the rifle out of its scabbard, then went inside to talk to the proprietor.

"Howdy," he said politely. "I'm expecting company from the west. You mind if I set up on the roof to keep an eye out?"

"Fine with me," the proprietor shrugged his shoulders. "But we close up in an hour. I can't have you up on the roof when no one's here." Thorn saw a stand of trees just west of the store. He figured he could keep watch there and still be out of sight.

"How about if I just leave my horse tied off in front of your store?" Thorn offered as an alternative.

"That's OK by me," the proprietor agreed.

Thorn rested his back against one of the pine trees, eyes trained on the western horizon. It couldn't have been 30 minute's time when he saw a lone rider approaching town from the west. He watched as the rider drew closer and closer. Thorn slipped around to the back side of the tree as the rider passed by not 50 feet away. It was Lonnie Jones without a doubt.

"How did he get here so fast?" Thorn wondered. "And where's Jim Whitley?"

Thorn was about to get to his feet when he heard the cock of a pistol and felt someone grab his collar from behind.

"Why Thorn Hickum," the voice said, shaking his collar. "Aren't you a long way from home." Thorn could not believe that anyone could get the drop on him. "How the hell did this happen?" he thought. The hand on his collar tightened and Thorn felt the barrel of a gun press against the back of his skull. He raised his hands away from his gun.

"Where's your partner, Mason? The two of you never go anywhere without the other," the voice sneered.

"He's eatin' dinner I expect," Thorn tried to make up a believable answer. His mind was racing. "Why doesn't he just shoot me? How did he get here ahead of Jones? What do I do now?" He felt for sure he was a dead man, and only wanted to be sure that his lack of awareness would not cause the deaths of any others.

"Let's go for a walk," Whitley ordered, as he pulled Thorn up to his feet by the collar. Whitley's horse was in a ravine a half mile north. He had ridden a wide circle around Springdale, in anticipation of just such a welcome, and walked into town ahead of Jones. He was standing in an alley when the four rode into town, and saw their every move. Now he had the drop on them.

When he let go of Thorn's collar and walked him to the ravine, Thorn knew Whitley had made his first mistake. They collected Whitley's horse and walked back to pick up Thorn's horse.

"That was your second mistake," thought Thorn. "You should have killed me when you had the gun to my head." They mounted up at the west end of town and slowly made their way down side streets to avoid any notice. But it was already too late. Capt. Thomas had been assigned the second watch, and was on his way to relieve Thorn when he saw Thorn and Whitley mount up and disappear behind the Main Street buildings. He ran back to collect Mason and Ed Randolph.

"They've got Thorn and they're heading out of town," he said to his companions. "I've got to blow the bridge." He ran out of the boarding house and mounted up. With a solid kick to his horse, he raced down Main Street and into the twilight east of town. Mason and Ed were right behind him.

Whitley met up with Lonnie Jones in the back alley behind the livery stable near the east end of town.

"Whata we got here?" Lonnie asked of his partner.

"We got a Montana lawman lyin' in wait for us," Whitley mocked Thorn. "His partner is Sheriff C.J. Mason – not one to mess with."

"What are you doin' with this pack of trouble?" asked Lonnie. "Why didn't you just shoot him where you found him?"

"Are you crazy? Gun shots will just draw attention. We'll keep this deputy for cover till we get way shed of town, then we'll shoot him and be on our way."

Whitley, Jones, and Thorn rode slowly through back alleys until they were well out of town. From the twilight shadows they saw Capt. Thomas riding like a bat out of hell, with Mason and Ed Randolph right behind. Thorn reared his horse up and shouted as loud as he could - "MASON!"

Whitley drew his gun and tried to get off a shot to silence Thorn, but Thorn's horse reared again, blocking Whitley from any decent shot. Capt. Thomas saw the commotion and drew his gun to engage the villains. They were about 50 yards away and lost between the rising moon and the cloak of night. He fired three shots as he continued to the bridge to cut off their retreat. Mason joined in the battle, to give Thorn enough time to seek cover. A nearby field of tall grass offered Thorn a place to duck and run. He leaped from his horse where he was far too visible, and dove into the field grass.

When Whitley saw Capt. Thomas bolt for the bridge he knew instinctively that he was cutting off their escape route. He had no idea that the bridge was set to blow.

"Stop that rider!" he yelled at Lonnie. From his saddle Lonnie turned and fired several rifle shots in the direction of Thomas. A lucky shot hit his horse, who collapsed under him, throwing Thomas to the ground. Mason continued firing in the direction of Whitley as Thorn scrambled through the tall grass to get out of firing range. Ed Randolph came to his rescue, firing his rifle in the direction of Whitley until Thorn could safely retreat.

"Thorn," Ed shouted. Thorn looked over to see Ed throw him a pistol. The gun landed about ten feet away, and as Ed resumed his covering fire, Thorn crawled over and grabbed the gun. Now he could be of some use, adding to the fire power of the lawmen.

Thomas rose to his feet and continued running to the bridge, with Lonnie on horseback in pursuit. Twenty yards from the bridge Lonnie stopped and dismounted. Pushing his horse aside, he took aim again and managed to clip Thomas with a bullet, who fell to the ground. Mason saw Thomas fall and knew he needed help. He ran towards the bridge, firing his pistol at Lonnie at the same time. His covering fire forced Lonnie's attention away from Thomas. He leveled a few shots at Mason to keep him at bay.

Thomas rose to his feet and managed to reach the bridge, but Lonnie pivoted and scored again with a bullet to Thomas's gut. Thomas dropped and rolled over the bank and under the bridge. Lonnie crossed over to finish him off when Mason took deadly aim and shot Lonnie in the shoulder. The impact spun him around and dropped him to the ground. From under the bridge Thomas felt his senses dimming. He knew he had to blow the bridge now or never. He rolled over on his stomach and began crawling up the bank.

Now Whitley realized he was outgunned and needed to make his escape. He ran for his horse, climbed aboard and bolted for the bridge. Mason knew he had only one good shot before Whitley would be out of pistol range. He took aim with his revolver, exhaled slowly and pulled the trigger. The shot hit Whitley in the leg, and the shock of the impact caused Whitley to reflexively pull back on his reins. In doing so, he yanked the horse's neck so far to the side that it lost balance and fell, sending Whitley sprawling to the ground. The horse promptly regained its footing and continued to run riderless over the bridge. It bounded across with a resounding beat of its hooves on the wooden planks and disappeared into the far glen on the other bank.

Lonnie saw his chance and got to his feet. He hobbled over the bridge, looking one side and then the other to see where Thomas was, with no luck. He finally reached the far side of the bridge, where he stopped to see if he could be of any help to Whitley. At that moment Thomas managed to find the fuse and lit it. He died before the fuse reached the dynamite.

The explosion blew the bridge to pieces. The blast knocked Lonnie to the north side of the bank. As fragments of the bridge rained down, he found Whitley's horse grazing several yards away, climbed aboard and rode east into the night. Whitley knew he was trapped for sure. He turned and raised his arms in surrender. Ed ran over to the splintered remains of the bridge and saw that there was no way to get to the other side to give chase to Lonnie. He searched for the body of Capt. Thomas, and found it among the rubble of splintered timbers. He dutifully carried the body of this brave soldier back to town for a proper burial.

Whitley was locked up for the rest of the night, while Ed made plans for his extradition back to Coulson. Springdale did not have a telegraph office, so Ed Randolph decided to ride on ahead in the morning to Big Timber to wire the news of Jim Whitley's capture, leaving Mason and Thorn to escort the prisoner back.

The horse ride back with Jim Whitley in leg irons was subdued. Thorn wore a scowl like an old maid at a barn dance. Before reaching Big Timber Thorn finally spoke his mind.

"Why don't we just dump Whitley with the County marshal in Big Timber and take the train back home?" he suggested. "I'm sick of the sight of this piece of shit." Mason made no reply. He just studied Thorn for a moment.

"And while I'm at it," Thorn continued, "I'm sick of sleeping on freezing ground and eating johnny cake and dried meat."

"Well, you brought it," Mason replied. "Yeah, but I didn't think I was gonna have to actually eat it," Thorn snarled. Mason gave the wounded Whitley a glance as he lumbered along with his horse in tow.

"Fine with me," Mason said. "We'll hand him off in Sweet Water County and be on our way."

The Showdown at Yellowstone

CHAPTER 6

The door to the sheriff's office kicked open as Mason walked in with an armload of firewood to feed the pot-bellied stove. He dumped the load in the corner of the office and noticed Thorn sitting at his desk with his boots perched on top and the Coulson Gazette folded in his hands.

"They strung up Jim Whitley in Big Timber last week," Thorn announced in disgust. Mason could tell by the tone of his voice that Thorn was spoiling for a squabble.

"Good – about time," Mason replied as he poured himself some coffee from the pot simmering on the stove.

"He was lynched without a trial," Thorn clarified. Mason sipped his coffee as he tried to decide how he felt about that. Thorn continued his rant.

"Seems the good folks of Big Timber weren't quite convinced that justice would be served and decided to speed things along," Thorn explained, waving the newspaper at Mason.

"Look, would you rather he got off with the help of some well-heeled cattlemen? 'Cuz what I heard, the smart money was on Whitley walkin' free" Mason said.

"There was no way he was gonna skate after what he did. Lynchin' those Swedes was never gonna set with a jury. But you read what happened – the town didn't even wait for a verdict. A mob broke into the jail, overpowered the deputies and dragged Jim Whitley out. He was kicking and screaming how they were all breaking the law – ain't that rich?" Thorn said. Mason stared at the floor, holding his coffee in his hand, not drinking it, just letting Thorn blow off steam.

"I don't hold with lynching, even a snake like Whitley, but nobody can say he didn't have it comin'," Mason admitted. Thorn exploded.

"Maybe so, but I nearly got my head blowed off so's we could bring him in all legal and such – and for what? To make it easier for some rabble to scoop him up and lynch him." Mason didn't know what to say.

"I'm sick of this job – lousy pay, god-awful hours, ungrateful citizens, and outlaws just itchin' to kill you," Thorn concluded. He lowered his head emotionally spent. "Nobody gives a damn," he muttered.

———

The last month of 1897 was dry and cold in Coulson. Snow flurries blew through town, leaving small piles to collect on the sides of buildings. Crime seemed to die out when the temperature dropped below freezing. Keeping warm just seemed to be a fulltime job even for scoundrels. While Mason disliked the cold he relished the peace and quiet. By mid-January he was caught up with most of his correspondence and finally got around to fixing the hinge on the back door.

Thorn's sullen mood lingered past Christmas and into the new year. Mason did not know exactly what the problem was, nor what the cure might be. At dinner with Sam at the Huntley Diner, he broached the subject.

"Thorn seem out of kilter to you?" He asked Sam. Sam savored his red wine for a thoughtful moment.

"I have been mindful of his surly affect lately," Sam nodded.

"You reckon I hurt his feelings?" Mason guessed.

"Not likely for Thorn. He's not sufficiently prone to self-awareness," Sam proclaimed.

"Well, then, what is it? He's like a wife who's mad at you but won't tell you why," Mason muttered in frustration.

"If I had my guess, I'd say he's experiencing a crisis of significance," Sam diagnosed.

"Whataya mean by that?" Mason asked.

"When a man gets to a certain age he wants to accomplish something, to feel like his life mattered, that he made a difference," Sam explained.

"Yeah?" Mason nodded.

"When the two of you got back from your little fracas with Jim Whitley and Lonnie Jones, he mentioned how he nearly got his head blowed off, and I could tell it affected him," Sam went on.

"Well, why wouldn't it?" Mason agreed.

"I mean to the core. When a man stares death in the face it changes him. He takes stock. He might figure he was spared for some reason, and now he's trying to figure out what that might be." Mason gave thought to that notion.

"Give him time. He'll sort it out," Sam concluded, as he raised his glass for another sip.

Mason didn't have long to wait. On January 25, 1898 the USS Maine was blown up in Havana Harbor and the United States was suddenly in a frenzy for revenge against Spain. As Mason read the accounts in the Coulson Gazette, his office door flew open and Thorn bounded in.

"I'm going to war," Thorn declared.

"You're doing what?" Mason asked.

"I'm joining the army and we're goin' to teach those sons-a-bitches which way the sun shines," Thorn said. Mason folded the newspaper up.

"You got a job here, ya know. Plenty of other fellas can take care of business down south."

"I can't just sit here and do nothin'. They're calling for volunteers to join a special regiment of US cavalry – men with experience with a horse and rifle," Thorn said. "That's me."

"And where exactly are you signing up? I don't recall any recruiting stations here in town," Mason asked.

"I'm goin' to San Antonio," Thorn answered.

"Texas?" Mason replied.

"Yeah. They only want fellas who can stand the heat down there in Cuba, so they figure to just take cowpokes from the southwest. I gotta get down there before it's too late. They're only taking about 1,200. They're gonna call us

Rough Riders. I kinda like the sound of that."

"That mean you're quittin' your job here?" Mason asked. Thorn thought for a second.

"I can't imagine it'll take more than a month or two to root out them trouble makers down there. I figure I'll be back before the devil knows I left. I'll be back shortly." And with that, Thorn marched to the depot for the next train bound for San Antonio.

The San Antonio recruiting office was overwhelmed with volunteers -- cowpokes, miners, hunters, gamblers, Native Americans and college boys -- all able-bodied and capable on horseback and in shooting. There were even some police officers, like Thorn, and military veterans itchin' to see action again.

Most of the rejects were tenderfeet - too old, too young, never been in a gun fight, or failed the rifle test. Thorn was among the lucky few to be chosen. They were shipped off to Tampa, Florida, in short order, where they underwent two months of rigorous training to improve their skills in riding and shooting from horseback. They also studied basic cavalry tactics and strategy and military protocol. By the end of May, the regiment was ready to board ship and set sail for Cuba. Unfortunately, the ship chosen for passage was already overloaded with supplies and equipment, and only three-fourths of the original 1,200 Rough Riders could fit on board. Most of the horses and mules had to be left behind. Another 200 men died from Malaria or yellow fever before even reaching Cuba, leaving only about 600 Rough Riders ready to fight.

On July 1, 1898 the heroic Rough Riders drove the Spaniards out of their trenches on the San Juan Heights, and by August 12 the Spanish Government surrendered to the United States. To spare any further ravages from malaria, yellow fever, and dysentery, Colonel Roosevelt ordered his Rough Riders shipped back to the United States, and two days later, on August 14, Thorn found himself in Long Island, New York. One month later, in September, the Rough Riders were disbanded, and the entire regiment discharged. Suddenly, Thorn's glorious military career was at an end. At the farewell ceremony Roosevelt gave a touching speech to his men, and shook each hand. Thorn discharged with the rank of Lieutenant.

As Thorn passed through the reception line, Roosevelt took him aside.

"What are your plans from here?" he asked.

"Don't know for sure." Thorn replied. Roosevelt leaned in a little closer.

"Let's talk."

The Showdown at Yellowstone

CHAPTER 7

With one eye closed and the other sighting down the 34-inch barrel of his Model 1874 Sharps rifle, he focused on his motionless prey standing 850 yards away. His Sharps rifle was ideally suited for the task. This legendary sniper rifle was lethal at 1,000 yards in the right hands. His rifle was equipped with a front globe sight and a tang mounted Creedmoor sight with windage adjustments.

The slightest wisp of a breeze sighed over the valley. He waited for it to pass. From his sitting position his rifle barrel rested at the vortex of two cross-sticks to help steady his aim, held in place with his left hand. Gently he pulled the lever down to open the chamber then slid in the brass cartridge. For maximum accuracy he loaded his bullets with black powder, which created very little velocity variations between rounds.

He knew his aim had to be true. At a distance of 850 yards, if your aim was off by a mere one half of one degree, the bullet would sail wide by a full 20 feet.

The sun tried to interfere, creating heat waves that made distant objects appear to shimmer and dance. A small bead of sweat formed on his forehead. He felt it trickle down to his eyebrow, then slid down the crease in his brow and into his open eye. The salty moisture burned slightly. He squeezed his eye slowly to clear his gaze, then opened it only so slightly. He exhaled gently and pulled the trigger.

A metal "PING" echoed across the valley as the metal target fashioned into the silhouette of a bison, fell backwards. "Hit," shouted the judge at the top of his lungs, and the waiting onlookers burst into applause.

With that bullseye the sharpshooting competition ended, and C.J. Mason proclaimed the winner. For the second year in a row he bested over 50 challengers from all over the state of Montana, in this annual long distance shooting challenge, held a few miles west of Coulson.

The two-day event, held every September, brought seasoned shooters seeking the $500 prize and the title of "Champion Marksman." The competition was simple in its design. A life-sized silhouette of a bison, cut out of solid iron, was painted black with a large white circle drawn in the center for ease of aiming. The target was propped up at a starting distance of 500 yards, and contestants were challenged to knock it down with a single shot from the rifle of their choosing. One miss and you were eliminated from the competition.

Once every contestant took his turn, and the losers were excused, the target was moved further back 25 yards and the next round of shooting began. Losers were again eliminated, the target was again moved back another 25 yards, and so on until the last two challengers were left. The two remaining shooters were each allowed to have their shot. If both scored, the target was again reset and the contest continued. If the first shooter missed, the second shooter had to hit the target to win the contest. If he also missed, the first shooter was given another chance to hit the target. If he was successful, the second shooter had to hit the target as well to stay alive, and the target was then moved another 25 yards.

Shooters from all over the state paid their $3.00 entrance fee to compete, which was used as part of the prize pool. The balance of the prize was contributed by the Coulson Rifle Company, who sponsored the event. Hunters, trappers, ranchers, farmers, retired military, and even soldiers from as far away as Fort Yellowstone traveled to Coulson for a shot at the title.

The event gave shooters of all stripes a chance to share tips, compare rifles, and swap stories. The field saw Springfields, Remingtons, Winchesters, Sharps, and Carbines, as well as some international rifles like the 1896 German Mauser and the Canadian Ross rifle. The night before the event, the Crystal Palace Saloon in Coulson was packed with contestants and spectators, full of swagger, and braggadocio. Bets were placed, and whiskey flowed.

Mason and Sam Stokes sat at a corner table.

"So, who are you betting on?" Mason asked.

"Since you won last year, you're the odds on favorite," Sam said.

"That's not what I asked," Mason said. Sam smiled.

"I got ten dollars on you," Sam said, "so, you're not drinking tonight."

"No drinkin?" Mason said. "Then what are we doin' here?"

"I didn't say I wasn't drinking – just you," Sam corrected. "You're supposed to be sizing up the competition, which I venture to say is prodigious," Sam continued. Mason scanned the saloon, where most of the contestants were getting pretty sloshed. One feller from Cody was so drunk he could no longer find his mouth to pour the next drink down. With his head tilted back, and his waiting jaw wide open, he was draining his mug of beer on the bar counter, all the while wondering why he couldn't taste anything.

"Well, judging by everyone's final preparations, I'd say my chances are lookin' good for tomorrow."

The next morning the throng gathered at the Ridley farm, where the contest was being held. Of the 60 shooters who paid to play, only 56 actually showed up. The other four were otherwise occupied. Two hungover shooters were found slumbering in the alley behind the Crystal Palace. Another had gotten into a fist fight a 2:00 a.m. With a swollen eye shut, he was in no condition to compete. The fourth "no-show" had slid under the tarp of a supply wagon to sleep it off, and was now well on his way to Bozeman.

By 10:00 a.m. the field was crowded with onlookers, each one charged 25 cents for the privilege of watching. Over a thousand folks lined the valley, with umbrellas to shade them from the sun, and picnic baskets to make a day of it. Three supply wagons full of water barrels quenched anyone's thirst, courtesy of the event sponsors. Ridley's water well kept the barrels filled.

"The contest will begin with the target set at 500 yards," announced the referee. "Shooters may fire their weapon either offhand or with the aid of cross sticks. We have drawn numbers, so everyone will follow that order in shooting. We will begin with Captain Joshua Kellerman from Fort Yellowstone." A stout army captain, in uniform, stepped up to the shooting line. He held a long range Creedmoor rolling block rifle .45-70 caliber with a 30-inch tapered octagonal conical barrel. It was deadly at 1,000 yards. He casually took his place, paused to measure windage, then raised his rifle in offhand position and fired.

A loud "PING" resounded as the bullet struck the iron silhouette and knocked it over. "Hit," shouted the field judge. Though it didn't matter where the bullet hit, so long as it knocked the target down, the judge noted that the bullet struck only 12 inches from dead center. The crowd cheered their approval.

The first round of shooting continued until all 56 contestants fired their shot. It took an hour and a half, but thinned the field by 19 shooters, leaving 37 still in play. The target was moved to 525 yards and new numbers were drawn so that each round everyone got a chance to draw a new number.

The day was ideal for shooting, with occasional clouds and only a slight breeze. Onlookers drifted in and out, some bored with the methodical tedium of these preliminary rounds. But as the target moved further away and more shooters were eliminated, the game got more and more interesting. By the end of the 10th round the target was moved to 750 yards, and was becoming more difficult to see. As Day One drew to a close, only ten shooters remained.

That night the Crystal Palace was again jammed and packed full. The bar was as crowded as a livestock feeder at dinner time. New bets were being placed and premature celebrations were underway with the remaining shooters. Captain Kellerman was still in the game, and his supporters rallied around him with predictions of glory.

Mason and Sam sat at their usual corner table and watched the jubilation unfold. One of the Kellerman supporters spotted Mason in the corner and shouted, "Mason, you got as much chance as a jackrabbit at a coyote convention."

Sam gently rested his hand on Mason's arm. "Let him blow. It's not the whistle that moves the train."

At 10:00 a.m. the competition resumed, with the target set at 750 yards, which every marksman hit with ease. After the second round, at 775 yards, two shooters missed. Now there were eight left. The crowd became increasingly awed at the incomprehensible accuracy of these shooters, who could hit a target barely visible to the naked eye. As each contestant stood to shoot, the audience fell silent in respect to these titans of marksmanship. With each "PING" of the bullet they erupted in applause and amazement.

At 800 yards the first five shooters failed to hit the target, and the crowd wondered if this was finally the limit of human capabilities. But then Mason hit the target, as did Captain Kellerman and the Swede called Hugo, and the crowd wondered if these men were not human at all.

The target stood at 825 yards, and Hugo drew the first number. He sat on the ground with the barrel of his rifle resting on the cross sticks provided by the judges. He paused, exhaled, and fired. Not a sound was heard down field. The judge called out "MISS", and suddenly the game was down to two. Both Mason and the Captain hit their marks, and the target was moved to 850 yards.

Kellerman drew the first number for this round, and took his place. He could end the match, he thought, if he could hit the target now. The crowd hushed, not daring to make a sound that might distract him. He lined up the distant target, now only a speck to be seen, in his sights and fired.

"MISS!" shouted the judge. The crowd heaved a collective groan at the first miss from Joshua the entire competition. Then everyone looked at Mason for his reaction. He was as stunned as the crowd, wondering if this man was even capable of missing. Now he suddenly realized the prize was his for the taking. Mason almost resisted the urge to look at Kellerman, but could not help but give him a glance.

Their eyes met. The Captain gave Mason a nod, and Mason returned the nod and took his place on the firing line. The entire valley was quiet as a tree full of owls. Mason heaved a sigh to calm himself. He loaded his cartridge before assuming his sitting position, and then wiped his brow.

Sam stood 20 yards behind Mason, wishing he had said something – anything - that might help at this moment. But no words came to mind. He had to just wait to see what Mason was capable of.

Mason rested his barrel on the cross sticks and looked down the sights to see a tiny dot of white nearly a half a mile away. He thought of how he had won last year's competition at only 750 yards.

"Can't think of that now," he urged himself. "Can't think of anything. Just breathe."

He felt that drop of sweat trickle down his brow and into his eye. He remembered squinting it away. He exhaled one more time. Then he gently pulled the trigger. For a second the echo of his rifle blast resounded, and time suddenly stood still. He didn't hear the usual "PING" and his heart sunk.

Then suddenly, "PING" rang out and the judge hollered from down field, "HIT!" The audience exploded with cheers, as much for Mason as for the deed itself. Kellerman came over to Mason and extended his hand. They shook hands. The Captain nodded his head with grudging respect, and left.

The award ceremony was short and sincere. The small crowd who gathered around simply could not believe what they had witnessed and did not want the moment to end. They would go home to their friends and families that night and try to share what they had seen, but they knew the incredible achievements they would try to describe could not capture the experience of seeing it in person.

Marshall Ed Randolph was among those congratulating Mason. With a handshake, he smiled and said, "You ready to earn your paycheck now?"

CHAPTER 8

"Whatcha got in mind?' Mason asked.

"We got word from a wolf trapper who works the Broadview Mountains that he saw smoke coming from the chimney of an old cabin back on the Musselshell River."

"Squatters?" Mason guessed.

"That's what he thought," Randolph agreed, "so he checked it out. What he saw was Lonnie Jones and another feller he didn't recognize," Randolph explained. "So he high-tailed it out and passed the word along."

"You're kidding me," Mason said. "Lonnie Jones? He's got a hell of a nerve showing up in these parts."

"I know," said Randolph. "You'd think he would stay clear of somebody whose already put a bullet in him. He's probably laying low till he heals up. Figures nobody's gonna know he's even up there."

"Well, if that don't beat the tar off a shovel," Mason said. Randolph got right to the point.

"Musselshell River is your jurisdiction. We let him slip away once. I suggest you go get him now while the gettin's good."

"I'm short a deputy," Mason said. "Thorn's been gone six months now."

"How much longer you figure?"

"Don't know," said Mason. "I Just got a letter from him. He may not be coming back." Randolph shook his head and sighed.

"Well, you can't wait any longer. Get yourself a new deputy, and get back to work." The marshal shook hands with Mason. "Oh, and nice shootin' out there today." Then he saddled up and rode back to town.

Mason knew he had to have help if he was going to bring in Lonnie Jones. He figured he'd better talk it over with Sam Stokes. When the crowds dispersed, he took Sam aside.

"Whatcha doin' for dinner?" he asked.

Sam thought Mason might be angling for a little celebration.

"Elinor's expecting me home before dark, but I might be tempted to join you if there is a steak involved and you're paying."

"I got prize money to burn," Mason smiled.

The two made their way back into town and found an open table at Huntley's Diner. While the cooks were building a couple of steaks, Mason got right to the point.

"I got a letter from Thorn," he began, pulling the envelope from his back pocket.

"You did? Why didn't you tell me?" Sam asked.

"I'm tellin' you now. It wasn't exactly good news, and I just needed to think about it before sayin' anything," Mason explained.

"Well, let's have it. Wha'd he say?" Sam said. Mason opened the letter and handed it to Sam to read.

The letter said...

Mase – If you're reading this letter, you obviously haven't got yourself killed yet from runnin' down outlaws, and I didn't get myself killed neither playing soldier. If you're still holding my deputy spot open for me till I get back, I might be a touch longer than expected. I'm done with soldiering, but Colonel Roosevelt must have a notion about me, 'cause he's gone into politics and offered me a job on his security detail. He intends to run for Governor of New York. If he can manage that state the way he handled his troops down in Cuba, I expect he'll do just fine. Leaving for New York in the morning. I'll wire you my new address when I get settled.

---Thorn

Sam closed the letter. "Well I'll be damned," he muttered. "Who'd of thought Thorn would take a job wet nursing a politician?"

"I know," Mason agreed. "It don't seem like him, but there you go."

"So, what are you gonna do?" Sam asked.

"I don't know. I've been holding his deputy position open kinda hoping he'd be back to claim it." Mason looked out the window of the diner as if searching for the answer on the other side of the glass. Then he drew Sam near.

"Lonnie Jones's holding up on the Musselshell River. I gotta go bring him in."

"Well, I'd offer to help, but I doubt that's what you need," Sam said.

"No, I gotta hire a deputy for this, but thanks," Mason smiled.

"Got anyone in mind?" Sam asked.

"I'm thinking Luke Cutter," Mason said. Sam nodded. "Good choice." Then he thought for a moment.

"I tell you what – why don't you mix a little business with pleasure," Sam began to scheme. "Lord knows I need to get out of the house, and we're overdue for a little elk hunting. Take me along on your manhunt and we'll make time for both." Mason squinted a bit.

"I'm not sure about that. Lonnie Jones's not God's little angel. He'll eat you up faster than a snake in a bucket of mice."

"I know, but this is not a two-man job. You need a third man to slam the back door shut so he can't sneak out again. That's me." Mason was not convinced. Sam made one more plea.

"You may not understand this, but when you get to be my age you'll discover that if you squeeze all the risk out of life, what's left ain't worth remembering." Mason chewed on those words for a moment then said, "I'll let you know."

Luke Cutter was a fearless young buck who was presently working as payroll guard for the Northern Pacific Railroad. It was his job to discourage train robberies with grit and guts. More than once he squashed evildoers with such courage that folks thought he had a little bit of a death wish. Off the clock he was as likable a feller as you could ever ask for, always ready with a joke and a smile.

Mason got to know him on the rare occasions Luke had to escort the few dunderheads who survived their ill-conceived train robbery attempt. He seemed slow to rile and quick to react, qualities that Mason prized. When Luke ended his shift at the Coulson train depot, Mason was waiting for him.

"Can I buy you a drink?" Mason smiled.

At the Crystal Palace Saloon Mason laid it all out for Luke.

"I don't expect you to fill Thorn's shoes, but I do need you to take his place."

"I never did ask why he left. Figured it was none of my business," said Luke. "Just tell me straight – what's my odds of living to 35?"

"I don't know – I ain't got there yet myself," said Mason. "Why don't we just figure it out together?" Luke nodded.

"I ain't askin' you to be reckless," Mason added.

"And I ain't lookin' to get killed," Luke said.

"Then I think we understand each other." They shook hands.

"You got yourself a deputy," Luke said. "So, what's next?"

Mason smiled and looked him in the eye. "How's about a little elk hunting?"

CHAPTER 9

Early Sunday morning Mason and his new deputy Luke Cutter rode up to the front yard of Sam Stokes house, just south of town, with their pack horse in tow. Mason had his Sharps '74 rifle and his Winchester slung in his saddle. Luke preferred his Henry rifle. The action was simple, reliable, and not prone to jamming.

Mason saw Sam's horse tied at the hitching post, saddled and ready to go. Neither bothered to dismount, expecting Sam to open the front door at any moment. Instead, Sam's wife, Elinor, opened the door and stepped out, wiping her hands with a small towel.

"Mornin', Elinor," Mason said with the tip of his hat. Elinor eyed him over and gave a look at the pack horse. Leg irons were hanging from the pack saddle.

"Elk hunting, you say?" She asked, glancing back at Mason. He gave her a sheepish smile.

"We hope so," he replied. Sam appeared at the front door with his rifle in hand and saddle bag over his shoulder.

"We set to go?" Sam asked.

"I expect," Mason said. Sam lashed down his saddle bag and slid his rifle into its scabbard, then mounted up.

"Mason," Elinor called out.

"Ma'am?" Mason replied.

She drilled him with a withering stare. "You be back by Friday. My husband and I are visiting my sister over in Glendive and I'm not going to miss that train," she said.

"Understood," Mason assured. She was not impressed with that answer.

"It has been my experience that with one boy there is one brain," She stated, then looking at Luke, she continued. "Two boys – half a brain." Finally eyeing Sam, "Three boys – no brains." Sam knew better than to reply. Mason gave her a polite smile.

"Always a pleasure, Elinor," he said. She was not finished. As if to further humiliate Sam in front of his friends, she issued a warning.

"Sam, if you're not back by Thursday I'm going to shred all of your books and burn them in the front yard." Then she smiled as if she were just kidding.

Sam made no reply. He merely gave her a nod, then tugged his reins and the three were on their way. Mason did not know whether or not to take Elinor's threat seriously. He knew that Sam kept an extensive library of reading material in his house. Now and then he sought to edify Mason with a quote from Shakespeare when the moment was fitting. Once they were out of Elinor's earshot Mason delicately turned to Sam.

"Sam, she was just kidding about burning your books, wasn't she?"

"My dear boy, many a true word is spoken in jest, for a man may say full sooth in game and play," Sam replied. Luke turned and gave Sam a quizzical look, expecting a translation, and Mason pondered for a moment.

"Shakespeare?" Mason asked.

"Chaucer," Sam said, and without further ado, they made for the hills.

SUNDAY - Mason decided to try to catch an elk before crossing over to the Musselshell River. He didn't know how cooperative Lonnie Jones might be if they chained him up first then asked him to sit tight while they hunted elk.

As they rode along the trail, Luke noticed Sam's Winchester slung in his saddle.

"You any good with that rifle?" he asked.

"I always hit my target," Sam replied.

"Really?" Luke was dubious.

"Yes, sir. I shoot first then whatever I hit I call the target." Luke smiled.

As the trail took them into the foothills, Mason gave Luke a few pointers.

"We'll mostly find elk in the mountains, but in the winter when food is scarce, they'll come down to the foothills. They've got good eyes and keen ears, but their sense of smell is their best defense. They can smell us coming, so you gotta keep your face to the breeze."

They rode deep into the back country where elk were known to thrive. Mason and Sam usually got lucky with spotting a herd before too long, which made choosing their prey easy. Not today.

The sun was about to dip behind the mountain peak, bringing the day's adventure to a halt. Near the bend in a creek the trio pitched camp for the night. Sam looked for dry wood while Mason made a fire and Luke filled their canteens.

After a dinner of canned meats and peaches, the three enjoyed some hot coffee and settled in for the night. Sam leaned against a rock near the campfire with his reading glasses on his nose and a book in his face. Mason tried to read the name of the book without Sam's notice but finally gave up.

"Whatcha readin', Sam?" Sam flipped the book closed and displayed the front cover.

"It's called T*he Adventures of Sherlock Holmes*, written by a British fellow name 'Arthur Conan Doyle." said Sam.

"What's it about?" asked Mason.

"You'd like it. It's about a fictional character with an amazing eye for observation and logical thinking that he uses to solve crimes."

"So he's a lawman?" Mason asked.

"Well, yes, kind of, in a way. He was what they called a consulting detective. He was quite brilliant."

"Was he handy with a gun?" asked Luke from underneath the brim of his hat pushed down over his nose.

"Well, yes," Sam replied, "but this Holmes fellow was more of a master of observation."

"How exactly does that compete with a Colt .45?" Luke pressed.

Sam smiled good naturedly as he turned to a page in

the book. "Here, in one place he explains the importance of observation to solving crimes—

'By a man's finger nails, by his coat-sleeve, by his boot, by his trouser knees, by the callosities of his forefinger and thumb, by his expression, by his shirt cuffs—by each of these things a man's calling is plainly revealed. That all united should fail to enlighten the competent enquirer in any case is almost inconceivable.'

Sam turned to Mason with a self-satisfied grin. "You see?" he said. Mason thought deeply for a moment, then finally shrugged his shoulders.

"See what?" he asked.

"That's what made Sherlock Holmes such an extraordinary investigator," he explained.

"Because he looked at people's finger nails?" Mason asked.

"Well, yes. The point is that the clues to solving a crime are all found in the details that are readily observable to anyone with an eye to pay attention."

Luke chimed in. "A bullet in the chest and a smoking gun in the hand of the man still standing – that's clues enough for me, and any judge and jury." Sam looked at Luke with a pitying gaze.

"Luke, I don't even know where to begin with you."

Mason smiled at Luke's formula to detective work, then turned to Sam.

"Toss me that book when you're done. I reckon I might just have a look," Mason said. Sam closed the book and handed it to Mason.

"It's all yours."

MONDAY - The next morning the trio decided to leave their horses tied off by the creek and work their way on foot up the heavily wooded hillside, hoping to drive any elk further up and into a woody draw. With rifles drawn, they carefully hiked through the trees and up the slope. Within an hour they spotted a big one - a bull elk six-by-six, maybe

700 pounds, poised on a distant hogback ridge.

"You take him," whispered Mason to Sam. Sam looked at his own Winchester then squinted at the silhouette on the ridge. It had to be over 300 yards away.

"I ain't hitting anything that far with a Winchester," he said. Then he nodded at Mason's Sharps rifle.

"He's all yours," Sam said. Mason eyed Luke, who held his Henry rifle at his side.

"Luke?" he offered. Luke sighed.

"My Henry's good for 200 yards, tops."

Mason nodded in agreement, settled into a sitting position and rested the barrel of his Sharps on top of a small boulder to help steady his aim. Then he exhaled slowly.

It wasn't long before Luke's horse was hoisting their prize with a rope from the branch of a tree to dress it properly. Sam did the honors. First he gutted it to remove the organs, then carefully skinned the hide. Elk leather was soft to the touch when properly tanned, and fetched a good price in town. From the elk's head he carefully removed the two upper back ivory teeth with pliers, which he liked to make into ear rings and necklaces as a peace offering for Elinor.

Then he removed the loins - some of the best eatin' parts to be had. Next he quartered the elk and wrapped it in breathable cheesecloth to protect it from pesky flies and insects, and to keep the meat cool. Then they loaded it all on the pack horse. He saved a large section of loin to cook over the camp fire.

Come dinner time they all carved a slice from the spit and sat down to enjoy a feast. Mason leaned back on a boulder to properly enjoy his cut of loin. He took a bite and let the flavor play around his taste buds. He sighed. "Is there anything better?" Sam opened the flap of his saddle bag and produced a wine bottle.

"Only if it's served with a proper Italian red," Sam smiled. He uncorked the bottle, took the first swig, and passed it around. Mason favored whiskey, but wine would do just fine in the wild. He savored a swallow, then turned to Sam, nodded and passed the bottle to Luke. Words were not needed. They all knew it just didn't get any better.

The Showdown at Yellowstone

CHAPTER 10

TUESDAY - The next morning, Mason rousted his companions early.

"Let's go, gents, we got work to do," he said as he nudged his sleeping partners. Luke lifted his hat from his eyes and squinted.

"What's up?"

"I saw a line of smoke on the other side of the ridge at dawn," Mason said, pointing to the east. "Chimney or campfire, not for sure which, but that's the direction of the Musselshell River. So, let's saddle up."

With their pack horse loaded, they rode single file over the ridge and down the valley until they reached the Musselshell River. It was a wide flowing river, mostly fed from snow melt, making it close to freezing most of the year. Its banks were mostly rocky, wrapped in tangled vines and hedge rows. The trail along the river's edge was narrow and uneven, giving the horses fits as they fought for solid footing. Mason had the lead, followed by Sam, then Luke with the tethered pack horse at the caboose.

"So, Sam," Luke broke the silence, "Mase tells me that you used to be sort of a doctor."

"I was indeed," Sam answered back. "I was what they might call an unlicensed physician," he offered good naturedly.

"That's good enough," Luke replied, "Cause I got a medical question that's been niggling me for some time."

"At your service," Sam said.

"I think I've got the sneeze, the cough, and the yawn

figured out, but what's the purpose of the hiccup?" Luke asked.

"The purpose?" Sam probed.

"Yeah, you know, what's it for? Why does the body suddenly decide to hiccup?" Luke amplified. Sam could tell by Luke's tone that he was asking in dead earnest, but he had never pondered that physiological question before, and he didn't have a ready answer. He thought for a moment.

"Let me get back to you on that," Sam said. From the front of the line Mason just smiled.

The three made steady progress until they came to a large fallen tree that lay across the trail. The trunk was almost too big for their horses to step over, but with the river on one side and thick vegetation on the other, they had no choice.

Mason dismounted and took his horse by the reins to lead it over the log. Sam attempted to follow suit, but as he began to dismount, his horse mistook his movement as a command to jump the log. The horse reared up to attempt the jump, throwing Sam out of his saddle and into the freezing river. He landed on his back, hitting his head on a cluster of boulders near the river's edge, dazing him into semi-consciousness. Immediately the current swept him up and took him downstream.

Luke saw the mishap and instantly knew that Sam was in grave danger. He leaped out of his saddle with his lariat in hand and ran towards Mason.

"Mase," he shouted, "grab the other end of this rope. I'm going in after him." He quickly took the noose end of the rope and lassoed himself tight, then threw the rope to Mason and jumped into the swift moving current. Mason grabbed the rope and fed it to Luke as he held the other end tight and ran down the riverbank to keep up.

In a minute Luke caught up with Sam's bobbing head and grabbed his collar, then wrapped his arm around him. Mason could see up ahead a tangled web of dead tree branches jammed across the river, almost like the makings of a beaver dam, capturing anything floating in the river and sucking it under. He knew he had to stop his partners before the current swept them into that deadly menagerie.

Running as fast as he could, he carried his end of the rope to a riverbank tree and tied the rope off. In a matter of seconds Luke and Sam slammed into the beaver dam. Now the current tried to suck them under. Mason tried to pull them to shore, but the strength of the current was overpowering. He sat down and wedged his boots against a shoreline boulder and arched his back, pulling for all he was worth, to no avail.

Luke and Sam were wedged against the tree branches. Sam had finally regained his wits and tried to crawl up the mass of branches to get out of the water, but the current would not let him out. Water was splashing over them, causing them to gasp for air. Mason knew they could not hold on for long before exhaustion would overtake them. He looked around frantically for a solution. He needed his horse to pull them out, but he had left it about 50 yards upstream where the incident began.

"I can't pull you out!" he shouted. "I need the horse!" he called out, pointing upstream where the horses quietly grazed on wild grass. Luke nodded and waved him on, as more freezing water splashed over them.

Mason never ran so hard in his life. Seconds counted. He reached his horse and grabbed the reins, turned and ran back to the rope. He scanned the river to see how his comrades were doing. Both were under water, their arms sticking out in a near death grip with the tree branches. Mason untied the rope from the tree, then looped it around his saddle horn, grabbed the bridle and quickly walked the horse back along the trail upstream. Suddenly Luke's and Sam's heads bobbed to the surface and they filled their lungs with fresh air. The horse kept pulling them closer and closer to shore, even as the current fought to hold them captive. In a moment Luke was able to gain some footing, and he hoisted Sam up. The two were finally able to stagger to shore.

They both dropped to the ground exhausted and freezing. Sam coughed up some water as he lay on his back. The two sat up soaking wet and shivering. They stared at each other, then at Mason, in amazement at how quickly fortunes can turn.

There was plenty of daylight left to reach the cabin, but Mason could see that his companions were spent physically and emotionally, so he decided to call it a day and get an early start in the morning. They found a small clearing along the river and set up camp for the night. Mason built a fire. Sam and Luke got out of their wet clothes and warmed themselves by the fire in their long johns. Words were not spoken for an hour.

Finally, Sam turned to Luke. Without speaking, he reached over and squeezed Luke's arm, holding onto it for a moment. That action spoke volumes between men. It said, "I was a goner. You saved my life." Luke gave Sam a firm squeeze on his shoulder in return. It was his reply, which meant, "Think nothing of it. Glad to help."

WEDNESDAY - At dawn the three were saddled up and back on the trail. The hunter's cabin was only a few miles further downstream, and they did not want to take the chance of accidentally running into their quarry, so they began leading their horses up the ravine to higher ground.

The cabin was easy to find. A thin line of chimney smoke could be seen for miles, and marked its location to anyone paying attention. By 8:00 am the three sat on the upper slope of a heavily wooded hillside overlooking the cabin and clearing below. Mason studied the cabin with his binoculars, waiting for a sign of Lonnie Jones.

"What do you see?" asked Luke.

"Someone's chopping fire wood in the front yard, but it's not Lonnie," he replied.

"He might be gone by now, if he was smart," Luke suggested.

"I put a bullet in him three months ago. He might be saddle ready, but--" Mason suddenly stopped talking. The door to the cabin opened and out walked Lonnie Jones, big as day.

"Wait a minute – there he is," Mason said. "I'll be damned."

Luke reached for the binoculars. "Let's have a look."

Luke peered through the lenses to see a tall burly man in

a red plaid shirt sauntering over to the creek to fill his bucket with water.

"So that's Lonnie," he muttered. They sat for several minutes to be sure of the number of people down below. When Mason was satisfied that it was just two, he laid out the plan.

"OK, Sam, you're going to slam the back door shut, just like you said. I want you to ride downstream about a half mile from the cabin. When you are set, fire two shots from your rifle. That will be the signal. Then sit tight and keep your eyes open. I doubt anyone's going to come your way, but you never know."

When Sam was out of sight, Luke turned to Mason.

"That's a mighty risky move to make. What's your plan?"

"You and I are going to make it seem like the 4th Montana infantry just arrived. As soon as Sam gives the signal, they're going to know something's up downstream. Then you and I are going to empty about 20 or 30 rounds into that cabin."

They waited for about 20 minutes for Sam to get into place. Suddenly the pastoral calm of the forest was broken with the distant echo of two ringing rifle shots in rapid order. Lonnie and Pete Sanders were just finishing coffee inside the cabin. Pete was a young kid who used to run with the Donaldson gang. The two met up in a bar in a small town on the Stillwater River, and hatched a plan to work their way east.

"What the hell was that?" asked Pete. Lonnie thought it might be a stray hunter. He went to the window and cracked opened the shutter, when the hillside came alive with rifle fire. Lonnie and Pete dropped to the floor as bullets tore through the window and started chewing up the insides. Suddenly the shooting stopped. Lonnie crawled on his belly to fetch his rifle, and waited.

From the hillside a familiar voice rang out. "Lonnie Jones, you are surrounded. Throw your guns out and step out of the cabin. This is C.J. Mason. You can give up now and turn yourself in, or you can die here. It's your call."

"Mason," Lonnie muttered.

"You know him?" Pete asked.

"We've met."

"Let's get out of here," Pete panicked. He opened the door a crack and was immediately met with five shots that splintered parts of the door. He slammed the door shut and crawled back to Lonnie.

"What are we gonna do? They've got a whole army out there." Lonnie considered his options.

"If I'm goin' down I'm takin' Mason with me," Lonnie said. He put a bullet in me. I owe him." He thought for a moment then set a plan in motion with Pete.

From the hillside Mason and Luke sat for several minutes, eyes and rifles trained on the cabin.

"What are we waiting for?" Luke asked.

"Someplace else you need to be?" Mason answered. He didn't know what to make of the sudden silence and wondered what Lonnie might be up to. They sat for a few more minutes, when they finally saw the cabin door slowly open and a figure appeared in the doorway wearing Pete's clothes.

"Hold your fire," Mason said. "This may be easier than I thought."

From the cabin window rifle fire suddenly erupted. The shots were blind, and seemed only to issue a warning. Luke decided to answer the shots with one of his own. He took aim at the motionless figure in the doorway and put a bullet right in his chest. The figure dropped in the doorway, face down.

"Well, that's one down," Luke said.

Then from the cabin, Lonnie called out.

"OK, I give. I'm coming out." A rifle and pistol were tossed out of the window and Lonnie slowly walked out of the cabin with his arms up.

"Let's go," said Mason. With leg irons in hand, Mason and Luke descended the hill and entered the clearing, guns drawn.

"Get on your belly," Mason ordered. Lonnie complied.

"Keep a gun on him while I cuff him," Mason told Luke. As Mason approached Lonnie, Pete, still very much alive, suddenly appeared in the doorway wearing nothing but his long johns and shot Luke, who spun around and dropped. Pete hastily snapped off a second shot at Mason, but missed. Mason turned and fired twice, both shots hitting Pete in the chest. Pete sank to the earth right beside the mystery figure already lying in the doorway. Mason quickly turned his gun on Lonnie, expecting more foul play. Lonnie just stayed put, cursing under his breath that their scheme failed.

When Mason had Lonnie properly shackled, he walked over to the mystery figure lying in the doorway. Heartsick, he could see close-up that it was nothing more than a stuffed scarecrow of clothes and dirty laundry. Pete and Lonnie had fashioned a prop to simulate a person with Pete's clothes, complete with hat and shoes. With a broom handle, Lonnie held the dummy up in the doorway while Pete fired a few shots from the window. When Luke's bullet pierced the dummy, Lonnie dropped it in the doorway and called out to Mason that he surrendered. He hoped that Pete would shoot Mason first, but he settled for killing Luke, even though it cost Pete his own life.

Mason was devastated at this act of treachery. He walked over and smacked Lonnie with the barrel of his pistol to wipe the smile off his face. Then he sat down and wept.

Mason wrapped up Luke's body in a blanket and loaded him on his horse, along with Pete's body on his horse. Then he placed Lonnie Jones on his horse, head still bleeding from the pistol whipping. He wrapped the leg irons under the horse's belly, with a second set of irons for his wrists, which he ran through the stirrups. With Sam, he made the slow mournful ride back to Sam's house. Not a word was spoken the entire trip home.

THURSDAY - Elinor met them as they arrived at the front porch Thursday afternoon, two dead bodies and a prisoner in tow.

"Well, at least you made it back in time for the train," she said. Sam was outraged at her callous comment.

"Shut up," he said to his wife, as he dismounted, threw his reins over the hitching post, and went inside.

When he got back from his trip to visit Elinor's sister,

Sam went in search of Mason. It took the better part of the afternoon, but he finally found Mason brooding in the 15th Street Tavern. He was sitting at the back table in the shadows. Sam waved down Harry, the bartender.

"Howdy, Sam," said Harry.

"How long's he been here?" Sam asked, pointing to Mason.

"Came in yesterday," said Harry. "I tried to get him to go home last night at closing, but he wouldn't move. What am I 'sposed to do? He's the sheriff."

Sam made his way over to Mason, who was sitting with his back to the wall, staring at his badge lying on the table.

"Been looking all over for you. You hardly ever drink here, but I checked every place else," said Sam, as he took a seat across from Mason.

Mason glanced at Sam for a moment, then continued to study his sheriff's badge on the table. He tried to get the badge to balance on two points unsuccessfully, then gave up.

"Mase, talk to me. I know what's eating you. It's not your fault," said Sam.

"It wouldn'ta happened to Sherlock Holmes," Mason muttered.

"What are you talking about?" asked Sam.

"The great master of observation…you know, that book you gave me. It's my fault Luke is dead," Mason said.

"Horseshit," Sam replied.

"I should have paid closer attention to that stupid dummy lying in the doorway. If I'd have just taken a closer look, you know, observed it. I'd have known it wasn't real, and Luke would be alive."

Sam sighed. "Mason, you do know that Sherlock Holmes isn't real - he's a fictional character. Nobody could do what he did, 'cause he's just made up. You did the best you could under the circumstances."

"Luke's still dead," Mason replied.

"That's because you're in a dangerous line of work. He knew that and he took his chances," Sam said.

"It shoulda been me," Mason sighed.

"It wasn't your time. Everything ain't up to you. That's

your ego talking," Sam urged.

Mason looked deeply into Sam's eyes with a sadness that rose up from the depths of his soul. "Don't you ever look at the bodies on your table and ask yourself why them and not you?" Mason implored.

"Every damn day," Sam nodded. "Some are easy to explain. Some make no sense. All I know is none of us gets out of this world alive. The best you can do is die trying, for to lose life is to lose a thing that only fools would keep."

"Chaucer?" Mason ventured.

"Shakespeare," Sam smiled.

The Showdown at Yellowstone

CHAPTER 11

Thorn followed Teddy Roosevelt around the state of New York in the fall of 1898 as he stumped for the governorship. Thorn provided minor body guard duties but mostly functioned as a glorified baggage handler; from carriage to train and train back to carriage. Thorn disliked his time out of the saddle. They were rarely in one city for more than a day as they criss-crossed New York. In November, Roosevelt won the election by a narrow margin and on January 1, 1899 he officially took office and moved to Albany where the governor's mansion was located.

Thorn was required to dress in suits, eat at the finest restaurants, stay in the finest hotels and sleep on beds with expensive sheets. The glad-handing and deal-making with forced smiles, back room maneuvers and outright falsehoods he observed began to wear on him. He especially rankled at this thing called 'quid pro quo'.

"What the hell is a quid pro quo?" Thorn asked Roosevelt one evening while traveling in their carriage to yet another dinner engagement.

Roosevelt chuckled.

"That, my good man, is the means by which all political rivals are able to function cooperatively with each other. It's a Latin term that means 'this for that'. I'll do something that you want, in return you do something that I want. I'll vote for your legislation, which I would otherwise oppose, if you will vote for my legislation, which you would otherwise oppose."

"Why would you do that?" Thorn asked.

"That's the only way we can get things done in politics," Roosevelt replied.

"Sounds like mutual bribery if you ask me," Thorn muttered. "Ain't you just selling your vote when you do that?" Thorn pressed.

"I hate to describe it in those terms but I have to admit that is exactly what it is," Roosevelt confessed. "In this town there isn't a single piece of legislation that could stand on its own feet. So you push it through with a quid pro quo."

Thorn just shook his head and stared out at the scenery.

"Where I come from we call that selling your soul one piece at a time," Thorn said.

In late fall of 1900 Roosevelt sat down with Thorn to keep him apprised of his political activities.

"I had thought to run for a second term as Governor, but McKinley's Vice President is in very poor health... bad heart. So McKinley needs a new running mate for the upcoming election."

"Don't tell me," Thorn sighed. "You're headed for the White House?"

"I go where I can do the most good," Roosevelt said. "I think I did some good for the state in the last two years, but if I can take my vision to the national level, we can tackle some big issues; monopolies, corruption, land conservation. I've got big plans."

"I respect your intentions," Thorn said. "But this is not what I had planned for my life. Don't you just wish you could get on your horse and ride to where there ain't a single building in sight?"

"I'll admit, I do, but I can't do the nation much good out there for long," Roosevelt explained.

Thorn sighed.

"I'll tag along for now. Maybe I'll find a way to get used to all this," Thorn offered.

Roosevelt campaigned vigorously through the fall. On November 6, 1900 the presidential election was held and McKinley defeated William Jennings Bryan in a landslide. Roosevelt turned his attentions to Washington, DC as the incoming Vice President. He had three months to prepare for his new job, which would begin March 4, 1901. Roosevelt sat down with Thorn with an offer.

"I know you've been restless," Roosevelt began. "But I'd like to persuade you to come with me to Washington in the spring. I need someone like you with roots in the west."

"I appreciate your offer but I don't even know what I'm doin' here. I'm not gonna carry your bags to the White House."

"It wouldn't be like that; how about a spot with the Secret Service?" Roosevelt asked. "It's a highly respected organization that demands very unique skills, but with your military background, and a recommendation from me, I can get you a slot."

Thorn heaved a sigh.

"I need to think about it. I ain't seen the sunrise on the Rockies for three years. I gotta take a few weeks and clear my head."

"Fair enough," Roosevelt nodded. "We got a big dinner coming up in a couple weeks then after that you go on ahead and take a break. Head back to Montana and soak it all up. Just get back here by the end of January to start your training."

"I reckon I can do that much," Thorn agreed.

In mid-December of 1900 a dinner was held in New York City at the Grand Ballroom of the Hotel Waldorf-Astoria to honor the visiting Winston Churchill. Every dignitary and government official who could buy his way in or wrangle a seat was there, including Vice President elect, Teddy Roosevelt. Thorn joined Roosevelt at his request. The evening was an elegant occasion with a full band and exquisite cuisine. These events always wore Thorn's patience thin as tinfoil; the fake pleasantries exchanged by political rivals were an exercise in hypocrisy that chapped Thorn to no end.

Samuel Clemens, the humorist, was in attendance, and after the meal Mr. Clemens stood up to offer a few remarks. Thorn knew the evening was about to get good when Mr. Clemens began by saying, "Ladies and gentlemen, I could not help but notice the extensive representation from the political class among us tonight, not the least of which is our esteemed governor of the state of New York."

He paused to allow the congregation to offer Roosevelt a polite round of applause.

"But tonight we are gathered here to honor Mr. Winston Churchill, who recently won a seat in the British House of Commons," Clemons shared with a nod to the guest of honor.

"Of course, you all know my estimation of politicians. They are much like diapers...both need to be changed often and for the very same reason."

The audience howled with laughter. Even the governor chuckled, though Thorn could not help but notice beads of sweat gathering on Teddy's brow.

Clemens went on.

"You all know my former vocation as a steamboat pilot but I think I might have developed into a very capable pickpocket if I had held public office for a year or two."

Again the crowd roared with laughter. But Thorn was no longer listening, as his thoughts strayed to the Lodgepole pines of Montana.

CHAPTER 12

"Hannah," Mason signaled to the proprietor of the Coulson Diner. "Sam Stokes and I will have our usual table and don't bother with menus. We're having steaks tonight. According to Sam the new century starts tomorrow, so make 'em thick and I want my cow still breathin'."

"Of course, Mr. Mason," Hannah smiled. She was a trim woman in her 50's, the sole proprietor of the Coulson Diner since her husband passed a few years back. She served good home cooking with a cheery smile. She had a soft spot for Mason, who reminded her of her son, who lit out for California to seek his fortune, but came down with a fever and died soon after. She ushered Mason and Sam to the front corner table with a good view of Minnesota Avenue.

"And, what are we drinking tonight to ring in the 20th century?" she asked. Mason suddenly turned to Sam and pointed at Hannah.

"I know we've gone round and round all year about this, Sam," Mason groused. "But it still don't seem right." Sam ignored Mason and turned to Hannah.

"I think the occasion calls for champagne," he winked. Hannah nodded and retired to the kitchen. No sooner had they got comfortably seated, Mason lit into Sam again.

"I know you've tried to explain it to me all year long, but I just don't get it," Mason began. "This whole year has been the year 1900. So, why was this year NOT the 20th century?"

"Well, the rest of the world and simple math says so," Sam replied. Hannah brought over a couple of champagne flutes and they took a sip. Sam savored the bubbly in his mouth for a moment, then smiled and nodded to Hannah his approval.

"I'm going to try to get through to you one more time," Sam began. "The beginning of the new century will actually start tomorrow, January 1, 1901, and here's why." Mason turned his head and stared out the window like a petulant student.

"Just listen," Sam continued. "A century is made up of ten decades, are we agreed?" Mason felt like it was a trick question, but he reluctantly nodded. "When the 10th decade is finished, we begin the new century," Sam reasoned with his confounded logic. "Just understand that the 10th decade began on January 1, 1891 and ends at the end of the year 1900. Therefore, it must follow that the new century must begin on January 1, 1901." Sam leaned back, fully satisfied. Mason turned and looked him in the eye.

"Everything you said may be true, but the fact remains, last year I dated my correspondence in the 1800's, but all this year I dated them '1900'. You can say what you like, but in my book, that makes the year 1900 the start of a new century. 1800. 1900."

With pitying eyes Sam looked at Mason and just shook his head.

"Suit yourself," Sam surrendered. "Doesn't really matter." Mason turned and continued to stare out the window with a vague feeling of discontent that he could not identify.

"What's eating you, anyway? You've been in a mood all day."

"I don't know," Mason grumbled. "This new year is kicking me in the ass. I'm almost 35 and look at me, I'm celebrating New Year's with an undertaker. No offense."

Sam had no words of comfort to offer until his gaze turned to the front door and saw Thorn Hickum standing there with a silly grin on his face.

"Well, lookie what the wind just blew in. If it ain't the prodigal." Sam declared. Mason looked over and saw Thorn looking back. Mason's face suddenly lit up.

"Thorn?" Mason uttered as if doubting his own eyes. "What the hell are you doin' here?" Thorn sauntered over to the table.

"I just happened to be in the neighborhood..."

"Did they run out of whiskey in New York?" Mason retorted.

"No, it just lacks the proper company to drink with," Thorn replied. Looking at the empty chair he pointed. "You got room for one more?"

"Well, we were saving it for the king of Siam, but he ain't showed up yet, so..." Mason shoved the chair over to Thorn with his boot.

"You just passing through?" Sam joined in.

"I had to babysit the governor over Christmas. So I told him I needed three weeks to clear my head someplace where you could smell pine needles. He laughed and told me he didn't want to see me till the end of January," Thorn explained.

"You sure you ain't gotten too soft for the west?" Mason asked. Thorn smiled.

"I ain't gonna lie to you, they got toilet paper on a roll back east now," Thorn confessed.

"We got drinkin' straws now here in Coulson," Sam offered in an attempt at one-ups-manship.

"The day I drink my whiskey out of a straw you can shoot me," Thorn declared. They all had a good laugh.

"Sam, why ain't you home with your wife instead of wasting your evening with this cactus needle?" Thorn asked, pointing to Mason.

"She's visiting her sister in Glendive, thank God." Hannah brought over the steaks Mason and Sam ordered and set her eyes on Thorn.

"Why, Thorn Hickum," she smiled. "You're a welcome sight and that's for sure. How you doin'?"

"Better now," Thorn smiled.

"You're lookin' good," Hannah gushed.

"And you're lookin' sweet as ever. How about a steak for me too," Thorn said.

"Are you sure all those New York City Delmonico steaks haven't spoiled you?" Hannah asked with a sly grin.

"Sweetheart, your steaks take me to church every time," Thorn replied. Hannah laughed.

"You are such a scamp," Hannah chuckled. "1901 is gonna be a good year…I can tell already," Hannah pronounced to the table, then turned back to the kitchen. She promptly brought back a bottle of Old Bushmills Whiskey and three glasses.

"Why, Hannah, you read my mind," Thorn smiled.

"And that's a short book. There ain't much else up there septin' this," she smiled as she poured three drinks.

"That's a fact," Thorn admitted. Like the Three Musketeers, this trio raised their glasses.

"Here's to drinking straws and toilet paper on a roll," Mason toasted.

"Here, here," declared Sam. They all shared a drink and a good laugh.

Whether the stroke of midnight simply announced the start of a new year or heralded the dawn of a new century, Coulson responded with the wildest scenes of raucous demonstrations ever witnessed. The noise of horns, whistles, cannon, guns, and fireworks from early in the evening was eclipsed by the quadrupled efforts of a similar nature that continued into the wee hours, with a steady series of explosions that the old Civil War veterans in town swore were as deafening as the cannonading on Seminary Ridge at the Battle of Gettysburg.

CHAPTER 13

The month of January, 1901 flew by like a dry leaf in a stiff breeze. By the third week Thorn said his goodbyes to Mason, Sam and Montana. On a Friday in late January he got off the train at Washington D.C.'s Union Station and carried his bags to the US Department of the Treasury Building where the Secret Service was headquartered. He stopped by the main desk to pick up a packet of information.

"Welcome to the Secret Service," smiled the receptionist. "We've made arrangements for you to stay at the Stevenson Boarding Home behind the Ford Theater on 10th Street."

"Much obliged," Thorn nodded.

"That packet should explain everything for you. Your training will start Monday. Just get settled in and enjoy the weekend."

Thorn walked over to the Stevenson Boarding Home and got acquainted with the landlord.

"Welcome to the Stevenson," the landlord offered.

Thorn unpacked his bag and opened the training packet for a preview of his life to come.

"Bailey Garrett will be your training officer," he read out loud. "Veteran of the Secret Service for 20 years."

Over the weekend Thorn acquainted himself with the Nation's Capital. He walked the National Mall, marveled at the Washington Monument, the world's tallest stone structure, visited the U.S. National Museum, the Botanical Gardens, walked the steps of the U.S. Capitol building and surveyed his new home town. By Sunday evening he was ready to start his training.

"Where can the condemned man go for his last meal?" Thorn asked his landlord.

"The off-duty agents generally gather around the Hamilton Club of an evening. Good food. Nice drinks. Friendly card games. It's a private club, so take your credentials."

The Hamilton Club was located off the National Mall in a fetching neighborhood. The building was unassuming, with an ivy-covered brick exterior, white window shutters and a handsome front door. A doorman halted Thorn.

"Members only," he advised. Thorn pulled out an envelope from his coat pocket and handed it over. The doorman scanned the document and returned it to Thorn.

"Welcome, Mr. Hickum," he nodded as he opened the door.

Inside, the lounge was warm and inviting. Tables around the bar allowed a gentleman to enjoy a fine meal or engage in card games. Stuffed chairs invited guests to read the newspaper or simply enjoy a cigar. Thorn decided to start at the bar go from there.

"Whiskey," he said to the bartender. Thorn turned around and rested his back and elbows on the bar counter as he surveyed the room. Twenty, maybe thirty gentlemen were gathered in this plush and cordial facility. The atmosphere was subdued and polite. As he sipped his drink, Thorn noticed a guest hunkered at a corner table, alone, nursing a nearly empty bottle of whiskey. Fashionably dressed and well groomed, he was squarely built with a muscular jaw. With a room full of people, he stood out as the only one unaccompanied.

"What's that fella's story?" Thorn asked the bartender, pointing at the solitary figure.

"Oh, that's Bailey Garrett," the bartender replied. "He's been here all day draining that bottle."

"Holy shit," Thorn thought to himself. "That's my training officer. He don't look so good." He held back and watched Bailey stare at the bottle, then pour another sip. His hands were unsteady and his gaze uneven. He appeared to be talking to himself. Thorn had been known to howl at the moon himself, and knew in those dark moments he was not fit for company. So, he decided it best not to intrude on Bailey's private party.

Suddenly Bailey stood up and lifted his glass, as if to make a toast to the entire room, then suddenly realized everything was spinning and began to drop like a freshly cut tree. Thorn leaped to his rescue and caught him on his way down.

"Whoa there…steady," Thorn called out, as he grabbed Bailey and propped him back up. "Maybe you better have a seat and think about it." He helped Bailey back into his chair. Bailey sat and stared back at Thorn.

"Who the hell are you?" he demanded.

"Nobody special," Thorn replied. He thought it best not to add to Bailey's embarrassment by revealing his identity as the very recruit Bailey was about to preside over as his instructor. Bailey squinted for a moment to make the room stop turning.

"Hang on," he said, as he grabbed Thorn's coat sleeve. "I'm not sure I got my sea legs yet." Then he studied Thorn's face. "You look about my age. You 40?"

"37," Thorn said.

"No," Bailey shook his head then sighed. "I'm 45. Can you believe that?"

"I'da never guessed," Thorn said to be polite. The truth was that Bailey looked like shit, the product of heavy drinking and self pity.

"37?" Bailey said. "Well, you got your whole life ahead of you. Me, I'm done. Finished. Twenty years with the agency and I'm still training rookies."

"Maybe I should go," Thorn tried to excuse himself. Bailey grabbed him by the lapel and sat him back down.

"You want to know why?" Bailey continued.

"No," Thorn politely replied.

"Because 20 years ago President Garfield had the misfortune of being shot and killed on my watch." That was a disclosure Thorn wished he had not revealed. Too much information shared with the wrong person.

"I'm sure it wasn't your fault," Thorn commiserated.

Bailey wagged his finger.

"Doesn't matter," he blurted out. "I am shit with the agency. I should have just quit 'cause my career was over." He poured himself another shot of whiskey and downed it. Thorn hoped that Bailey was through talking. But he was wrong by a mile.

"My wife finally had enough of me and I've had enough of me, too." He suddenly turned morose. "She wanted me to work for her father in the clothing business but my father used to make furniture and I was sick of business. I shoulda listened to her but it's too late for me now." He picked up the whiskey bottle, which was now empty, and set it back down.

"I'm 20 years with the agency. I should be section chief by now but you know what I'm doing starting tomorrow morning?" Thorn winced at what he was about to hear. "I've got to start training some damned war hero handpicked by the Vice President. Who the hell does he think he is?"

"I don't know. I really don't know," Thorn muttered.

"So, I'm here getting myself ready for training day," Bailey forced a smile. "I think one more bottle should do it." He raised his hand to get the bartender's attention when the room started to spin again and his arm felt too heavy to lift. A fog settled over his brain and his senses started to dim.

"You OK?" Thorn asked. Bailey tried to stand up, but his balance failed him and he sank to the floor like a boxer who had just been K.O.'d. The bartender came over and helped Thorn pick up Bailey.

"What do we do with him?" Thorn asked.

"Just help me put him in the back room. He'll sleep it off. He probably won't remember a thing in the morning," the bartender said.

"I should be so lucky," Thorn whispered. He wasn't.

CHAPTER 14

Monday morning at 7:45 Thorn sat waiting in the Secret Service classroom. Two other recruits joined him. No one spoke to each other. Thorn half expected Bailey to be a no-show after draining the Hamilton Club's liquor inventory. They all watched the hands on the wall clock slowly move minute by minute. It was so quiet you could hear the shadows creeping along the floor as the sun rose in the sky.

At the stroke of 8:00 a.m. the door flew open and Bailey Garrett marched in like a race horse shot out of a starting gate. With a stack of folders under one arm, he breezed to the lectern where he dropped the folders down, picked up a stick of chalk and turned to the chalkboard. With his back to the class he wrote his name in bold capital letters…'BAILEY GARRETT'. Then he turned and eyed his pupils. When he set eyes on Thorn, he was visibly stunned.

"What the hell are you doing here?" Bailey asked.

"I'm one of your recruits," Thorn replied.

"The hell you are," Bailey responded.

"The hell I am," Thorn shot back. Bailey could not dare let the other two recruits know the self-pitying drunken stupor Thorn had witnessed the night before. But he was furious that he had unwittingly shared such personal history and feelings with an actual Secret Service rookie. Only one thing could make it worse.

"You wouldn't be Thorn Hickum, would you?" Bailey ventured, praying it wasn't so.

"Yes, I am," Thorn calmly replied. Bailey nodded his head.

"Of course you are. Who else could you be?" Bailey bit his lip. The other two recruits looked at each other mystified. Bailey's head was still throbbing from his hangover and he needed this class to be over soon. He turned to the group as a whole.

"Welcome to the Secret Service. My name is Bailey Garrett. I'll be your training officer during your orientation. For the most part you were selected from a large field of candidates because your qualifications set you above the rest. You already come to this agency with skills and experience. We're gonna build on that. Your training is going to be individualized; one-on-one with me. What I say to each of you will be in strict confidence. For now all you need to know is each other's names."

Pointing to the first recruit, Bailey spoke.

"This is Stewart Oakley." Stewart nodded to the other two candidates. He was in his early 20's, lean, clean shaven, and clear-eyed. Bailey continued. "Stewart hails from Virginia, where he just graduated from the Military Academy." He stepped down to the next introduction.

"This is Anthony Howell," Bailey continued. Anthony was in his late 20's, stocky with a thick mustache. "Anthony is a Yale graduate and the son of Brigadier General Nathan Howell." Thorn and Stewart were suitably impressed. Finally, Bailey stepped beside Thorn.

"This is Thorn Hiccup, oh, I'm sorry, I mean Hickum," Bailey began, waiting to see how Thorn would react. Thorn made no reply. Bailey continued. "Thorn comes from cattle country," Bailey scanned Thorn's personnel file, "...where he quit as a wrangler, tried his hand as a deputy and quit, joined the army and was let go after only three months." Thorn was seething on the inside but would not give Bailey the satisfaction of an outburst. You couldn't put a worse face on facts than Bailey just did with Thorn's work history and he knew it.

"All right, then," Bailey concluded, "...I will meet with each of you individually today starting with Mr. Hiccup. Tomorrow we will meet on the gun range, so bring your weapon of choice. Thorn at 8:00, Stewart at 11:00, and

Anthony at 2:00. The two of you are excused." With that, Stewart and Anthony gathered their things and left the classroom. Bailey and Thorn were alone. Bailey sat across from Thorn.

"Why didn't you tell me last night who you were?" Bailey demanded.

"I tried to excuse myself to spare you what little dignity you had left," Thorn snapped back. Bailey could see Thorn was no pushover.

"What was that slimy introduction all about?" Thorn asked.

"I need to know your temperament. How easily you can be offended. Agents have to be in complete control at all times," Bailey answered. Thorn nodded.

"Don't worry. You held up better than most," Bailey added. "Last year one recruit took a swing at me when I made fun of the clothes he was wearing. He flunked his first test and didn't even know it."

Bailey opened Thorn's folder. "I read your file," Bailey continued. "Rough Rider under Roosevelt, marched up San Juan Hill."

"Kettle Hill, actually," Thorn interrupted.

"You think you're something. Well, I think you're just a cocky little bastard. You got a free ticket to the agency 'cause you got connections, that's all. Well, that may have gotten you in the door, but let's just see how well you can cut it. You think you got something on me because of last night. But you don't got shit. But here's what I got…you don't make the grade and I'll see to it you get sent packing. Roosevelt or not. You understand?"

"Yes sir," Thorn said.

"Tomorrow morning at the gun range. Bring your piece, and I got a little assignment for you tonight. I want you to bring with you a list of the five most important things you think you need to win a gun fight," Bailey said.

Thorn stood to leave.

"See you at the Hamilton Club," Thorn saluted as he left.

The next morning Thorn arrived at 8:00 with a Colt .45 and his list.

"Let's have a look at your piece," Bailey said with his hand extended. Thorn had already been through this little exercise with Mason years ago; he was ready. He passed his gun over to Bailey, who examined it, checked the chamber and barrel, all clean and well oiled.

"I can see that you know how to take care of your weapon. And, you've been to war, so I know you aren't shy about killing. How good are you with a pistol?" Bailey asked.

"Set'em up," Thorn replied.

"We'll start at 10 feet and go to 50 feet. You aren't gonna be shootin' anybody farther away than 50 feet in this line of work," Bailey assured Thorn.

"Where have I heard that before?" Thorn mused to himself. The target assistant set up a row of six life-sized wooden human silhouettes with bulls eyes painted on their chest.

"OK," Bailey said. "You've got ten seconds to clear leather and hit the bulls eye in each of the six targets."

"From ten feet?" Thorn asked just to be sure.

"That's right," Bailey said. "On three, two, one, GO!"

Thorn drew his gun and quickly dispatched his six targets. And, he did the same at 20, 30, 40, and 50 feet.

"OK, so you can shoot," Bailey admitted. "How about when they're shooting back?"

They moved to a firing stall with a back stop that absorbed pistol fire.

"Now, I'm going to be shooting at you, to your right and left. Try to keep from getting rattled and still hit your targets." Thorn reloaded and waited for the signal to begin. Bailey nodded and Thorn drew his gun. While he shot his targets, Bailey returned fire from a bunker above the targets, coming within a few feet of Thorn. It was enough to rattle even the steadiest of hands, but Thorn drew on his battlefield experience to remain calm and maintain his concentration. Bailey was impressed.

"You scored higher than most, I'll give you that," Bailey admitted. "Let me see your list." Thorn handed Bailey his list of essential gun fighting rules, drawn on his seven years as a lawman. Bailey read them out loud:

1. *There is no such thing as cheating in a gun fight. Winning is all that counts.*
2. *There are only four things you should be doing in a gun fight – shooting, reloading, communicating with your opponent, or seeking cover.*
3. *Watch their hands. In God we Trust. Everyone else keep your hands where I can see them.*
4. *Don't stand still for very long. Keep moving – side to side if possible.*
5. *A gun fight is not a game. Shoot to kill.*

Bailey nodded his approval. "Best list I've seen so far. Now, come inside with me. I want to show you something." They walked inside the building to a demonstration room. On the table were experimental items that all agents needed to become familiar with.

"Take a look at this," Bailey said as he picked up a padded vest. "This here is a bullet-proof vest. Ever seen one?" Thorn was incredulous.

"What do you mean?" he asked.

"I mean bullet-proof," Bailey repeated. "This vest is made of 30 layers of silk. It will actually stop a bullet from penetrating."

"You must be joking," Thorn frowned.

"I'll prove it," said Bailey. He put on the vest as Thorn looked on in utter skepticism. Bailey handed Thorn his pistol and took his position in a shooting stall.

"Go ahead – shoot me in the chest," Bailey said, as he put his hands behind his back.

"NO – are you crazy?" Thorn said. He lowered his weapon and backed away.

"Do it!" Bailey demanded.

"No. I don't care for you much but I ain't gonna shoot you," Thorn confessed. Bailey gave up and took the vest off and put it on a hanger, and hung it on the wall.

"All right, you damn sissy," Bailey sneered. He took the gun out of Thorn's hand, turned around and fired at the vest. The impact of the bullet knocked the vest and hanger off the wall. They both walked over to the vest to inspect it. Sure enough, the bullet never passed through the silk barrier. Thorn was amazed.

"I wouldn't have believed it if I hadn't just seen it with my own eyes."

"Are you convinced now?" Bailey chided.

"I s'pose," Thorn said.

"Gangsters are starting to use these now, so you need to be aware of them." Bailey explained. Then he put the vest back on and took his original position at the firing wall. "OK, now shoot me," he ordered. Thorn could hardly make himself aim his pistol at Bailey, but he slowly leveled the barrel at his instructor, then hesitated.

"Shoot it!" shouted Bailey. Thorn grit his teeth and pulled the trigger. The impact of the bullet knocked Bailey back a few feet, but he was otherwise unharmed.

"See!" he said. Thorn breathed a sigh of relief that he had not killed his training officer. Bailey laughed and took the vest off and handed it to Thorn.

"Now you put it on," he said. Thorn thought he might be kidding.

"I don't think so," Thorn replied with a nervous chuckle. Bailey became serious.

"I said put it on. It's not a request." Thorn stared into Bailey's eyes to be certain that he was deadly earnest. "Every agent has to do this."

Thorn slowly put on the vest and fastened it tight around his chest. His mind began to wonder if this was just an elaborate scheme to permit Bailey to kill him in a training "accident" with no consequences. "How stupid am I going to feel if he kills me?" Thorn thought to himself. But it seemed his manhood was at stake, so he took a deep breath and waited for the moment of truth.

He didn't have to wait long. Bailey pulled the trigger and the shot knocked Thorn off his feet. It felt like he had been kicked by a mule, and he got back on his feet wondering if he broke a few ribs. He hadn't, but he knew he was going to ache for a few days.

The session was almost over, but Bailey had one more item to show Thorn.

"Follow me," Bailey said, as they walked to an adjoining building. Inside this building was a large collection of tables where experimental explosive devices were in various stages of assembly.

"Take a look at this," Bailey pointed to a suitcase. "What do you see?" Thorn thought this might be a trick question.

"I think I see a suitcase," he ventured.

"You're right – that's what it looks like, but open it up," Bailey said. Thorn opened the lid to the suitcase to reveal explosives packed tight with wires and a timer clock. He was intrigued by the intricacies of this deadly creation.

"This is the kind of stuff we're dealing with now. It's a suitcase bomb that's triggered with a timer," Bailey explained. "You just set the clock's alarm for when you want it to go off, close the lid and carry the bomb to wherever you want it to do maximum damage. Slide it behind a couch. Then leave." Thorn was speechless. He looked at Bailey.

"You gotta keep your eyes open. Tick tock," Bailey smiled.

The Showdown at Yellowstone

CHAPTER 15

The training continued for the next few months. It included tactical training, hand-to-hand combat, procedural instruction, and a review of departmental policies and procedures. Thorn was taught methods of observation, searching a crowd for potential threats, how to disarm a suspect, and if needed protecting the President with his very own body as a shield. Little did he know, those skills would be put to the test much sooner than expected.

Thorn's training ended in May, and he was assigned to various security details for President McKinley; luncheons, speeches, visit to schools and hospitals. McKinley saw no need for such tight protection, and feared the public would misinterpret his wall of defense as crass elitism. At times he insisted that he be allowed to mingle with the crowds, which made it virtually impossible to protect him.

Bailey met with Thorn in late August.

"We're going to Buffalo," he announced. "The President intends to visit the Pan American Exposition for a few days in September, and we've been assigned to his security detail."

The Pan American Exposition of 1901 was envisioned to be a good will event to create better understanding among the American republics, and to showcase the latest technology and innovations destined to make life better for everyone in the 20th century. Buffalo, New York, was chosen for the event because it was such a huge tourist destination, with Niagara Falls nearby, and the enormous population in the area. Buffalo was the 8th largest city in the United

States, which promised to provide a throng of visitors. The selection of Buffalo ultimately exceeded all expectations. In the six months the exposition was open, over 8 million visitors passed through its gates.

President McKinley insisted on attending the event, which he thoroughly supported. He called such expositions "the timekeepers of progress. They record the world's advancement. They stimulate the energy, enterprise, and intellect of the people; and quicken human genius."

The newest inventions were on display in the exhibit halls. Thomas Edison's new x-ray machine amazed visitors, and the new electrograph made telegraphing pictures over the wire possible. The event was truly a cavalcade of mechanical marvels that offered a glimpse of an exciting future.

———————

Leon Czolgosz knew only one thing for sure, President McKinley had to die. He sat in his small boarding room with nothing to do but stare at the ceiling and think. He fancied himself an anarchist; a political philosophy adhered to by recent killers of foreign leaders. In secret meetings with fellow sympathizers, he agreed that McKinley was the national symbol of oppression. Alone in his room, Czolgosz could think of no other way to end his own suffering than to take the life of the leader of the country that was responsible for all his miseries.

Leon was born in Detroit in 1873, the son of Polish immigrants. As an adult, Leon worked in a Cleveland factory until he lost his job in a labor dispute in 1893. From there, he worked off and on, attending political meetings, trying to understand the reasons for the economic turmoil of the day. He and his compatriots concluded that the government was to blame and should be abolished.

Leon thought of ways to get close enough to the President to finish him off. Two previous Presidents had already been shot at close range; Lincoln and Garfield. The method seemed fool proof. He began following McKinley around Washington, from a distance, observing his routines. He noticed that McKinley walked to church on Sunday alone, and occasionally took rides with his wife in a carriage without any guards. Still, Leon found it almost impossible to anticipate McKinley's moves with enough advance notice to be in position at the key moment to do the deed.

That's when he read in the newspaper the President's plans to visit the Pan American Exposition. He knew why such announcements were published; to entice more people to attend the exposition and swell ticket sales. He sneered at the foolish recklessness of these corrupt capitalists.

In late August, Leon moved to Buffalo and began plotting assassination scenarios. He thought he might catch the President in an unguarded moment when he and his wife disembarked the train upon their arrival in Buffalo. With his .32-caliber revolver he sat at the Buffalo train station on September 4 waiting with the crowd for the presidential couple to arrive.

Bailey Garrett and Thorn rode the train with McKinley, part of the security detail from Washington D.C. A cannon was positioned on the Buffalo platform to fire a salute to the President upon his arrival. Unfortunately, it was set too close to the track. When the train pulled into the station and the cannon was fired, the blast concussion blew out several windows in the train, terrifying everyone. A dozen people on the platform thought the explosion was a bomb, and shouted 'Anarchists!' sending the Secret Service swarming.

As McKinley stepped down from the train, Bailey and Thorn followed close behind. Czolgosz eased forward. He weaved his way through the masses with his gun hidden in his coat pocket, looking for an unguarded moment. The President was busy greeting well wishers, shaking hands and chuckling, with Bailey and Thorn on either side. Leon stopped a few yards away and waited, watching. Those damned secret service men were circled around him like a sheep fence. They were so easy to spot, all so smartly dressed, he thought. As Thorn scanned the crowd he noticed Leon just standing and staring, and became suspicious. Without taking his eyes off of Leon, Thorn's gun hand slipped down to his revolver as he took a few steps in Leon's direction. Leon saw him approaching and quickly ducked behind a clutch of ladies, then crisscrossed his way through the crowd, off the platform and down an alley.

Leon cursed himself for missing his moment. He would have to wait for another opportunity. He knew he had only one chance, because he would certainly be caught and killed even if his attempt on the president failed, so he had to get it right. He returned to his boarding room to plot his next move.

"Damn! Damn! Damn!" he hissed as he slammed his fist repeatedly on the small desk.

Once they were off duty for the evening, Bailey and Thorn found a nice restaurant in downtown Buffalo.

"You mind if I ask you a question?" Thorn said.

"Yeah, what?' Bailey answered.

"What happened with President Garfield? What went wrong?" Thorn asked.

"Why? So you can pile on me like everybody else?" Bailey frowned.

"Hey, I ain't taking sides. I just figure if I could learn by it, then something good could come from it," Thorn explained.

Bailey eyed Thorn for a moment. The request seemed reasonable, he concluded. Bailey finished his drink and thought for a moment, trying to decide where the story should begin.

"Let's just say for starters that 20 years ago Presidential security was shit compared to today," Bailey began. "We got almost no advance notice on his whereabouts or travel plans. He might decide to go for a walk to church or a ride in a carriage through the park. And these fools think because they won the election the whole country loves them. They don't much care for us trailing them around or stepping between them and the crowds. But I got my orders, see. Guard the President. Well, that's all fine until the President refuses protection. Then I have to decide who's my boss – the agency or the President. 'Cause either one could fire me if I fail to obey an order." Thorn sat quietly, taking it all in.

"I was just a rookie back in 1881 - 25 years old and just

trying to do my job. It was July 2, 1881, a Saturday. Garfield was scheduled to leave Washington by train that day for his summer vacation. And the news of that was splashed all over every newspaper so's everybody could know his business – friend and foe. It was the weekend so it was my shift. I met the President at the White House to escort him to the train station and beyond, and he had a fit. Refused protection. I didn't know what to do. I begged him not to do this on my shift, but he insisted that this level of protection was intrusive and absurd. He warned me that he would have me fired if I shadowed him."

"What did you do?" Thorn asked.

"They did not cover this in my training. I had no idea, so I let him go. While he was waiting at the train station he was shot twice by a stalker who had already written letters to Garfield and Gen. Sherman threatening to kill the President. And those letters were ignored."

"So, what happened?" Thorn asked.

"In the inquiry I pled my case, and my attorney argued that the agency shared the blame for ignoring the assassin's threats," Bailey said. "In the end I kept my job but the agency never forgot the shame I brought to it, and made it clear I'd be better off just quitting."

"What did they do?" Thorn asked.

"I was overlooked for promotions, given menial jobs, disrespected, ignored, barred from meetings," Bailey listed off the abuse.

"Why didn't you just quit?" Thorn asked.

"At first, I thought it would all blow over and be forgotten, but after a few years of it, I started to get pretty chapped about the abuse, and decided not to give them the satisfaction of leaving. Eventually I knew too much about the agency's dirty laundry, and they couldn't afford to let me go. So here I am today – too miserable to stay, too dangerous to fire."

"You're just a powder keg with a lit fuse," Thorn said.

"I tell you, it wouldn't take much to push me over the edge," Bailey muttered.

The Showdown at Yellowstone

CHAPTER 16

The next morning at 6:00 A.M., Bailey Garrett awoke to a knock at his hotel room door. Half asleep, he cracked the door open. It was John Hawkins, the Secret Service Exposition team leader. He was a 15-year veteran of the agency and straight as an arrow. Well respected by the other men and a good strategist, he focused on solutions when others were content to point out the problems.

"Meeting downstairs in 15 minutes," He said. "We got a situation."

The hotel meeting room was full of agents barely dressed and searching for coffee. Hawkins hushed everyone. Thorn stood along the back wall.

"The original program called for President McKinley to greet the public at a reception at the Temple of Music later today," Hawkins began. "I've tried twice to cancel that event and each time the President has put it back on the program. We've told him over and over again that the venue is not safe but he is not taking this seriously. This morning I urged him one last time to cancel the reception but his answer was, 'Why should I? No one would wish to hurt me.'"

The agents shook their heads and murmured to each other. Hawkins raised his hand.

"I know…I've done everything I can. Now, we are just going to have to do what we're paid to do…protect the stupid son-of-a bitch."

"How we gonna do that?" asked one of the agents. "This damn 'meet 'n greet' has been advertised in all the papers for weeks. The whole country knows he's gonna be here.

Everybody with a grudge and a gun is gonna line up for crack at him."

The others mumbled their agreement.

"Everybody just shut up," Hawkins growled. "The gates open at 8:30. I've already asked for extra help from the Buffalo Police, the military and the County Sheriff. We've pulled in agents from three states for extra manpower. I want two men at every gate to watch for weapons."

Another agent interrupted.

"What are we supposed to do? Frisk 100,000 people?" he griped.

"You're gonna stop anyone who looks suspicious and turn 'em around, that's all there is to it," Hawkins answered. "Then we're gonna surround the President with so much protection he's gonna gag."

"Good luck with that," Bailey muttered under his breath. Hawkins went on.

"The worst of it is gonna be that damn reception line this afternoon, where every Jack Henry and his dog are gonna try to shake the President's hand," Hawkins said. "I want agents behind him and agents in front of him. I want agents all the way down that reception line, out the building, and down the street."

The agents could see it was going to be a long day. Hawkins got very sober.

"I'm only gonna say this once, so listen good," he said. The room hushed. "Twenty years ago this agency made a fatal mistake by allowing the President to walk unescorted to a train station."

He paused to study the faces in the room. Every eye was on him, even though Bailey felt like every eye was on HIM...and not in a good way.

"Now we know better, even if the current President doesn't. We're gonna get through this day and we're gonna go home tonight with pride knowing we safeguarded the symbol of our nation's greatness. Now, let's get to work."

The meeting ended and everyone shuffled off to get dressed and man up. Bailey took Thorn aside.

"Don't forget to bring your vest...we drew bodyguard

duty," Bailey said. Thorn knew what that meant; they would be side by side with the President, the last line of defense against an attacker. Bailey saw this moment as his opportunity for redemption. Thorn saw it as a possible suicide mission.

"I can do it," Thorn gave himself a kick in the pants. "If I could run up San Juan Hill, I can sure as hell do this."

The temperature was in the 80's and humid, and the heavy bullet-proof vest added to Thorn's discomfort. He began sweating before noon, wiping his forehead with his coat sleeve until it was soaked with perspiration. By the afternoon the entourage moved to the Temple of Music, where the reception was scheduled. This monstrous ornate brick structure was designed after the Italian Renaissance with a concert hall that seated 2,000 and a flamboyant dome that rose 180 feet above the ground.

Inside the Temple, McKinley took his position in front of a speaker's platform, draped from behind with American flags. Gregarious and charming, he extended his hand to one and all. Bailey and Thorn were assigned to watch the President's back, to prevent anyone from sneaking up from behind. So, essentially their backs were to McKinley, leaving other agents to watch the action from the front.

Leon Czolgosz stood in line and counted the people between him and the President. Dressed in a dark suit and wearing an innocent expression, he looked younger than his 28 years and blended in with all the other well wishers. He had waited for more than two hours in 82 degree heat for his turn to shake hands. The humidity brought out everyone's handkerchief to wipe the sweat from their brow. Ordinarily, strangers approaching the President were required to clearly show their empty hands, but today that rule was suspended to give everyone permission to hold their hanky for last minute preening. Leon observed this violation of protocol, and took advantage of it by slipping his gun out of his pocket and wrapping his handkerchief around it. Amazingly, no agent was the least bit aroused at the sight of his wadded handkerchief wrapped around his hand.

Other conditions conspired to place McKinley at

his greatest peril. A close friend of the President stood to his immediate left to introduce him to any dignitaries, blocking Thorn's peripheral vision of McKinley. Soldiers and detectives clogged the aisle looking for danger, making it ironically impossible to spot the assassin approaching.

McKinley shook hands at the rate of 50 people per minute, gripping their hands first so as to both guide them past him quickly and prevent his fingers from being squeezed. The Secret Service men looked suspiciously at a tall, swarthy man who appeared restless as he walked towards the President, but breathed a sigh of relief when he shook hands with McKinley without incident.

The next in line was Leon. His right hand was wrapped in a handkerchief, as if injured. Seeing this, McKinley reached to shake his left hand instead. As the two men's hands touched at 4:07 pm, the assassin shot McKinley twice in the abdomen with a .32 revolver concealed under the handkerchief. Thorn heard the muffled shot and immediately recognized the sound.

"Gun!" he shouted, as he turned around to see McKinley lurching forward. As onlookers gazed in horror, Czolgosz prepared to take a third shot, when Thorn and several other agents leaped on him and took him to the ground, wrestling the gun away. Bailey ran to McKinley, who staggered backwards and to the right. Bailey grabbed him to prevent his falling, and guided him across the stage to a chair. McKinley turned his head to see a pile of men punching the assassin, some hitting him with rifle butts.

"Don't hurt him," McKinley mercifully called out. Bailey struggled to control the hefty bulk of McKinley's frame. He called out to Thorn.

"I need some help." Thorn unraveled himself from the pile and raced to Bailey's side. The two laid McKinley gently to the ground. Bailey turned savagely to Thorn.

"How could you let this happen?" he blurted out. Thorn looked back at Bailey, dumbfounded.

CHAPTER 17

Once McKinley was settled comfortably in the hospital, the steely-eyed director of the Secret Service, John Wilkie began an excruciating inquiry to understand how this catastrophe could have occurred right under their noses. He was a well groomed man; almost what you might call a dandy, with a handlebar mustache and his hair parted in the middle and slicked down behind his ears. He knew that, rightly so, the American public was going to crucify the Secret Service for yet another Presidential security failure. It seemed that about every twenty years or so a President was getting shot and for damn sure, not only was the shooter going to pay, but somebody in the agency was going to jail too.

Wilkie called a general meeting with all the agents assigned to the Presidential detail that day.

"First, before we get started, this was found on Bailey Garrett's desk," Wilkie began. He held up a colt .45 revolver with a wooden grip for everyone to see. The wood handle had two large notches carved into it; obviously commemorating two kills, Garfield and McKinley. Bailey was not amused by the anonymous prank gift and neither was Wilkie.

"If I find out who did this, he'll be sorry he ever joined the agency," Wilkie stated. "Now, let's get down to the business at hand. I want to know who did what, where and why."

At first, the field agents wanted to blame McKinley himself and his blatant disregard for caution. One agent pointed out that they had repeatedly tried to cancel the public reception, but McKinley insisted on it.

"The old blowhard was convinced that nobody would want to hurt him," said one agent.

Wilkie knew that blaming the President for getting shot wouldn't quite wash with the American people. He began probing into any protocols that might have been overlooked. Finger pointing and name blaming commenced, as every agent on duty that day made excuses for his conduct and offered up his fellow agents as incompetents. Front line agents blamed the back line agents, and back line agents displayed righteous outrage at the bungling of the front line agents. And the reception line agents blamed everyone and everything from the angle of the sun to the pavilion florist to the food venders.

One agent recalled that Bailey and Thorn were the closest to the President and should have been able to stop the assassin. All eyes turned to Bailey and he suddenly feared for his job, if not his life. He had already suffered shame and professional stagnation in the wake of the Garfield assassination twenty years earlier. He quickly came to his own defense.

"Yes, Thorn and I were the closest to the President but we were standing behind him watching his back. We were in no position to see anyone approaching him from the front. That would have been Agent Saunders' job."

Saunders, a veteran agent with his own reputation to protect, shot back.

"Now wait a minute. Wasn't Thorn actually to the side of the president? He should have been in the best position to see."

Bailey suddenly saw the scapegoat everyone was looking for. Even though he knew Thorn was in no better position to spot the shooter than himself, he was ready to sell Thorn down the river to protect his own neck.

"You're right," Bailey agreed. "Thorn was more to the side of McKinley and should have seen it coming."

Thorn was not in the meeting to defend himself. He was still at the President's bedside in the hospital. No one explained to him the rules of the blame game. He who is not in the room takes the fall. The inquiry ended with the designation of the sacrificial lamb; Thorn Hickum. Bailey took Mr. Wilkie aside with a request.

"I would appreciate it if you didn't name me as the agent who reported his dereliction of duty. I worked with Thorn during his training and naming me might make it impossible for the two of us to continue a professional relationship."

The request seemed reasonable and Wilkie nodded his head in agreement.

John Wilkie brought Thorn into his office to deliver the verdict.

"Mr. Hickum, please have a seat," he began with a solemn tone. Thorn took a chair opposite Wilkie's desk. "Your place here with the Secret Service was at the recommendation of Mr. Roosevelt and your military record gave us great hopes for your future here. But after your failure to adequately protect the President at the Pan American Exposition, I am forced to take disciplinary action."

"Now, hold on a minute. Are you saying it was my fault?" Thorn asked.

"There are two rules that are necessary to protect the President when he is greeting the public," Wilkie explained as if he were a high school teacher. "The first is to keep the crowd away. The second is that anyone approaching the president should have both hands empty and visible. Both of those rules were broken at the exposition which put the Secret Service at its most ineffective disadvantage. Now, I don't blame you for crowd control but you should never have allowed Leon Czolgosz to approach the President with a handkerchief wrapped around his hand."

"With all due respect, I was standing behind the President and was not in a position to see the assailant approaching. Besides, it was a hot day and people were allowed to carry handkerchiefs to wipe the sweat off their brows," Thorn offered in his defense.

"My investigation confirms otherwise. I am not here to dicker with you. Some of the more vocal members of the agency want to see you in jail, and frankly, the public expects someone to be held accountable," Wilkie continued.

"This is horse shit and you know it," Thorn fumed.

Wilkie chose to overlook Thorn's outburst. He continued.

"Because of your outstanding military record, you are not going to jail. I am prepared to offer you two choices. You can accept a transfer to our counterfeiting division or you can simply resign for reasons of your own choosing."

"Does Roosevelt know about this?" Thorn asked.

"He's been briefed," Wilkie said.

"I think I'll just pack up and leave," Thorn said, "with one request."

"And that being?"

"Mr. Roosevelt and I are personal friends and I would appreciate the chance to say good-bye to him."

"I think we can arrange that," Wilkie nodded.

Roosevelt had been in Vermont with Senator Proctor on the day of McKinley's assassination, but when he heard the news, he raced back to Buffalo, New York, to find McKinley in stable condition. When he was informed that Thorn Hickum was forced to resign over the incident, he smelled a rat, and gladly accepted Thorn's request to meet. They sat together in his Vice Presidential office.

"Before you say a word, understand one thing…I do not believe for a second that you deserve the blame for this disaster," Roosevelt began. "I've never seen a more brave nor a more loyal soldier in my life."

"You know what, they did me a favor," Thorn sighed. "This is not my world. This town is choking with sharks, back-stabbers, liars, and leeches. Where I come from, if a snake's goin' to bite, at least he shakes his rattle first. Around here you can't tell a snake from a cow pie."

Roosevelt chuckled. "Can't argue with that, and if you leave, we are all the worse for it."

"You need to get out too," Thorn said.

"And if I leave, who's left to fix it?" Roosevelt answered.

"I don't think it can be fixed," Thorn sighed.

"And nobody thought we could make it up San Juan Hill, either," Roosevelt winked.

Thorn couldn't argue that logic.

"Just do me one favor," Thorn continued. "Whatever you do, please keep my name out of the papers."

"I'll make it like you were never here," Roosevelt agreed. "Where are you headed?"

"Back to Montana," Thorn replied.

"God Almighty, I love that country," Roosevelt sighed. "I need to get back out there and hunt some pronghorn bucks." The two shook hands.

"Let me know when you're coming, we'll have 'em lined up and waiting."

The Showdown at Yellowstone

CHAPTER 18

It seemed anytime Marshal Ed Randolph showed up, he either carried bad news or a dangerous assignment. This day it was a friendly warning. He tied off his horse and stepped into Mason's office where his sheriff was enjoying a hot cup of coffee and reading the newspaper.

"Ed, pour yourself a cup and come on over," Mason said, as he folded the newspaper over.

"I believe I will," Ed nodded as he walked over to the coffee pot.

"I been reading about the McKinley shooting. Looks like he may recover. Lucky for him," Mason noted. Ed brought over his cup of coffee and sat across from Mason. His countenance was rather sober. He was having trouble making eye contact with Mason, which did not go unnoticed.

"OK, let's have it. What's eatin' you?"

"I got some bad news," Ed began. "I wouldn't give it too much thought, but still you need to know."

"Now you got my attention. What's up?"

"Well, I'll just say it. Lonnie Jones just broke out of the Deer Lodge Penitentiary." Mason turned and stared out the window, then studied the color of his coffee. Finally he looked up at Ed.

"How'd he get out?"

"They got some prison ranch program to try to control over-crowding. A couple three prisoners over powered the guards and busted out. Two prisoners were shot but two got away. One of 'em's already been recaptured, but Lonnie's still on the loose."

Mason shook his head and stared out the window again.

"I wouldn't give it a thought," Ed went on. "Except he made some threats against you if he ever got out. He swore a vow of blood vengeance."

"I shoulda just killed him up there on the Muscleshell."

"He's probably long gone," Ed said. "He'd be crazy to show up here."

"But that's the thing of it...he IS crazy," Mason said. Ed just nodded.

"Well, there you go. Just keep your eye out," Ed said as he rose to leave. Mason stood up to walk him out. When Ed mounted up Mason gave him a smile.

"Sometime you need to come here with some cheery news or you're gonna wear out your welcome." Ed smiled back and rode off. As Mason turned to go back inside, he saw Tommy coming his way.

"Telegram, Sheriff."

"Who's it from?" Mason asked, examining the envelope.

"Mr. Thorn Hickum," Tommy replied. Mason thought to himself, "I don't need any more bad news today."

"You want me to wait for you to write a reply?" asked Tommy.

"No," Mason said. "I'll stop by if I need to." Tommy excused himself and closed the door behind him. Mason opened the telegram. It read:

"Leaving Washington on the 6:30 train. Stop. Should be in Coulson on Sunday the 15th. Stop. Have a hot bath ready. Stop. I need to scrub this city off me. Stop."

Mason smiled at the thought of seeing Thorn again but puzzled over the circumstances that might have prompted his departure. Was he fired? Quit? On vacation? No matter. He marked his calendar and gave thought to a welcome home party. He decided a nice steak at the Coulson Diner would do just fine - just like last New Year's night.

He meandered over to the Undertaker's Office to share the good news with Sam Stokes. Sam was finishing up on a poor unfortunate drunk whose liver finally gave out. The family paid extra for Sam to give the deceased a shave to look presentable when he met St. Peter.

Sam had already read the account of the assassination and feared the prognosis for the President was bleak.

"You know, a gunshot to the abdomen generally guarantees death by infection," Sam said, as he wiped his hands with a cloth. "I don't know who his doctor is, but I'm afraid he's been dealt a losing hand."

Mason noticed the fine shave Sam had just given his customer.

"You should set up a barber chair in here," Mason said. "I think you missed your calling."

"Well, I prefer shaving dead people to live ones," Sam said. "They don't complain if you nick'm, and they don't bleed none either."

Mason smiled as he headed out the door.

Sure enough, Sam's prediction bore fruit. By September 13 the President's condition turned for the worst and on morning of the 14th he died. Within minutes the news spread worldwide, just in time to make the evening edition of the Coulson Gazette. Sunday afternoon the 15th, with newspaper in hand, Mason stood at the train platform waiting for Thorn's arrival. The station was full of families waiting along with him for their loved ones.

Mason had always thought that the train station was about the happiest place in town, always the sight of hugs and kisses and happy greetings. Unfortunately, Mason felt mixed emotions at this particular reunion. He didn't know if Thorn had the chance to learn of McKinley's death en route, and did not look forward to breaking the news.

The Northern Pacific rolled in on schedule amidst a waiting crowd. As passengers poured out, Mason scanned the masses in search of one familiar face. And finally, there he was. Thorn stepped down to the platform wearing his familiar cowboy hat; a Stetson with the classic Montana crease in the crown, and a saddle bag slung over his shoulder. Mason couldn't help but smile as their eyes met.

"Damn, it's good to see you," said Mason. Thorn grinned.

"You're a pretty welcome sight yourself," Thorn replied.

They weaved through the crowd as they talked.

"How long you here for?" Mason asked.

"For good," Thorn said. Mason gave him an inquisitive look. He didn't exactly know what that meant but he figured Thorn would explain it when he was good and ready.

"That deputy job still open?" Thorn asked.

"It's all yours," Mason said, glad to know the team was back in business.

"You heard the news about McKinley dying?" Mason asked. Thorn's grin faded.

"Yeah, read about it this morning," Thorn said.

"Were you in Buffalo when he got shot?" Mason asked.

"Yeah, pretty close. About three feet away," Thorn replied, looking straight ahead as they walked into town. Mason didn't ask another question. Thorn changed the subject.

"You ain't gonna believe some of the new inventions back east."

"Like what?" Mason asked.

"Like an actual sugar cone to put your ice cream in," Thorn smiled.

"Well, ain't that handy," Mason said. "That it?"

"Oh, no," Thorn shook his head. "Get this; electricity to light up a whole city, machines to send pictures over the wire, candy in the shape of a wad of cotton, ice-making machines, and water power that turns machines to run trolleys with electrical wires underground," Thorn said. "I just can't describe it all."

They stopped at the sheriff's office where Mason kept Thorn's mail in a pile. Thorn sat down and began sifting through the envelopes.

"I usually sent your mail to you in a bunch. This is from the last two months. When I got word you were comin' home I figured I'd just hold this batch till you got here."

Thorn nodded as he sorted through the pile until he came across a letter from Elsworth Riley, the city attorney. He opened it up and read the letter to himself. Mason waited patiently. Thorn turned and looked at him.

"You're not gonna believe this," Thorn said. "It looks like

I inherited a ranch."

"You what?" Mason wasn't sure he heard right.

Thorn met Elsworth Riley in his office to learn the details.

"You remember a fella by the name of Horace Blunt?" Riley began.

"I sure do," Thorn nodded. "I helped him out of a bind ten years ago, and spent a few Sundays gettin' his ranch back on its feet."

"Well, Mr. Blunt passed away a few months ago," Riley continued. "He left a will. He never married and had no kin to leave his ranch to, so he left it to you," Riley stated as he handed Horace's will to Thorn for proof.

"I don't know if you realize, but it's quite a spread now; 500 acres of farmland, over 300 head of cattle, 50 horses, eight wranglers and a foreman, all waiting orders from their new owner." Thorn was at a loss for words.

"If you'll just sign here, we'll register your name with the county clerk and you'll be on your way," Riley pointed to the deed.

"I just helped him a little bit and pointed him in the right direction. I really don't deserve this," Thorn stammered.

"No matter. If you don't take it, it'll just get auctioned off on the courthouse steps," Riley explained.

Thorn signed the papers and rode out to the ranch to meet his wranglers. As he rode, he let the enormity of this good fortune sink in. He was now a rich land owner. He would never have to work again a day in his life. He was free to travel, relax, do as he pleased, even stay on as deputy just for the hell of it.

He rode through the main gate of the property to see a handsome prairie ranch house with a wrap-around veranda, and two stone chimneys. The barn was a beauty, with bales of hay stacked inside and a first rate corral attached. He tied off his horse as one of the workers rode up to greet him.

"Howdy. You must be Thorn Hickum," he said as he shook hands. "Just call me Hank. I'm the foreman here. If you don't mind, I'd sure like to have a few words with you."

Hank dismounted and the two went inside. They sat at

the kitchen table and Hank began.

"I been working here for six years, been foreman for three. And I heard about you since the day I started."

"Is that right?" Thorn said.

"Yes, sir. Mr. Blunt never stopped talking about you and how you saved his ranch. Why to hear him speak you were sent straight from the Almighty."

"Not to speak ill of the dead, but I was actually sent to him straight from the sheriff's office," Thorn admitted with a big grin.

"Just the same, I'm mighty proud to finally meet ya."

"The pleasure's mine." Hank cleared his throat to get down to business.

"It's your ranch now and whatever you say goes. If you got somebody else in mind to run it, I got no right to object. If you don't, then I'd sure like to stay on. You've got a helluva spread here, and I'd be proud to take care of it for you."

"I'll be honest, I did some wrangling in my day, and I respect those who do it for a living, but it's not my game anymore," Thorn admitted.

"You don't got a thing to worry about. I been takin' care of the place without any direction since Mr. Blunt passed, and I'd be honored to do the same for you. Everything hums along pretty nice here. We got plenty of water, lots of land, cattle to take to market and farmland that brings a good harvest every year. You can ask around, but I'll tell you up front I'm as honest a man as you'll find. I'm a church-goer, and I got roots here. You can depend on me. You give the orders and I'll make it happen. All I ask is that you and I meet at least once a month to go over the books and settle accounts, go to the bank and take stock of your earnings."

"That's a tempting offer. I like everything I seen so far, and no doubt it's because of you," Thorn nodded. "But there's one part that don't sit right with me."

"What's that?" Hank asked.

"I don't care to have a hired hand runnin' my spread," Thorn explained. Hank swallowed hard, figuring he was about to get the boot, but made no reply.

"So if you don't mind, I'm gonna make you a part

owner... 50/50 if that's OK," Thorn declared. Hank did not expect that. He stood up with a grin as big as a kid on Christmas morning.

"I don't know what to say," Hank sputtered. He shook Thorn's hand like he was priming a water pump. "I'll do you proud. I'll do us both proud."

The Showdown at Yellowstone

CHAPTER 19

"Thorn! Come over here," bellowed one of the locals who made the Crystal Palace their unofficial home. "I got some friends from out of town. I'll buy you a drink if you'll tell us all one more time how you made that run up San Juan Hill."

"How many times I gotta tell you. It was Kettle Hill," Thorn corrected him for the 20th time.

"Yeah, right, right. Kettle Hill," he nodded. Then to his buddies he promised, "You're gonna love this story."

The Coulson bar flies embraced Thorn as a returning war hero. Even though it was now 1902, and the Spanish-American War ended four years earlier, he was a bona fide celebrity at the Crystal Palace, where he regaled the patrons with tales of his brief exploits in Cuba. Whenever he walked in the doorway he got a rousing 'hail fellow well met', a drink on the house, and yet another request to share his death defying stories of the Rough Riders glory days.

After six months of free drinks and tales of daring do, Thorn found himself avoiding the Crystal Palace in favor of just hanging around the sheriff's office with Mason. One late summer day he found himself sitting at Mason's desk, legs crossed with his feet propped up, balancing on the two back legs of his chair, fingers laced behind his head. Softly whistling to himself, he lazily scanned the bulletin board on the far wall for anything of interest. The very picture of contented leisure or idle boredom, take your pick. Mason, on the other hand, lived by the old bromide 'Get it done – do it now'. He occupied his free time sweeping the office and emptying the trash basket. Thorn's whistling finally got on Mason's nerves.

He stopped and stared at Thorn, holding his broom limp in his hands. He held Thorn in the grip of his gaze for a full two minutes, waiting to see how long it would take for Thorn to notice. Thorn gave no indication that he was aware of the sudden stillness, or that Mason was eying him disapprovingly. Then he saw it; a poster on the bulletin board that read "Wild West Show" coming to Coulson. It was scheduled to appear on Saturday at the fairground's arena. Thorn strained his eye sight to read the poster from where he was sitting, rather than actually get up and walk over for a closer look. Mason finally spoke his peace.

"Nobody likes a whistler, particularly one who is sitting on his ass while his boss is sweepin' up the place. Why don'cha go empty the spittoons or put some extra wiping paper in the outhouse?"

Thorn was not ready to hog-tie his curiosity over this coming attraction just yet. Out of consideration for Mason's work ethic, he stopped his whistling, but continued to read the ad, lips silently forming the words as his eye scanned down the poster. Mason gave up trying to shame Thorn into some housekeeping, and renewed his sweeping.

All of a sudden, like a man inspired, Thorn dropped his chair back down on all four legs, walked over to the poster and laid his finger on it.

"Hey Mase, you got any interest in going to see this?"

"What is it?" Mason asked.

"Colonel Dooley's Wild West Round-Up Show. It's gonna be at the arena fairgrounds on Saturday."

"That so?" Mason muttered.

"Yeah. Says here they're gonna have a grand parade down main street at noon, then put on what they call a Wild West Show in the afternoon. Ever seen one of those?"

"Nope. Heard about 'em. Buffalo Bill Cody used to take his show all over the country, but last year a freight train accidently crashed into Cody's show train, killed most of his horses and put Annie Oakley in the hospital."

"Well, that's a damn shame," Thorn lamented. "But lookie here," he pointed to the small print. "Says they're gonna hold a dance that evening. They promise three girls for every fella that attends. I kinda like those odds." Mason stopped sweeping again.

"With three girls for every fella, even a guy like you's got a chance with a pretty filly," Mason jabbed. Thorn ignored the remark. "Says here they put on displays of trick riding, trick shooting, they re-enact a stagecoach robbery, old west kind of stuff. What do you say, wanna go?" Mason began sweeping again, thinking it over.

"Naw, I been livin' the old west all my life, can't see paying 2 bits to watch somebody else doin' the same thing," said Mason. Thorn persisted.

"Come on, let's go. Let's do something besides sit around here cleaning our guns. I'll buy your ticket."

"All right," Mason surrendered, "I guess I can't turn down a free look."

Saturday noon, and the parade started right on time. It began with a mounted military color-guard, followed on horseback by the show cowboys waving and smiling. Next came the girls that did the trick riding and the trick shooting. Some of 'em not bad looking, Mason thought. For a flickering moment Thorn caught the eye of a young brown haired girl who flashed him a smile as she rode by. Finally, some worn out looking Indians trudged on by, dressed in outlandish and exaggerated costumes meant to portray plains Indians in all their finery. These were some pretty poor specimens by Mason's figurin'. He'd seen real Indian warriors in his day. These looked like they were hired out of Crow Agency, beat down domesticated Indians.

When the last of the Indians passed in review, a lone street sweeper brought up the rear. With his manure scoop, he dutifully removed the evidence of 100 passing horses from the town's main street.

"Not sure about the rest, but that there's a man who is doing some good," Mason remarked, nodding with approval.

Mason and Thorn walked over to the ticket office and, true to his word, Thorn ponied up the two bits for Mason's ticket, and they stepped through the gate and into the arena to find a good seat. Thorn bought a bag of fresh roasted peanuts to snack on. They settled on two seats about 12 rows up and on the aisle, in case they got bored and decided to leave early.

Colonel Dooley stepped into the center of the arena. Raising his hands to hush the audience, he picked up his megaphone and announced all the exciting events in turn. Mason and Thorn were impressed with the skills of the bucking bronco riders, but after the bull dogging and calf roping events, Mason began to yawn. He could appreciate the determination it took for a cowboy to ride a knot-head mustang that took a notion to start crow-hopping when a sudden gust of wind blew a tumbleweed in its path. But he had little interest in displays of common ranching activities. It wasn't' so much fun to do, and less fun to watch.

Mason elbowed Thorn in the side, "C'mon, let's get out of here. I seen all I care to."

"Yeah, okay," Thorn said. He was getting restless too. Besides, they needed to change into something presentable for the dance in the evening. They both got up and moved down the stairs. As they turned to leave, Thorn caught a glimpse of the cowgirls assembling for the trick riding. And then he saw her, the brown haired girl from the parade.

Sadie Mcginty was 22 years old. Born in Ogallala, Nebraska, Sadie was raised with horses, and learned to ride astride instead of side saddle as was the custom for most young ladies. With flowing auburn hair, apple cheeks, and sparkling eyes, she stood out as the prettiest gal in the show. When she was 18 years of age, she saw her first Wild West show and was mesmerized; the excitement, the costumes, and the romance of it all. Without a doubt, she knew this was the life for her. After the show, she ran back stage and begged the manager for a job.

"Can you do any trick riding," the manager asked. Without batting an eye she answered, "Of course I can." She surprised herself at how easy it was to lie about such things. She had never even seen trick riding, much less done it, but she knew how to ride horses better than most boys her age and figured she could learn fast enough.

"All right, missy. Bring your horse around this afternoon and let's see what you can do," the manager said. "If you can impress me, then we'll talk."

Sadie arrived at 3:30 pm and found the manager inside the arena, going over the program with a few of the other buckaroos. Sadie sat mounted a few yards away, waiting for the manager to begin the audition. A small knot of cowboys noticed Sadie waiting, and thought it would be a good joke to fire off a pistol loaded with blanks. Two shots were fired into the air and Sadie's horse began to lurch. Whirling around at the unexpected gunfire, the manager turned and saw Sadie expertly handling the startled horse, anticipating its every attempt to unseat her. After about 20 seconds of the horse's jumping, leaping and twisting six different ways, Sadie continued to stick like glue to the saddle. The cowboys watching couldn't believe their eyes and soon found themselves cheering her on. Walking over to Sadie after the horse settled down, the manager looked at her for about a minute without speaking. Finally, a smile began to creep across his face.

"All right. You're hired," and walked back to the wagon that doubled as his office.

For the next four years Sadie amazed crowds in every town she performed. She picked up tricks from her fellow cowgirls, but also learned long forgotten stunts from old Indians who shared with her some unbelievable feats they saw in their youth by daring braves steeped in the horse culture of the plains. She learned how to hook one foot around a horse's tail, and with one hand grab a knot of its mane, then slide to the side of its torso, and while the horse was in full gallop she rested her rifle on its back and with one hand shoot a china plate out of the hand of her assistant. She was utterly fearless and her acrobatics on horseback became the climax of every show. Six months earlier she left the troupe and signed on with Colonel Dooley, where she became one of the show's headliners

Mason was already halfway out of the arena when he noticed that he was alone. Turning, he saw Thorn sitting on the arena railing talking to one of the cowgirl performers. Idly coiling her rope, Sadie was bashfully looking down as Thorn engaged her in conversation.

"What's your name, Lassie," Thorn grinned.

"Sadie." Then putting her arm around the girl beside her, she added, "And this is my friend, Sarah."

"You both do trick riding?" Thorn asked. The two girls smiled.

"Guess you'll just have to wait and see," Sadie answered. Then the three laughed at Sadie's boldness.

Mason decided to fetch his partner before he got in over his head. Truth be told, he was actually feeling a little jealous that these girls had Thorn's devoted attention with so little effort.

"You comin' or stayin'?" Mason called out. Thorn turned and gave the two girls a wink.

"I think I'll stay and watch the show. It's just gettin' good. Why don't you stay too?" Mason looked at the two girls who awaited his decision. Thorn could not believe that Mason was even hesitating.

"What else do you need to do that's better than this?" Thorn prodded.

"I guess nothin'," Mason shrugged with a smile. The two girls giggled with glee.

"We gotta get ready. We're on next," said Sadie, as they scampered back to the other trick riding girls. Thorn turned to Mason.

"C'mon, let's get a good seat down front."

The two made their way to the low fence that separated the grand stands from the arena. The seats were all filled, so they just stood along the edge.

"Ladies and Gentlemen," Colonel Dooley proclaimed through his megaphone, "Now, for your viewing pleasure we present our own Sadie McGintey and Dooley's Daring Dillies." With that, the gate at the far end flew open and ten fearless girls on horseback, with Sadie in the lead, galloped in single file along the fence line, waving to the audience as they blew by. They were wearing tassels and shimmering rhinestones, with rifles that glittered to match. The audience cheered and whistled with approval. After making a full revolution around the ring, they lined up in a row at the far end.

Again the Colonel spoke.

"We need a brave volunteer from the audience who'd be willing to hold the targets for our Dillies to shoot."

Thorn was the closest to the arena and couldn't resist the urge to get into the act. He leaped over the fence before Mason could grab him.

"Here's a brave buckaroo. Let's all give him a hand," shouted Dooley. The crowd roared. The Colonel positioned Thorn in the center of the arena next to a small table full of stacked china plates.

"Just hold these plates in your outstretched arms, and stand perfectly still," the Colonel explained as he demonstrated. Thorn followed along, holding two plates at arm's length.

"And now our Dillies will ride past the grandstand while standing in their stirrups and shoot the plates out of the hands of our brave assistant," the Colonel heralded to the crowd.

Suddenly the grandstand hushed with anticipation. The distance from the edge of the ring to the center, where Thorn stood, was a good 50 feet, a test of marksmanship for anyone standing still, much less riding horseback. And, these girls were going to do it standing upright in their stirrups.

Mason held his breath. Surely these girls had done this before, he thought. Even so, anything could go wrong. Mason dreaded the possibility that after all his years of deputy shoot-outs and military action, Thorn might die at the hands of a sweet little rodeo gal.

At the sound of a starting gun, the first girl stood up in her stirrups and with a pistol in one hand and the reins in the other, jiggered her horse into a full gallop. At just the right moment, she fired two rapid shots, shattering the two plates with ease. The audience erupted with applause as the next girl set her horse into motion. Thorn quickly grabbed the next two plates and assumed his position. The second girl fired twice with amazing precision and the two plates exploded. Again the crowd cheered this sensational exhibition of marksmanship.

Sadie was next, and bolted into the arena with reins and pistol in hand. Thorn was ready with his plates just in time for Sadie to hit each one dead center with her .22 caliber revolver.

This was high entertainment for the spectators, who had never seen such a feat of trick shooting. A couple of rowdies in the grandstand fired their pistols into the air in typical cowboy approval. Sadie's friend, Sarah, was the next rider to go and had already begun her run when the shots went off. Her horse did a little stutter step in momentary confusion. But that was just enough to cause Sarah to lose balance and the heel of her boot slipped through the tread of the stirrup as she fell. Mason and Thorn knew immediately what she had done. Mason had caught his boot in exactly the same way years ago at a bucking bronco contest, and could not get free; it took Thorn's quick thinking and instant reflexes to save his life.

In the confusion, Sarah's horse took off running, dragging Sarah in the dirt, her leg trapped in the stirrup. The audience all stood up and gasped in unison, hoping she could wiggle her boot free. Without hesitation Thorn leaped into action. He ran to the side of the arena where a few riderless horses were tied off. He leaped on a horse from the rear, yanked its reins, and gave it a swift kick. Off they surged in full gallop to head off Sarah's runaway horse. Luckily the arena kept her horse from heading down the road. As the horse turned along the fence Thorn leaped on its back and yanked its reins so hard the horse's neck jerked back and it fell to the ground. Thorn went down with it to make sure it stayed down, while others grabbed Sarah's stirrup and freed her boot.

Sadie ran up to help in the rescue, which was already complete. Sarah was shaken and bruised and covered in dirt, but otherwise okay. She got to her feet and waved to the crowd to let everyone know she was all right. As Thorn helped the horse back to its feet, Sadie looked at him with gratitude and a new respect.

"Thank you," she said with all the earnestness she possessed. "How can we ever repay you?" Thorn smiled.

"Would you come to the dance with me tonight?"

CHAPTER 20

The dance was held at the Coulson Livestock Auction yard at the far end of town across from the railroad depot. A floor of fresh cut pine boards served as the dancing surface under a canvas tent hastily thrown up for the event. The sides of the tent were rolled up to take advantage of the late summer warm evening. Concession booths for the sale of spirits completed the venue. "Colonel Dooley's Wild West Roundup" was strictly a profit driven enterprise. The tickets for the dance ran six bits for gents. Women were admitted free of charge, hence the bold promise of "three girls for every fella".

The potential for revenue simply doubled when the festivities were capped off with an evening dance social. The sale of intoxicants also helped separate these western folks from their coins. Whatever money Colonel Dooley expected from Coulson would have to be wrung out in one day since the show was packing up and moving on to Bozeman before sun up.

Social events were always well attended in Coulson. The opportunities for entertainment and diversion were scarce. A large crowd had already gathered when Mason and Thorn arrived. A lively cowboy band, with fiddle, guitar and bass, filled the air with tunes to swing your partner.

"Good thing they rolled up the sides of the tent," Mason said to Thorn as they stood in line to pay their six bits. "Some of these boys smell like they ain't bathed in a while."

"And some of 'em smell like they already got to drinking before they got here," Thorn added. "Which I ain't complainin' about. A sweaty beer-stinking cowboy just means less competition for us."

Thorn scanned the crowd for Sadie. He suddenly worried that she only agreed to meet him at the dance to be shed of him earlier in the day. His fears abruptly melted away when he spotted her, looking as fresh as a lemonade, standing near the bandstand with a bodyguard of three girlfriends. He felt a fluttering sensation in his chest and a smile crept widely across his face. Safety in numbers Thorn thought, and he began to navigate his way through the crowd towards her.

Mason watched as Thorn angled his way thru the couples on the dance floor. He felt somewhat deflated, not sure if he should follow his pard and maybe meet some of Sadie's girlfriends or just keep out of the way. He decided the easiest thing to do would be to lay back and see what transpired. Relegating himself to wallflower, he joined a crowd of about twenty other fellers too shy to ask a girl to dance.

As Thorn was making his way to meet Sadie, he rehearsed some clever words he might say. He was about to step up to Sadie and her friends when a big rough looking guy suddenly pushed in front of him.

Trot Molesworth was his name. He wasn't exactly a wanted outlaw but only for lack of imagination. Too lazy for ranching, he worked at various odd jobs around town, usually in the vice district. Because he was a big man, he got jobs as a bouncer in the tenderloin. Regular cowpokes stepped wide of him. He could make a fist all right and had some meat in his swing, but had never been tested in a real fight with a man who knew his elbow from a gopher hole.

Tonight he was dressed in a suit too small, wearing a city hat perched forward at a rakish angle. He smiled his tobacco stained teeth at Sadie.

"Howdy ma'am," he tipped his hat. "I reckon I'll claim the first dance. And if your card ain't already filled, well, I'll do those honors as well." Trot removed his hat, leaned forward and extended his arm toward Sadie for her to take. Sadie was disgusted at the sight of him. She and her three friends folded their arms and stuck their jaws out, teeth set in defiance. Sarah spoke out first.

"Thank you, no, we are already otherwise engaged for the evening." Trot's smile vanished as he leaned forward into Sarah's face, close enough to smell alcohol on his breath.

"Shut up squirt, ain't no one talking to your ugly self."

Sarah was outraged.

"Well, I never!" she declared.

"And besides, ain't you that one what fell off your horse today at the show? Ugly and can't ride neither."

Then he laughed and looked around for approval, proud of himself for his clever retort. The girls' expressions changed from defiance to loathing at this crude brute. Sadie stepped in front of Sarah and slapped Trot across the mouth. The dance music stopped and all eyes turned to the sound of the slap. Trot looked back at Sadie, first in disbelief, then rage at this most public humiliation. Sadie's friends stepped back slowly, fearful of what might happen next.

Sadie held her ground, pointing to her friend Sarah, and loudly demanded, "You will apologize to my friend for your rude insults and then you will leave this dance immediately or I will have you thrown out."

Trot had never been challenged like this by anyone, much less by a little girl.

"Get out," Sadie repeated, again pointing to the exit to emphasize her demand.

Trot felt this affront to his masculinity must not go unanswered.

"By god I'm gonna whip you like your daddy should have," Trot snarled at Sadie as he reached out to grab her hair.

Sadie ducked and stepped back, doubled her fists in both hands and braced for action. Trot couldn't believe this little squirt was actually going to go toe to toe with him.

"Trot!" Thorn yelled from behind.

Trot turned quickly to see Thorn thrust the palm of his hand into Trot's nose. Thorn heard the cartilage in Trot's nose crack and blood began streaming out. Trot's eyes immediately flooded with tears, the salt stinging his eyes making vision impossible. Blinking hard, he grabbed his nose with both hands.

"You son of a bitch," Trot screamed as he swung a blind haymaker in Thorn's general direction.

Thorn easily sidestepped it and returned a precision punch to Trot's breadbasket, knocking the wind out of him. Trot sank to his knees then laid flat on is back, blood flowing from his smashed nose, fighting to get his wind back. As quickly as it started, the fracas was all over. Thorn kneeled down beside the fallen hooligan and spoke closely into Trot's ear.

"Trot, you know better than to behave this way in public and you damn sure know better than to treat a woman like that. I've spoken to you before about this. Now, why don't we both get up and walk out of here like men. You go home and I'll fetch the doc to come fix up that nose and we'll say no more about this, okay?" Trot finally got his wind back.

"Yeah, sure, okay Thorn, sure," he whispered. Trot slowly rolled himself onto his hands and knees, remained there for a moment as he cleared his head. Then he rose to his feet with Thorn at his side to steady him. Mason came over to see if he could help.

"Le'me give you a hand," he said as he reached for Trot's other arm.

"I got it," Thorn said. "Just keep an eye on Sadie till I get back."

"Sure thing," Mason agreed. Thorn turned back to Trot.

"Ready?" he asked as he put Trot's hat back on his head. Trot nodded. Thorn turned to Sadie and winked.

"I'll be back in a jig and a hop." Turning with Trot, the two left the tent arm in arm.

Sadie stared at Thorn in amazement.

"That's twice in one day he's saved a lady in distress," she whispered to herself.

CHAPTER 21

Thorn couldn't sleep that night after the dance. He'd had a wonderful night; borderline magical, in fact. He had never given any serious thought to settling down with one woman before. Oh, he liked the pursuit, the attention that he got from women. He enjoyed the way it made him feel when they smiled at him or laughed when he joked. But getting married and settling down just wasn't in the cards. Maybe someday, but that was way off to the horizon. But last night, with Sadie in his arms, dancing, her hair flying, the smell of her skin, her laughter. The way she smiled and looked at him, MAN! He'd never felt like that before.

Thorn rolled over in the bed of his new ranch home and looked out the window...dawn breaking to the east. Suddenly, it hit him like a thunderclap!

"I gotta go get her, talk to her before the show pulls out."

He was suddenly frightened of not ever seeing her again. Throwing the blankets off, he rolled up into a sitting position and frantically pulled his boots on, struggled into his jacket, grabbed his hat and flew out the door.

He rode into town. The middle-aged shopkeeper was out sweeping the boardwalk in front of his place, cigarette idly dangling from his lips. He paused from his early morning chore to give Thorn a wave. Thorn waved back and kept on cantering. He rode to the fairgrounds, fearing the worst. Maybe the Wild West show might have already pulled out, leaving nothing behind but trash and debris.

To his surprise and relief, Colonel Dooley's Wild West Roundup hadn't even begun to pull up stakes. Lantern lights could be seen here and there in the early morning, indicating that the occupants were beginning to stir.

He hadn't given any thought as to which tent belonged to Sadie, or how he would go about finding her.

"If I go sticking my head into a bunch of different tents I'm liable to get my damn head blowed off,'" he thought.

He considered standing in the middle of the tent area and shouting out Sadie's name.

"No, that would cause a commotion…start a lot of loose talk that might embarrass Sadie." Then his mind strayed to the worst.

"What if she already has a beau? That could start a fight. But then why would she dance with me all night if she already has a man. Maybe he ain't around just now. Hell, she probl'y aint even thinking about me at all in that way."

He was feeling as helpless as a calf in a mudbog.

"Why would she want to marry me?" he thought.

But there it was, he shocked himself at saying the very word - marry!

"Well, by godfrey, I'm gonna find out right now!" he said to himself. He tied his horse off and decided to look for Colonel Dooley's wagon.

He found Colonel Dooley pacing back and forth outside his wagon, puffing on his cigar, making more smoke than a wet wood fire. Muttering out loud, he read the telegram in his pudgy fist, crumpled it in disgust, then opened it up again. He noticed a cowboy walking purposefully towards him out of the early dawn. He turned to face Thorn and waved the telegram up in the air.

"Sorry, buster, I ain't hiring just now. Can't use anymore acts at the moment. These damned cancellations will be the ruin of me. How's a man supposed to make a living if he has to fight God, government, and the weather, too? I ask you, how? Hell's bells and damnation!" he thundered.

Thorn pulled up abruptly.

"Take it easy, I'm not looking for work. What are you so riled up about anyhow?' stammered Thorn.

"This telegram I received from Bozeman a few hours ago. Damned hailstorm just blew chunks of ice so big you could choke a horse with 'em. Smashed up their rodeo arena so bad they canceled our appearance. They tell me the arena is an absolute quagmire, take a week before they can put things back together to let the arena dry out." Then he zeroed in on Thorn.

"You get what I'm sayin'? We're stuck here. I just sent a rider out to Big Timber to see what their situation is. Maybe they might book a show in the meantime. I can't just sit here not making any money."

Dooley turned and continued to pace around his wagon, chewing on his cigar. Thorn followed the Colonel, hoping he'd cool down enough for him to ask about Sadie. Dooley stopped abruptly and Thorn bumped into him. Turning quickly, he adjusted his jacket and straightened his lapels.

"Well, what is it now?" Dooley sputtered.

"I was going to ask you where Miss Sadie McGinty's tent is," Thorn explained. Colonel Dooley leaned forward, took the cigar from his mouth.

"Who?" he nearly shouted. Thorn took a half step back.

"Miss Sadie McGinty, one of your trick riders and sharp shooters." Thorn replied. "I just want to talk to her."

The Colonel turned to walk away and stuck his cigar back in his mouth.

"Yeah, you and every other Jack Do-Da," he said dismissively. Without looking back, he hooked his thumb over his shoulder and pointed backward.

"The women's tent area is over there."

Thorn looked back in the general area where Dooley pointed, but saw nothing that looked anything like a female bivouac. Realizing he would get no more from Colonel Dooley, Thorn shoved his hands in his pockets and walked back to the tent area, feeling slightly defeated. He scanned the area to see if any other workers could help him.

Turning around, he bumped into a woman who was carrying two buckets of water. Without looking up, he touched the brim of his hat to apologize.

"Pardon ma'am" he said.

"Certainly" the young lady replied. Thorn froze...he recognizing that voice. He looked up to find Sadie, smiling brightly at him.

The Showdown at Yellowstone

CHAPTER 22

"Thanks, Jesse," Mason said as he studied his reflection in the mirror. "Nice job, as usual."

"What's the occasion?" asked Jesse.

"Not sure. I got my suspicions," Mason replied. He hopped out of the barber chair and tossed Jesse an extra coin for good measure. Preoccupied with thoughts of the festivities ahead, he failed to notice a pair of hellish eyes studying him from a distance as he emerged from the barber shop. Sitting under the veranda of the Broom Tail Saloon, the stranger was obscured by the evening shadows. Quietly puffing on a cigarette, the figure panted at the delicious thoughts of revenge.

Mason walked in the direction of The Prairie Star, the finest hotel and restaurant in Coulson. It was patterned after the ornate architecture of the New Orleans French Quarter; lavish and expensive. All he knew for sure was that Thorn told him to be there for dinner.

"Ah, Monsieur Mason, how grand it is to see you!" gushed Paul, the Maitre d', in his thick French accent. "You do not come in to see us enough." He took Mason's hat and coat. The lilting sound of a romantic tune drifted through the dining room, courtesy of the tuxedoed piano player.

"Are we dining alone tonight?" he asked.

"We are not," Mason smiled.

"Ah, Monsieur, you make with jokes again," Paul replied laughing.

"No, Paul, I'm going to be dining with the Thorn Hickum party," replied Mason. "I believe he has a table reserved."

"Ah, yes. Right this way my friend. A member of your party has earlier arrived."

With menus in hand, Paul pointed Mason to the table where Sam Stokes was sitting, glass in hand.

"Howdy, Sam," Mason said.

"Howdy Mase", Sam smiled back.

"Didn't know you were coming, Sam... an unexpected pleasure."

Just as they got comfortable, Thorn and Sadie entered the Prairie Star. Sam noticed them approaching and signaled Mason to turn around.

"Here they come, Mase." Mason turned and saw Thorn all dressed up and was about to josh him a little, when his eyes shifted to Sadie. His mouth dropped open.

"Now, that's a handsome woman," Mason said to no one in particular. Mason looked at Sam. Sam was speechless at the sight of this extraordinary couple. Sam had not known a happy marriage, his had been miserable for many years. When he saw this couple, it was obvious how joyful they appeared. He was both pleased for them and envious. Still, he would never let that sad fact diminish the thrill he had in seeing true romance in bloom.

"Gentleman," Thorn announced, "I want you both to meet Miss Sadie McGinty. Sadie, this is my pard, Mason. He's the sheriff here in Coulson." Sadie smiled and extended her hand to Mason.

"Mason, so pleased to finally meet you. Thorn has told me so much about you, and not all of it bad either." she smiled good naturedly. "Mason, is that your first or last name?"

Mason took her hand and warmly shook it.

"Mason is my last name, ma'am, that's what I go by mostly." Thorn continued the introductions.

"Sadie, I would like to present Samuel Stokes. He is the town undertaker and one of our leading citizens."

Sam smiled to himself at that last little flourish. Leading citizen, he thought. He smiled and took Sadie's hand, bent forward and kissed it.

"Why, Mr. Stokes!" Sadie flushed with pleased

embarrassment, "how gallant!" Sam looked up at Sadie.

"Miss McGinty, I am honored to stand in your favor." Thorn and Mason gawked at Sam's sudden acts of chivalry. Paying them no mind, Sam stepped around the table and pulled Sadie's chair out. "Allow me, Miss McGinty," and he seated Sadie at the table.

"Thank you, Mr. Stokes," Sadie gushed as she settled in at the table. Sam stepped back around to his chair.

"May I propose a toast? To Miss Sadie McGinty, the fairest flower on the prairie."

"Here, here" responded Mason. "Couldn't have said it any better," replied Thorn. The four drained their glasses.

Dinner was exquisite. Sam had the beef bourguignon, Thorn had the filet, Sadie dined on chicken fricassee, and Mason requested a bowl of chili. Sadie was utterly charming. It was clear that she had learned to conquer all with a wink and a smile. Thorn squirmed with nervous anticipation that was visible to all.

When the meal ended, the table fell silent in anticipation of the big surprise.

"OK, Thorn," Mason began. "Don't keep us in suspense any longer. What's the big occasion?" Thorn stood up.

"I have an announcement to make," Thorn declared, his face ablaze with incandescence. Sadie, also glowing and smiling, nonetheless buried her face in her hands in joyful embarrassment as Thorn prepared to utter the words they had previously rehearsed. Mason and Sam waited for Thorn to say something. Thorn cleared his throat then tried to recall the first few words of his prepared speech.

Giving up, he finally blurted out…"Sadie an' me are gettin' married."

Sadie looked at Thorn, smiling and laughing, then turned to Mason.

"Don't he have a way with words!" she gushed.

Thunderstruck, Mason's astonishment slowly gave way to a look of pleasure. Smiling, he playfully shook his head.

"You two… are a perfect match," He proclaimed. Sam stood up and raised his glass in a toast to the couple.

"May the Lord keep you in his hand, and never close His

fist too tight." Thorn, still standing, felt contentment that his pard approved of their matrimonial plans. Mason raised his glass in a second toast to the couple.

"And may you live to be a hundred years, with one extra to repent." The table erupted into laughter.

"Now, how about a word from the groom?" Sam declared. All eyes turned to Thorn. He felt a sudden flush, then just turned to Sadie, raised his glass and spoke from the heart.

"Sadie, you take my breath away like the sunrise on a canyon wall," Sadie blushed and replied.

"I hope you always feel that way," she said.

Suddenly, for Thorn the room faded from view, and all he could see was Sadie, as if they were completely alone.

"Life just ain't long enough for it to ever be any other way," he answered.

"How did we get so lucky?" Sadie whispered.

"It was just our turn," Thorn answered with a certainty that surpassed night following day.

"Bravo," declared Mason, with his glass raised, and they all drank to love eternal. Then Mason took Thorn aside for a moment.

"Not that it's any of my business, but what are you gonna do about her job in the Wild West show?" he asked. "I mean it's a dangerous line of work, and, well, you saw what happened with that other girl at the rodeo."

"We're workin' on that," Thorn confided. "But I'm pretty sure she can take care of herself."

"Are you sure?" Mason pressed.

Thorn had no time to answer, for just at that moment, the door to the restaurant burst open. The man who'd been watching Mason from across the street could wait no longer.

"Goddamn you, Mason," the man shouted as he swung around his Winchester rifle and snapped off a quick, poorly aimed shot at the table. The sudden unexpected attack caught everyone by surprise. Thorn shoved back from the table and reached inside his suit jacket for his Colt revolver. In stepping back, Thorn's boot got caught in the leg of his chair, causing him to trip backwards, hitting his head on a table in back of him. Momentarily stunned, he dropped his revolver. The shooter worked the lever on his rifle to load a new cartridge and continued firing indiscriminately. Upon hearing the first rifle shot, Sadie dived for the floor. She knew enough about drunks and rowdies to grab for the floorboards when bullets started flying.

Mason hit the floor too when he saw this degenerate raise his rifle. He jerked his pistol from his shoulder holster and returned fire, hitting the assailant's rifle stock with a chance, lucky shot. Mason recognized him and knew in an instant that it was Lonnie Jones come back for revenge. The man threw away his now useless rifle and grabbed his pistol, one of those German automatics, and began firing at the table recklessly. One slug hit a diner one table over, sending him sprawling. Mason crawled under the table while the man wildly emptied his clip. He was also counting the number of shots fired. But when the hoodlum exceeded his six shots and kept on firing at a rapid rate, Mason knew Lonnie was using a gun he was not familiar with.

Sadie crawled along the floor towards Thorn, to make sure he was okay. He was too far away from her for her to reach him safely but she could see he was only dazed. The screams of the other restaurant patrons and the gunfire created pandemonium. Sadie knew she had to do something to protect Thorn. She looked around and saw Thorn's pistol lying on the floor within reach. She crawled to the fallen pistol and grabbed it. Lying on her back, she quickly opened the chamber and counted six unused bullets. She closed the barrel and felt the revolver's weight in her hand. It was heavier than her .22 but not that much. She closed her eyes and took a deep breath, waiting for the right moment. Suddenly and deliberately, she opened her eyes, exhaled and got up on her knees, her head just appearing over the table's edge. The brute was splintering a nearby upended table with pistol fire. She leveled the colt and thumbed the hammer back.

"HEY!" she shouted. The vicious gunman suddenly looked her way as she squeezed off a level shot, hitting him square in the chest just like it was a big fat china plate. The impact threw him backward through the front door and out into the street. Suddenly it was silent. The terrified diners slowly got off the floor where they had sought cover. The air was thick with gun smoke. Everyone's ears were ringing as people tried to make sense of what just happened. Sadie dropped the gun and ran to Thorn, who was rubbing the back of his head and twisting his neck.

"Who shot him?" Thorn asked.

"I did," Sadie answered, dabbing some blood from the back of Thorn's noggin with a napkin. Mason quickly dashed out the door to make certain Lonnie was finished. The man was groaning as Mason stood over him, his pistol aimed directly at Lonnie's head.

"That's the second time you put a bullet in me," he whispered.

"I didn't shoot you," Mason replied.

"Who did?"

"A girl."

"A girl? No shit? Figures," Lonnie muttered. His breathing stopped and his lifeless eyes stared up into the night sky.

Mason walked back inside to reassure the customers the danger was over. He saw Sam slowly turning chairs back up. Then he walked over to Thorn, who was just getting back on his feet.

"You were saying something about Sadie not being able to handle a dangerous job?" Thorn said. Mason surveyed the room.

"Never mind."

CHAPTER 23

Thorn and Sadie sat in a small booth inside the Oasis Cafe the next morning, holding hands and sipping coffee. Still keyed up over the previous evening's excitement, they were in high spirits. Sadie leaned across the table and gently massaged the goose egg on Thorn's head.

"You poor thing" she soothed. "You were so brave last night, the way you jumped up from the table. You'd a plugged that sidewinder for sure if you hadn't tripped and hit your head. Poor baby...does it hurt much?" Thorn just smiled.

"Only my pride," he thought. Thorn wasn't used to this kind of attention from women, and he was getting to like it. Mason walked in for some mid-morning coffee and spied the two of them.

"Just want you two to know that little fracas last night kept me busy most of the night and all morning. Picking up after you two is getting to be a full-time job," he smiled.

"He came gunning for you, ya know," Thorn reminded him. Mason sat down and ordered a cup of black coffee.

"Hot, black, and strong enough to float an anvil," Mason declared with a smile as his coffee was poured by the waitress. Tipping the brim of his hat back, he picked up the cup and held it with both hands. He savored the aroma then slowly sipped the strong brew.

"Why'n cha two just get on with it and be on your way to Niagara Falls or something? I might get a little peace and quiet around here for a spell," Mason smiled.

The suggestion set Sadie's heart a flutter.

"Oh, lets, Thorn," Sadie urged. "But not to Niagara Falls, I'd love to honeymoon in Yellowstone Park instead, go camping there." Thorn looked at Mason and grinned.

"Now you see why I love this gal? Only my Sadie would rather go camping out west than go back east to Niagara Falls." Thorn winked at Mason.

"Then it's settled," declared Sadie. "But before we do anything else, I want to sit for a photograph, Thorn. Just you and me. You know, one of them formal portraits in a studio so's that when we're sixty years old, we can look back and see what we used to look like when we was young and had the world at our feet. And, I want to do it now, today, this minute."

Sadie was nothing if not impulsive. She got up and playfully pulled Thorn's arm to get him to stand up.

"We got a photographer right here in town," Mason offered helpfully, smiling at Thorn. "You know, the Osborn Studio. It's just up the street. Bet he could fit you in right now." Thorn scowled at Mason.

"Thanks, Mase," he managed to squeeze out a smile to mask his gritting teeth. Searching for an escape route, he turned to Sadie.

"Sadie, don't you want to get fixed up a bit and put on some frilly clothes before we sit for a portrait?" But she would not be dissuaded.

"What's wrong with the way we look right now?" she asked. "You look perfect; young, tough, and handsome. Fancy clothes won't improve on that."

Thorn knew any further resistance was futile. He shrugged his shoulders to signal his surrender, got up and fished around in his pocket for some change to pay their tab. Mason slapped Thorn and his back and flashed a big grin.

"Thanks for paying for my coffee too, pard," Mason said. Then he turned and offered his arm to Sadie.

"C'mon, Miss Sadie, I'll escort you to the photography studio while this cowhand pays the check." She giggled and took his arm, and the two exited the cafe with Thorn still counting out the change for the bill and enough left over for the tip.

Thomas Osborn Photography Studio was a short distance up and across the street from the Oasis Café. It took all of two minutes to walk there. Entering the studio, they found the proprietor at his desk, Thomas Osborn, feet up and leaned back with a newspaper in his hands, snoozing.

"When does the busy season start around here?" Mason loudly inquired. Startled, Tom Osborn almost fell out of his chair, dropping his paper as he quickly awoke from his nap. Thomas was a tall lean man in his 30s, with a wild head of hair and a full beard. He had that flare about him that couldn't be bothered to dress like a businessman…he was an artist.

"Why the hell don't you knock before you bust in on a feller? Like to scare me to death," Osborn growled. The he saw that it was Mason. "Oh, sorry, Sheriff… didn't recognize you."

Then he cleared his throat and checked his tousled hair in the mirror. It was beyond repair. He shrugged his shoulders and turned to button his vest.

"What can I do for you?" Osborn asked, clearing his throat.

"Got a couple of young turtle doves that want to be immortalized on film. That is if you're not too busy." Tom Osborn's expression immediately changed from annoyance to delight.

"And, it'll be my treat," Mason added, with a wink to Sadie, whose eyes suddenly got big at Mason's generous offer.

"Then let's get started," Thomas proclaimed.

Thorn and Sadie busied themselves choosing the proper background for their portrait while Thomas set up his camera equipment. Mason idly looked around the studio at all the modern and scientific looking photography equipment.

"Holy Moses" he thought to himself, "how many years must it take a feller to study up on all this to get the knack of it?" he wondered.

Thorn and Sadie settled on an outdoor scene for their background, and Osborn busied himself attaching lenses, adjusting tripods, moving chairs into position. Mason couldn't help but notice Osborn's long and delicate fingers nimbly at work. Then he noticed brown stains on each of Osborn's finger tips. His curiosity got the best of him.

"Why are your fingers all stained brown?' He asked. Osborn suddenly stopped what he was doing and looked at his own hands.

"Oh, that," he shrugged, and went back to work. "That's just from the chemicals I use to develop the photographs. They have a staining quality that discolors the skin when it comes in contact with it. I should use tongs instead of my fingers, but, oh well. There's not a serious photographer alive who doesn't have stained fingers. Occupational hazard I suppose." Then he turned to the wedding couple.

"Are we ready?" he asked. The two love birds nodded.

"Okay. Now, if you two will take your positions. Madam, if you will sit here in the chair, and sir, you will stand behind and slightly to her right, placing your left hand on her shoulder."

Osborn adjusted the head braces behind the heads and necks of the couple, designed to keep them from moving while the picture was being taken. With everything in readiness, Osborn ducked under the camera drape and held the flash pan high while he focused in on the happy couple.

"All right, now. Don't move." Osborn triggered the flash pan which ignited in a brilliant flash and pop.

Sadie, Thorn and Mason were temporarily blinded and began blinking and rubbing their eyes.

"Damnation!" exclaimed Mason. "How do you keep from blowing your hand off?"

The picture was a keeper.

CHAPTER 24

After only five days of knowing each other, Thorn and Sadie met at the Coulson Courthouse to be joined by the Justice of the peace. The ceremony was supposed to be brief, with Mason standing up as the witness and best man. Sam Stokes was given the honorary task of usher. Only one personal invitation had actually been sent out; to none other than the President of the United States. Roosevelt politely declined, citing pressing national business that made his attendance impossible. In his telegram he wished Thorn and Sadie a long and happy life.

No one was really expected to attend, since only a brief mention of the nuptials appeared in the Coulson newspaper the previous day. Dressed in his Sunday suit, Sam stood at the door of the courthouse, arms folded and tapping his boot idly against the door jamb.

"I got the job they figgered was so unimportant it wouldn't matter if I made a hot mess of it or not." He looked at his pocket watch. "Nobody's comin'. I might as well just go inside and have a seat myself."

He started to turn to the door when he saw Trot Molesworth approaching, with a small bouquet of flowers in his hand. He was unshaven, as usual, dressed in an ill-fitting suit.

Sam blocked the door to the courthouse as Trot approached, demanding to know his intentions.

"We don't want no trouble, Trot, so if you mean to disrupt things, then you can just keep on walking or by god you'll have to deal with me." Sam braced for a fight, which he knew he would lose, when he saw Trot back down.

"You got every right to prevent my attendance," admitted Trot. "I just wanted Thorn to know I bear him no grudge for that little altercation at the dance the other night. He was just so goddamned decent to me after I made a ass outta myself, I just had to attend his weddin' an wish him well."

Speechless, Sam extended his hand and led Trot to an empty seat. When Thorn saw him, Sam just shrugged his shoulders and returned to his post. He got there just in time. A large crowd was making its way to the courthouse.

"What's this?" Sam thought to himself. He suddenly recognized the pudgy figure of Col. Dooley, dressed in all his Wild West show plainsman regalia, leading a large contingent of his show performers. Dooley stepped up to Sam.

"The family and friends of the bride, sir!" he announced with the flourish of a circus ringmaster. "You needn't bother to escort us, we know the way."

With that said, Col. Dooley led the forty or so Wild West show 'family' to the courthouse seats. Right behind them, half the customers from the Crystal Palace Saloon marched up the courthouse steps to share in the wedding of their very own war hero. Now Sam began to worry that there would not be enough seats for everyone.

He stepped back out to the door when he saw what looked like half the town approaching the courthouse.

"Hope we're not too late," said Howard Wilkins, the local barber. Rockwell Stevenson, the owner of the dry goods store followed right behind, along with Thomas Osborn, the photographer, and the mayor himself. Just as it seemed that everyone was present, County Marshal Ed Randolph stepped into the courthouse, hat in hand, to offer his blessings.

Thorn was overwhelmed by the show of affection from people he barely know. It didn't matter. They knew him and knew that he had protected them as deputy, and they owed him a debt of gratitude. Sadie was not surprised at all by the turnout. She beamed as she scanned the crowd, proud to say that she was soon to become the wife of one of the pillars of the community.

The service was simple but touching. Once they both pledged "I do" and the justice of the peace uttered those magic words – "I now pronounce you man and wife" – the room erupted into a throng of celebration. Col. Dooly stepped up and hushed the crowd for a surprise.

"Thorn and Sadie, just to show you how much we adore the two of you, we passed the hat around the Wild West show employees, over at the Crystal Palace, and around town." He pulled out an envelope thick with cash and smiled broadly.

"We want to help you get your new life off to a glorious start by presenting you with a wedding gift of $950 in cash." He handed the envelope to Thorn as the room joined in a thunderous applause. Thorn and Sadie were simply overwhelmed at the generosity of everyone. Sadie burst into tears of joy and Thorn felt like he couldn't take much more happiness for fear of exploding. Dooley concluded with one final announcement.

"If everyone will join us over at the Prairie Star Restaurant for a surprise reception, the drinks will be on the house, courtesy of the Col. Dooley Wild West Show."

The dancing and music lasted into the night. Thorn and Sadie had made reservations for the night at the Coulson Grand Hotel, expecting to catch the train the next day for Yellowstone to begin their honeymoon. Once the night was winding down, Col. Dooley took the happy couple aside for a more serious topic of conversation.

"I know the two of you have plans to light out tomorrow for a splendid honeymoon, which you are certainly entitled to," he began. "But I'm going to prevail on you to hold off on that trip for five short days. And before you say anything, let me explain. Our show in Bozeman was cancelled, as you know, due to weather, which is why we stayed here in Coulson as long as we did. That cancellation cost me dearly. But we intend to make that up. The day after tomorrow our show opens in Missoula, and we're expecting a big crowd. Now, Sadie here is one of the headliners in the show, and one of the reasons we attract so many female customers." He paused to let that sink in.

"I'm going to ask a big favor of both of you. I need Sadie

for the opening night. We advertised her by name before even knowing the two of you were getting married, and people have paid money to see her." Sadie spoke up.

"But Colonel, we've got train tickets for tomorrow. And besides, I'm a married woman now, and I intend to start a new life here in Coulson. So, I need to end things with the show. You've got plenty of good female trick shooters. You'll do fine without me." Thorn felt no need to add anything to Sadie's reasonable explanation. But the Colonel was not ready to give up yet.

"Let me make this offer to you...I will reimburse you for the cost of your tickets and replace them with first class passage in five days. In addition, I will pay you triple your usual rate for the inconvenience." Thorn saw that he needed to speak up.

"Colonel, we don't need the money," Thorn said.

"You may not need the money, but I do. There's no telling how many people will want refunds if Sadie doesn't show up," Dooley explained.

"It's just that Sadie is leaving the show, whether it happens now or a week from now. It don't really make any difference. So, thanks, but no thanks." The Colonel saw that he had to play the only card he had left. As gently as he could, he applied the iron hand with a velvet glove.

"Let me remind you that Sadie is under contract with the Wild West Show, and failure to appear will result in legal consequences." Thorn suddenly got serious.

"What the hell are you talking about?" he asked in a low growl.

"Ask Sadie. She knows. It's a one year contract, which I am willing to tear up if she'll just be in Missoula on opening night the day after tomorrow. You do that for me and I will consider her contract satisfactorily fulfilled and tear it up. Otherwise, you'll be speaking to my lawyer." Thorn heaved a heavy sigh.

"Give Sadie and me a minute to talk this over," Thorn said to Dooley. Dooley nodded and stepped over to the buffet table to refill his champagne flute.

"What do you want to do, Sadie?" Thorn asked.

"I did sign a contract. We don't need to begin our marriage with a big legal battle. I say just let me do the opening night show, then we are done for good and we can be on our way."

"One night," Thorn insisted. "Then you get on that train and I'll meet you in Livingston." Sadie nodded in agreement and the two gave each other a hug and kiss.

They spent their first night as husband and wife in the honeymoon suite of the Grand Hotel, pampered decadently by the hotel staff. In the morning Thorn woke up slowly and turned over to see Sadie wide awake with the look of love in her eyes.

"You look happy," he said, as he put his arm around her. She snuggled up to him and put her head on his chest.

"What's on your mind?" Thorn asked as he stroked her hair.

"I was just thinking about your name, 'Thorn'. At first I thought it was a very odd name," she said.

"Really?" Thorn replied.

"But once I got to know you, I think it's perfect," she explained.

"And, why's that?" he asked. Sadie put her head on the pillow beside Thorn's ear and caressed the side of his face with her soft hand.

"Just like the beautiful rose has its thorns to protect it, now I have my own 'thorn' to protect me," she whispered. "That's what you do best...you're a protector." Thorn smiled and gave her a soft kiss on the forehead.

"Ain't you just the sweetest thing," he whispered back. They held each other for a moment.

"What about Mason," Thorn asked. "Ain't that kind of a funny name?" Thorn challenged Sadie.

"Not at all. I've thought about that, too," she exuded. "Now don't laugh, but here's how I see it. He's like the mason jar, septin' instead of preservin' fruit, he's preservin' the peace." She looked at Thorn for approval. He just busted up laughing.

"I gotta tell Mason next time I see him...he'll just love that," Thorn grinned and pulled the bed sheets over the two of them.

After a leisurely breakfast in bed, they got dressed and Thorn escorted Sadie to the train station to leave with the rest of the show cast. Thorn waved to Sadie from the platform, and Sadie leaned out the window, blowing him kisses. He watched the train until it disappeared from sight, then slowly walked back to town to wait four long days. He counted them out.

"She'll do the show in two days, then she'll pack up and board the train in three days, and I'll see her in Livingston in four days," he calculated. A wave of joy washed over him. He was unable to recall a time in his life when he had felt so happy, content, and optimistic about the future.

On Day Four Thorn was packed and ready to leave for Livingston. He stopped by Mason's office to say good bye. While there, Tommy stopped by with two telegrams for Thorn.

"I'm sorry I didn't get these to you sooner. One of these came yesterday, but I couldn't find you. The second one just came this morning."

"That's okay, Tommy," Thorn said.

"You want me to wait in case you have a reply?" Tommy asked.

"No," Thorn said. "I'm leaving town for a couple weeks for my honeymoon. Whatever it is can wait."

Tommy nodded and left. Thorn took the first telegram and opened it. He smiled at Mason.

"It's from Sadie," he said. He scanned the rest of the telegram. "It's from two days ago. She's in Missoula getting ready for the show. It's a sold-out crowd. She loves me and misses me and is looking forward to our honeymoon in two days." Mason sipped his coffee and nodded his approval.

"You're starting to make me ill. Just go get on your damn train and be on your way," Mason chuckled.

Thorn folded up the first telegram and opened the second one. As he read it to himself his face suddenly paralyzed with shock.

"What's wrong?" asked Mason. "What's it say?" Thorn struggled to utter the words on the paper he was holding. His hands began to tremble. He handed it to Mason. It read:

We regret to inform you that Sadie died last night in an accident on stage. Stop. Two horses collided and she was thrown to the ground and trampled. Stop. Please advise. Stop.

The Showdown at Yellowstone

CHAPTER 25

Thorn awoke slowly from a deep sleep in his ranch home bed. How he got there he didn't remember. He slowly sat up, putting both feet on the floor and waited for the room to stop spinning. He bent over and put his elbows on his knees, held his head in his hands, and rubbed his temples. His drinking bout from the previous night was intended to dull the pain, but the stabbing hangover ache in his head now only compounded the devastation of his soul. His misery was complete. The thought of living without Sadie consumed him with a melancholy previously unimaginable. Overcome with crushing grief, he slowly looked up and spied the empty bottle of rye whiskey on his night stand. He slowly stood up, grabbing the headboard and reached over, just in case he'd overlooked a drop or two. Not a chance. It was clean empty. Angry that he hadn't saved a swig for himself later, he hurled the bottle across the room and watched it shatter.

Thorn staggered into the kitchen and rummaged through the cupboards for more alcohol, anything to silence the demons. He discovered a bottle of rum he brought home from Cuba. He had planned to preserve it untouched it as a memento of his military glories with the Colonel. He fumbled with the cap and opened it, and went back to bed.

Colonel Dooley's Wild West Roundup Show was well known around the country and news of the accident quickly made the newspapers in the larger towns and cities. Eventually, the story traveled east and caught the attention of President Roosevelt himself. His heart felt a stab of pain as he read about the death of his friend Thorn's wife. He immediately cancelled a meeting and sent his condolences to Thorn by telegraph.

Sadie's folks in Ogallala were notified of her death by telegraph. They requested that her body be shipped home by rail for burial in the family plot. Nobody dared at this point to ask Thorn for his permission.

"It should be Thorn's decision," Sam said to Mason. "Somebody needs to go out and see what he wants."

Mason knew his pard' well enough to know that any intrusion right now would not only be unwelcome, but possibly fatal.

"Just ship the body to her family. I'll take responsibility," Mason said.

Two weeks passed. Mason checked in on Thorn daily, bringing food and gentle words of encouragement. He usually found him in various stages of desolation. At the end of each visit Mason made sure Thorn's weapons were unloaded and the bullets locked away.

On one such visit Thorn broke his silence.

"Where's Sadie?" he asked with a pitiful stare at Mason. Mason thought for a moment, trying to decide what to say. Finally he decided the truth was the only option.

"They shipped her back to her folk's home in Nebraska." Mason searched Thorn's eyes for a reaction; good or bad.

"Who gave permission to do that?" Thorn asked. Another long pause as Mason braced himself.

"I did." Mason waited to reap the whirlwind. Thorn stared at him with sad soulful eyes.

"You did the right thing," Thorn finally uttered. "She belongs with her family."

One morning Mason was in his office taking delivery of some groceries from Jim Proctor, delivery boy for the Stillwell General Merchandise Store.

"The coffee you ordered won't be in till next week, but the rest of your list is all here," Jim explained, unpacking the box of items he just brought in. Suddenly the door opened and Thorn walked in slow and easy, almost like he was lost. Mason took it as a good sign. It was the first time he'd seen

Thorn out and about.

"Thorn, good to see you. How you doin'?" Mason asked. Thorn made no reply. Mason turned to Jim.

"This'll be fine. Thanks, Jim. Tell Stillwell I'll be by later to settle up."

"OK, Mr. Mason," Jim said, then excused himself. Mason turned back to Thorn, who was standing in front of the bulletin board, surveying the wanted posters.

"Been worried about you," Mason said. "You look good."

His small talk made no impact on Thorn, who continued to stare at the wanted posters. He finally pulled one off the board and held it up to Mason.

"Where's he at?" Thorn asked. It was a poster for the capture of Warren Stanton for the Red Lodge stagecoach robbery. Mason thought about it for a second.

"Last I heard he was seen somewhere around Fishtail. Why?" Mason said.

Thorn made no reply. He folded up the wanted poster and tucked it in his pocket, then turned for the door.

"You ain't thinkin' about goin' after him, are you?" Mason asked, but the door closed before he could finish his question. Mason looked out the window and saw Thorn mount his horse and ride out of town.

The trail left by Warren Stanton was easy to follow. He splashed his thievin' money around pretty recklessly. Thorn rode into Fishtail, which led him to Nye, and then to Greycliff, where Warren was waist-deep in a poker game at the local watering hole. Thorn stepped into the saloon and walked over to the poker table. The players took note of his aggressive posture, with his side arm strapped and ready for action. The game stopped and the players eased their chairs back. Warren had just finished a drink when he noticed Thorn staring at him. Warren's hand was pretty good; aces up, which he didn't exactly want to lay down. Holding his cards in one hand, he gave Thorn an aggravated look.

"Somethin' I can do for you, mister?" Warren growled. As he waited for Thorn's reply, he let his free hand ease down under the table to his holster. Thorn slid the lapel of his coat back to reveal his deputy star.

"Warren Stanton, I'm takin' you in for the Red Lodge stagecoach robbery," Thorn said loud enough for all to hear. "You can take your hand off that holster and come quietly..."

That was as far as Thorn got with his little speech, because Warren made his play. He barely cleared leather when Thorn outdrew him and put one in his chest. The impact of the bullet knocked Warren back. His cards went flying and he crashed to the floor.

"...Or you can resist and die right here," Thorn finished his either-or speech to the dead man. He stood over the body for several seconds as the gun smoke cleared, then holstered his piece.

A week later Thorn rode into Coulson with a dead body slung over the previous owner's horse. He tied it off in front of the sheriff's office and walked inside. Mason was stunned to see him.

"Thorn, where you been?" he asked. Thorn made no reply, but simply walked back over to the bulletin board in search of his next prey. "Is that Warren Stanton out there?" Mason asked, pointing out the window. Thorn found a suitable challenge on the board and pulled off the wanted poster for the Fallon brothers.

"What about these two?" Thorn asked. "Any word on them?"

"Now, hang on a second," Mason cautioned. "What's goin' on here?"

"Doin' my job," Thorn replied. "You got a line on their whereabouts?"

"Look, you're not going after the Fallon brothers by yourself," replied Mason. His irritation at Thorn's behavior was growing.

"I don't need no help. Just point me in the right direction," Thorn insisted.

"This is not a one man job. I'll go with you if you'll just let me close up shop," Mason said. Thorn paused for a moment.

"All right, get your gear and let's go," Thorn agreed. Mason heaved a sigh of relief.

"Now you're talkin' sense," Mason said. He grabbed the box of groceries off his desk and headed for the storage room in the back. "Just let me get these goods put away."

He carried the box with both hands down the hall, and Thorn quietly followed behind. As they walked, Thorn softly lifted a chair from the office and continued to follow Mason. As Mason entered the storage room Thorn shut the door and wedged the back of the chair up underneath the door knob, then kicked the two back legs tight against the floor. From inside the storage room Mason tried to open the door then put a shoulder into it and knew he'd been had.

"Thorn, open this door," Mason shouted. "I mean it. Do not go out there by yourself." He paused to listen, and heard only the sound of Thorn's boots leaving the building.

"Damn you, Thorn," Mason shouted. Then he pounded his fist on the door again, mostly to register his own anger at being so easily hornswoggled.

Thorn rode east about 10 miles to Ballantine. He knew the Fallon brothers hailed from there and figured it to be a good place to pick up the trail. Finding outlaws in Montana wasn't the hard part. They were never very shy about their whereabouts. They just depended on their reputation as killers to insure they wouldn't be molested…even by lawmen. With a couple of dead deputies to their credit, the Fallon brothers got a lot of respect wherever they chose to hole up. Few lawmen had the guts to run 'em down and rid the earth of their villainy. What they didn't count on was somebody like Thorn Hickum, who didn't much care whether he lived or died.

Thorn pulled up at the Lodge Pole Saloon to talk to someone he knew. Slip Conway was kind of a shady fellow; he was the saloon swamper at the Lodge Pole. He took payoffs from outlaws to help them stay hid, then turned around and betrayed them to the law for the right price. Thorn knew his reputation as a double dippin' sidewinder that would trade his own sister for a cold can of hash.

It was mid-afternoon when Thorn stepped into the Lodge Pole. He spotted Slip jawboning with one of the saloon gals over by the piano. Slip noticed Thorn walk in for no good reason. He knew when a lawman showed his face in a strange town he's on the prowl. Well known snitches like

Slip were essential to lawmen and Slip didn't particularly want to be helpful at this moment. He ducked out the back door into the alley. Thorn just shook his head and followed Slip out the back door just in time to see the outhouse door shut easy-like. Thorn walked up to the outhouse and tapped on the door.

"Slip?" Thorn spoke to the door. A shaky voice from inside responded.

"No one in here by that name."

"Lookin' for the Fallon brothers, Slip, you got any sign on 'em?" Thorn asked, then stepped to the side of the door and waited. And sure enough, a gun discharged from inside the outhouse and a bullet flew through the door where Thorn was recently standing. Quick as a flash, Thorn squared himself in front of the outhouse door and kicked it in, smashing Slip's knees. Thorn reached through the doorway and grabbed Slip by the collar and yanked him out of the outhouse and sent him sprawling to the ground. Thorn rolled Slip over onto his back and kneeled onto Slip's chest and pointed his pistol at Slip's forehead.

"I ain't seen the Fallons, Thorn," Slip squealed pitifully. Thorn thumbed back the hammer of his Colt to full cock.

"I know they're in this district, Slip," Thorn said. "You know you're gonna tell me. Just do it now before I cripple you.

It came to Slip all of a sudden that the Fallon brothers had rode into town that very morning to resupply.

"Where are they?" Thorn insisted. He pressed the barrel of his Colt into Slip's mouth. "You don't even need to talk. Just nod if I get it right. Are they still in town?"

Slip reluctantly nodded his head yes.

"Good," Thorn said approvingly. "North end of town?" he probed further. Slip made no head motion. "South end?" Thorn continued. Slip paused a moment then slowly nodded his head yes. Thorn considered the possibilities.

"Saloon?" He asked. No reply. "Livery stable?" he guessed, as he pushed the barrel of his gun a little deeper down Slip's throat. Slip's gag reflex kicked in and he coughed a bit. Then he nodded urgently.

That's all he needed to know. Thorn rapped Slip on the top of his head with the barrel of his pistol just hard enough to keep him still for a few minutes while he walked down to the livery to pay his respects to the Fallons. Thorn pulled the 45-70 Winchester out of his saddle scabbard, worked the lever to open the action and check his loads.

"Five rounds" he thought, "two apiece and one extra just in case two aren't enough." Thorn levered one round into the chamber and kept the rifle on cock. Pulling his Stetson down low over his eyes, he walked down the middle of the street to the livery so the Fallons could see him coming.

Tom Fallon was standing by his pony tightening up the cinch strap when he looked up and noticed a figure walking down the middle of the street with a Winchester slung over his shoulder. Tom Fallon wasn't the brightest outlaw in Montana, but he did know trouble when he saw it. And this was bad business no matter how you sliced it. Tom called over to his brother.

"Todd!" he shouted. Big Todd Fallon was checking a split hoof on his horse's left rear leg when he heard his brother Tom call out his name. He looked over at his brother and saw him nod up toward the street. Big Todd turned his head to see what looked like a lawman coming their way, rifle at the ready.

"Company's coming," Tom said as he pulled a 12-gauge pump shotgun from his horse's saddle boot. Big Todd pulled his Winchester from his saddle and worked the action to lever a round into position.

"You know this guy?" Tom asked, as he squinting his eyes at the figure approaching.

"No," said Todd. "But he looks like he means business." Big Todd, standing behind his horse, took aim at Thorn, resting his Winchester across the seat of the saddle to steady his aim. Just as Big Todd squeezed the trigger, his horse shifted its balance, causing the shot to miss by a wide margin. The unexpected sound of the gunfire caused the horse to rear back and bolt from the corral, knocking Big Todd to the ground, leaving him an exposed target.

Thorn swung his 45-70 into position and fired at Big

Todd as he was getting up. The heavy slug tore into Big Todd's chest with the force of a freight train, knocking him backward several feet. Landing on his back at his brother's feet, Big Todd was dead before he hit the ground. Tom looked down at his dead brother in disbelief. Todd had always seemed invincible and the master of every tight spot. Who was this stranger that bested his brother in a heartbeat? Clutching his 12-gauge pump, he knelt beside his dead brother.

"Todd?" he muttered.

Fear and anger welled up within Tom as he stood up and faced the stranger coming towards him, still 50 feet away. Tom worked the action of his pump shotgun, racking a shell into its chamber and aimed at Thorn, cursing him as he stepped into the street. Thorn saw his danger and dived behind a nearby water trough just as Tom fired. The buckshot tore into the wooden sides of the trough, sending up a spray of water. Unharmed, Thorn continued to use the water trough for cover. Tossing away his Winchester he drew his colt's revolver from its holster. Lying prone behind the trough, Thorn peeked around the corner to see Tom advancing towards him, firing his pump action as he closed the distance. Each shot tore into the trough, shattering Thorn's tiny fortress. One more shot from that pump action and Thorn's shield would be gone. Before he could make a move the shotgun blew the trough to pieces and Thorn was fully exposed. His only chance was to beat Tom in a draw down between a pistol and a shotgun. A lopsided match-up at best, but Thorn had no other play.

Tom leveled his shotgun as Thorn rolled away from the shattered trough. Before he could take aim at Tom, a rifle shot rang out from behind him, striking Tom squarely in the chest and dropping him to the ground. Thorn swung around to see Mason on the boardwalk with a smoking Winchester in his hands. Mason looked over at Thorn.

"How'd you get here?" Thorn asked.

"I crawled out the window," Mason replied.

The ride back to Coulson was ugly.

"I know what you're doing," Mason said. "Trying to get

yourself killed playing a fool's hand going up against thieves and killers. You think you can stop that ache in your gut by killing men, or them killing you?"

"Truth to tell?" Thorn responded, "I don't much care if they surrender or make a fight of it. I'd rather they try to shoot it out and see who wins – and I don't much care who does."

At that point conversation trailed off, and the two rode in silence.

The sun touched the western ridgeline and tree shadows extended their long fingers across the valley. Mason chose to make camp rather than try to follow the road home by moonlight. They built a fire, bedded down their horses, and broke out a can of beans. Campfire chatter, which usually came easy between the two, went begging. Thorn threw a blanket around him as he stared at the fire's embers. After a painful hour of solitude, Mason spoke up.

"I never told you about a deputy of mine that got killed," he began.

Thorn cut him off.

"I don't want to hear about it," he muttered.

"Just give me a second. Let me say this," Mason countered. Thorn gave his silent consent by staring into the campfire with no reply.

"You'd gone off to war and I didn't know if you were ever coming back. I deputized a kid name Luke Cutter, and we lit out to bring in Lonnie Jones, who was hiding out on the Muscleshell." Mason glanced at Thorn, who sat as still as a granite rock.

"We had him dead to rights, cornered in a cabin. Thought we had his partner shot and killed. But I was wrong. My fault. I shoulda made sure. When Lonnie surrendered and we had him spread out on the ground, his partner busted out of the cabin and killed Luke. Almost killed me too, but he missed and I finished him off."

Mason paused, overcome with old feelings of pain and guilt. Thorn tilted his head and gave Mason a glance. Mason cleared his throat and continued.

"I was a wreck. That kid had his whole life ahead of him,

and within a week of working for me he was dead. Nobody could make me believe it wasn't my fault. I drank myself sick and just about threw my whole career away. Then someone smarter than me, who cared enough, sat me down and made me understand that everything in this life ain't up to me. Now I'm gonna do the same favor for you."

He focused his gaze on Thorn.

"I want you to look at me," Mason said. Thorn hesitated. "I'm serious. I want to make sure you hear me, so look me in the eye for what I'm about to say." He paused again and waited for Thorn.

After a few heavy moments, Thorn turned his head and looked right into Mason's eyes.

"Sadie's death was not your fault. I know that my sayin' so ain't gonna take your pain away, but that guilt you're carryin' on your shoulders, you gotta lay it down. Put her memory in a special place in your heart and keep her there. Then get on with livin'."

Thorn turned his gaze back to the fire and let Mason's words find a resting place in his brain. Then he spoke.

"Partner, you saved my life today. Not sure it was worth savin', 'cause the way I see it, I ain't been nothing but a failure in this life. Couldn't cut it as a wrangler, quit the deputy work, soldiered for less than three months, carry the blame for the death of the President, and couldn't stay married for more than two days. I ain't sure what I'm gonna do next, but I'm gonna relieve you over worrying about me anymore. I quit."

CHAPTER 26

The news of Thorn's resignation spread around town faster than if the parson had gotten caught with a whore. Most folks were shocked but the City Council couldn't have been more pleased with the timing. For more than a year the Coulson city fathers conspired to replace the sheriff's department with a full-fledged police department. But each time they broached the subject with Mason, he got his back up.

"You don't need no east coast system out here in the west. It ain't gonna work like you think," Mason insisted. "We need to keep it simple out here."

"Not for long," the Mayor rebutted. "We got a population of 5,000 and it's growing every day. You can't wrap your arms around much more than that."

Coulson was in no position for a showdown with its own sheriff. If he walked out, they'd be in a pickle and they knew it. They needed to insert someone into the sheriff's office who could learn the ins and outs of the current organization, such as it was, so they could be in a better position to make a change when the time was right. With an opening for a new deputy, the City Council saw the opportunity to install their own man in that post…and they had just the right candidate in mind.

The Mayor stopped by Mason's office.

"Mason," the Mayor said with a hearty hand shake. "I'm ashamed that I don't tell you as often as I should what a splendid job you do here. You are a credit to this community."

"I 'preciate the kind words," Mason replied, smelling a rat.

The Mayor continued.

"I couldn't help but notice you're shy a deputy and I told my missus just the other day that it's not right to put the burden of finding a replacement entirely on your shoulders, what with everything else you have to say the blessing over."

"I manage," Mason reassured the Mayor. "But thanks for caring."

"I intend to do more than just care...I intend to help," said the Mayor.

"Really?" puzzled Mason.

"Yes," smiled the Mayor. "I convened some of our forward-thinking city leaders together and we assembled a field of potential deputies until we winnowed the list down to the most promising individual to fill your opening."

Mason tried to mask his ingratitude.

"I generally like to do that myself," Mason said.

"And, I expect you to give him a thorough going over. But we're so certain you will be as impressed with him as we are, you'll thank us," said the Mayor.

"Well, if you'll give me his name, I'll contact him and set up an interview," said Mason.

"No need," said the Mayor. "We already brought him up from Denver. He's actually right outside the door," gushed the Mayor.

"He's not even from Montana?" Mason cringed. "You didn't think there was any talent to be found in this entire state?"

"He brings a special set of skills that are not likely to be found locally," the Mayor explained.

"Such as?" Mason asked.

"His organizational skills for one. He helped organize the entire Denver Police Department. And, whether you like it or not, we're headed in that direction one day."

Mason groaned audibly.

"For now, you'd be smart to let him run the office while you're out catching renegades and lawbreakers. That would allow both of you to do what you do best."

"Sounds like you've already hired him," Mason said.

"Not without your final okay," the Mayor clarified. He

could see the look of resignation on Mason's face.

"Mason, I'm serious when I say you're the reason this community is growing. You've made everyone feel safe and secure for many years now. But I'm afraid your success is your curse. Coulson's growing…you gotta grow with it," said the Mayor with as much candor as he could muster.

Mason sighed.

"What's his name?"

"Sebastian Huntley," said the Mayor. "I'll fetch him in." He opened the door and waved Sebastian in.

He was a tall stocky man with dark hair, deep piercing eyes, and a push-broom mustache. Smartly dressed, he certainly looked business savvy. None of which struck Mason as lawman qualifications.

The Mayor beamed with pride.

"I'll leave you two to get acquainted," he said. He eased out the door, and the room fell silent. Mason broke the ice. He extended his hand and Huntley gave it a firm shake.

"Welcome to the Sheriff's Office," Mason began.

"Thanks," Sebastian nodded. An awkward silence followed.

"You got a gun?" Mason asked.

"No," Sebastian said with a diabolical smile. "I won't need one." A cold chill ran down Mason's spine.

The hiring of Sebastian as deputy was a surrender to the inevitable on the part of Mason, who wearied of dodging the relentless political maneuverings of the city council. Over coffee at the Oasis Café, He explained his thinking to Sam Stokes.

"I never seen a less qualified lawman in my life who actually wanted the job," Mason said. "I know what they're up to."

"What would that be?" Sam asked.

"They're grooming him to replace me," Mason explained.

"That's horseshit," Sam snorted. "He can't do a better job than you…he doesn't even own a gun."

"Oh, you don't need a gun for the way his kind operates. I seen it in the big cities. First, he'll surround himself with a loyal gang of roughnecks who'll do the usual police work.

But his specialty will be the political dirty work that I refused," Mason said.

"Like what?" Sam asked.

"Selective enforcement, for starters. The power to choose which crimes to punish and which ones to ignore is a powerful political tool. One that I would never abide," Mason explained.

"And, you think Sebastian is that sort?" Sam asked. Mason nodded.

"He strikes me as a total political creature, just what the mayor wants," Mason said.

"They'd have to fire you first," Sam said, "And, that'll never happen. The town wouldn't stand for it."

Sam was only half right. On the other side of town in the mayor's office, the conspiracy was taking shape. The mayor, the leading councilman, and Sebastian convened.

"How long before you could be in a position to take over?" asked the councilman.

"Not long. A few months," Sebastian said. "The organization isn't complicated, it's just inexplicable. I've got to make sure I understand the filing system and to know what sort of law enforcement network is in place, so that when Mason's gone we don't miss a beat."

"Let's make one thing clear. We are not firing Mason," the mayor insisted. "We will find a place for him in this new police department. He may quit before it's all over, but we are not tossing him out on the street."

"That's a sentimental gesture that you'll regret one day," Sebastian said. "He will be a sore that will fester and demoralize the department for as long as he stays. I promise you, there will come a day when it's either him or me."

CHAPTER 27

"If somebody doesn't put a stop to that confounded Roosevelt, he's going to put us all out of business," Henry Oswald grimly predicted. The other three conspirators were not so sure yet.

"I don't know if I'm ready to sign on to this," said the portly Danford Langley, owner of the American Beef Company. "I've got my stockholders to think of."

Squeezed into his custom tailored wool gabardine suit, he looked like he had personally eaten all the profits of his enormous livestock corporation.

Oswald was sick of his vacillation.

"You saw what they did to Northern Securities," Oswald reminded him. "Picked apart and carved it up into 34 little companies. You want them to do that to you? I can tell you how J.P. Morgan feels about it, he's been spitting nails ever since."

Langley grimaced at the thought. His eyes wandered up to the portrait of Cornelius Vanderbilt hanging overhead, scowling down at them. In fact the room was full of portraits of the insufferably rich tycoons of business. It was the Grand Lounge of the Union Club, where portraits of America's royalty were on display; captains of industry, titans of government, and members of the nation's beloved military heroes.

The Union Club of New York City was the most prestigious and exclusive gentlemen's club in the country. It was a haven of retreat for the elite of the nation to share a libation with fellow achievers and converse with like-minded thinkers. The membership was highly selective, and included the likes of Winston Churchill, William Randolph Hearst, J.P. Morgan, Winthrop Rockefeller, Cornelius Vanderbilt, and John Jacob Astor.

Tonight in one corner of the Grand Lounge, a handful of national industry leaders quietly huddled together, conspiring to take care of business the old fashioned way.

Henry Oswald, owner of the American Telegraph Company, marshaled this little nest of scorpions. He was in his late 50s with receding grey hair, van dyke beard, dark suit and silk cravat. He was joined by J.G. Peters, chairman of Harvesters Consolidated, the nation's largest manufacturer of motorized farm equipment. He was prim with wispy grey hair, a neat mustache, and wire rim glasses. Alongside him sat Nathaniel Forsythe, CEO of Eastern Electric, which provided electrical power for most of New England. Forsythe was the most senior of the group, sporting a dark suit with a white waistcoat and dotted necktie. He was visibly nervous at the entire nature of the conversation.

"Maybe they're done trust-busting," suggested Peters.

"Are you kidding," snapped Oswald. "They're going after Standard Oil next."

"Are you sure? I just had dinner with Rockefeller last week," muttered Langley. "Does he know?"

"He's Rockefeller," said Oswald. "Of course he knows."

"Well, why doesn't he stop it?" asked Peters.

"He can't...don't you understand?" Oswald was becoming impatient. "We're dealing with a fanatic who doesn't understand business."

"This is just outrageous. We spend our entire lives building a company to be the biggest and best only to have it called a monopoly, like that's a bad thing," said Forsythe.

"Precisely," added Langley. "If we can't manipulate our prices to drive our competition out of business, then what's the point?"

"Don't kid yourselves. Any of us could be next," Oswald warned. Pointing to each man, he ticked off the obvious targets. "Beef, tobacco, sugar, oil, coal, transportation." He stopped and sipped his brandy.

"We're being treated like criminals. I for one am not just going to sit and take it." He paused to gauge the mood of his compatriots.

"Where does he get off thinking he can tell us how to run our companies?" Oswald continued. Then he tapped his finger on Peter's knee. "We run America, not Roosevelt. If he doesn't understand that, then maybe we've got the wrong man in office."

"Well, we're stuck with him for at least another year, unless he wins re-election," said Forsythe.

"Maybe not," whispered Oswald.

"He can't be fired. He's not one of your employees. He's not going to be impeached and I doubt he's going to have a heart attack anytime soon," Peters shot back.

"There are other ways for a man to die," hinted Oswald. The group suddenly fell silent. "Oh, come on, we've talked about this before. We are long past the point of debating whether or not. It is time to decide when, where and how he needs to go."

"Good god, Oswald," Forsythe raised his voice and was immediately hushed by the others. He lowered his tone. "I never thought you were really serious."

"Why not?" Oswald whispered. "If you recall your history, for the good of the republic, Caesar had to be removed."

"Do you realize what you're saying?" asked Peters.

"What would you do to save your company? To save the country?" Oswald challenged the group. He searched every face. No one could look him in the eye. "When he takes down Standard Oil, what will you do then? Then when he takes down beef, tobacco, fertilizer, harvesters, then what?"

"He won't go that far," Peters said.

"I was in Washington last week and I spoke to the Attorney General," Oswald replied. "He told me Roosevelt's got a list of over 40 companies he intends to dismantle. We're all on the list."

"You're kidding," Langley gasped.

"That cuts it. I'm in," said Peters. Oswald turned to Forsythe.

"Don't look at me. I'm not going to shoot him," he declared.

"We're not going to do anything, you fool," Oswald shot back. "There are people who will do these things for the right price. It can be arranged. No one will ever know."

"And if he gets caught?" asked Forsythe.

"He won't get caught. The right man will make it look like an accident," said Oswald, "Not a damnable assassination like McKinley."

"Sounds like you've already thought this out," Forsythe said.

"I have someone in mind," said Oswald. "We just have to decide which of us will make the offer." Oswald looked at his companions for a reply. Then he scanned the surroundings quickly and spotted a deck of playing cards sitting on an end table. He picked up the deck.

"We'll decide the same way we choose who pays for dinner…we'll cut cards. Low card makes the offer. Are we all in?" The others slowly nodded in agreement.

"Okay, then," Oswald said as he shuffled the deck a few times then set the deck face down on the end table. "Forsythe, you draw first."

Forsythe thought for a moment, then reached over and pinched off the top quarter of the deck and turned them up to reveal the bottom card…a ten of diamonds. Oswald looked over at Langley, who reached over and pinched off about ten cards and turned up the bottom card…a queen of clubs. He breathed a sigh. Peters took his turn and showed a six of hearts. He grimaced slightly at the sight of it.

"Okay, here we go," Oswald said, as he reached over to make the final draw. He pinched off most of the remaining deck, and held them up to show the bottom card…a four of spades. The others three gentlemen breathed a sigh of relief. Oswald gave the others a determined look.

"All right, then. It's on me. The decision is made and we are all agreed. Just remember what Benjamin Franklin said at the start of the Revolution…'Either we all hang together, or we will all surely hang separately.' "

CHAPTER 28

The train from Washington, D.C. rolled into New York's Grand Central Station shortly after lunch. The 220-mile trip took about five hours, and carried mostly business travelers. Today one of its passengers arrived courtesy of the American Telegraph Company. As soon as he disembarked, a driver collected his baggage and directed him to the company's newly imported 1903 Mercedes Simplex luxury car, the latest in elegant transportation, for the 30-mile drive out to Long Island. The chauffeur driven ride took an hour, made utterly decadent by the extensive array of alcoholic beverages and exotic hors d'oeuvres on board. It was late in January and a sip or two of whiskey helped subdue the chilly air. The bare trees and patches of snow along the road reminded him of holiday trips to the relatives when he was a lad.

By early afternoon the limousine rolled onto the estate of Henry Oswald, owner of the American Telegraph Company. The mansion was truly a breathtaking marvel of elegance and charm. It was designed in the French Châteauesque style with three stories, 250 rooms, and served as the luxurious family home of Henry and Mary Oswald. The grounds were impeccably landscaped to the absolute detail and the views of the Long Island Sound were nothing less than stunning.

Once the limousine came to a stop, the chauffeur opened the back seat door and out stepped Bailey Garrett, senior agent for the US Secret Service. By special invitation and with all expenses paid, Mr. Garrett's presence had been requested by Henry Oswald.

"This way, please," pointed the chauffeur to the butler waiting at the front door. Garrett turned to grab his baggage but saw that they were already being wheeled into the house by other attendants. The butler showed him to his quarters, a spacious bedroom and lounge with its own fully functioning bathroom.

"Dinner in the banquet hall will be at 6:00 pm," instructed the butler.

"You wouldn't have a map, would you?" Bailey asked, not entirely tongue-in-cheek.

"I will collect you," replied the butler. "Would you care for anything in the meantime?"

"Anything?" echoed Bailey.

"Anything," insisted the butler.

"Nothing now, thank you."

At 6:00 pm the butler ushered Garrett to the banquet hall and seated him at the massive table.

"Mr. Oswald will join you shortly," he assured Bailey, then excused himself. Bailey sat alone at the table, scanning the cavernous dining hall, with its 20-foot wide stone fireplace, vaulted ceiling rising 25 feet high, enormous crystal chandelier descending from the rafters, and the imported Italian marble flooring. The excess was starting to numb his senses, when Henry Oswald entered.

"I apologize for the delay," he offered. "How was your trip over?"

"It was probably the most expensive trip I never paid for," Bailey joked. "I'm still catching my breath at how the other side lives, so you'll have to excuse me." Bailey glanced around the room again in wonder. Oswald chuckled.

"How do you like the place? This is our country retreat. Our regular home is in the city."

"Pardon me for asking, but what do you do with 250 rooms out here?" Bailey said. Oswald laughed sheepishly.

"I don't know. I just wanted a bigger house than that insufferable Vanderbilt and this is what I ended up with." Bailey had no words for this kind of staggering exorbitance. He could only shake his head and gasp.

The wait staff set the table for dinner as Bailey and

Oswald made small talk, and Bailey noticed that only two plates were set.

"Aren't we expecting anyone else?" Bailey asked.

"No. Just you and me."

"Just you and me," Bailey repeated, to be sure he heard right.

"That's right," Oswald confirmed. "What do you drink? Brandy or whiskey?"

Bailey was becoming uneasy at these endless courtesies lavished on him. The invitation was rather vague. He had no idea this was going to be a one-on-one event.

"Uh, make it a whiskey," Bailey replied.

He'd been around long enough to know something was amiss. There was no good reason for a wealthy business magnate to be courting an aging civil servant like himself, but he didn't want to be so rude as to demand to know Oswald's intentions.

Dinner progressed with the usual small talk about the weather, life in New York, family vacations, and favorite past times. The meal itself was by far the most elegant and superb dining experience of Bailey's life. He asked the server for the name of the dish, and all he could recall was that it had a French name of some kind.

"Do you always eat like this?" he asked Oswald.

"Oh, this? They just threw this together at the last minute. I hope it was to your liking."

"Well, the beef thing...that was beef, wasn't it? It was just, well, it was simply indescribable," Bailey stammered.

"Wonderful. I'll take that as a 'yes'. What do you say we retire to the study?" Oswald suggested. They walked down a long ornate hallway framed in crown molding to a large double door of deep stained cherry wood. Oswald opened the doors and invited Bailey to enter. The study was as big as Bailey's house. It was two stories tall, lined with books organized by language and century. The room featured rare sculptures and ancient vases that would take Bailey twenty lifetimes worth of salary to buy. Oswald sat himself behind his desk and invited Bailey to sit across from him.

"Make yourself comfortable," Oswald insisted.

Bailey sat down with a heightened sense of anticipation. He figured he was about to find out the price tag for this little adventure. His mind started racing. Perhaps Oswald wanted a special favor, like an introduction to someone in Roosevelt's cabinet, or a back stage pass to the next inaugural ball.

What could I have that he wants? Bailey pondered.

After a momentous pause, Oswald began.

"What would you say is the main source of America's greatness?"

Say what? Bailey thought. What kind of a question was that? He remembered as a lad being quizzed by his father with metaphorical questions like "What do you need to climb a mountain?" simply for the purpose of making some obscure point. Oswald's question struck him as that sort of query. No right answer. No wrong answer. Just the one that the inquisitor was looking for and he didn't want to play this game.

"I don't know. Why don't you tell me."

With smug delight that he had stumped his guest, Oswald smiled.

"Freedom," he replied. "One of our inalienable rights, along with life and the pursuit of happiness."

Bravo, so what's your point? Bailey thought. Oswald continued.

"The freedom to choose, the freedom to speak, the freedom to worship as you please." Bailey could hardly disagree.

"Okay," he nodded.

"But what happens to this country when our freedoms are eroded by the very government that was created to ensure them?" Oswald explained.

Bailey began to squirm a bit in his seat.

"I think you lost me," Bailey said. "What freedoms are we talking about?"

Oswald tried to explain.

"What line of work was your father in?"

"He ran a furniture store," Bailey said.

"Perfect," Oswald proclaimed. "Now, suppose he worked

diligently to grow his business, producing a good product at a fair price. So he expanded. Opened stores in several towns."

"He just had the one store," Bailey explained.

"Yes, but suppose he became the largest furniture company in the country. Wouldn't that be magnificent? Something to pass on to your children?"

"Yeah. I guess."

"Should government have the last word as to how much he charges for his furniture?" Oswald continued.

"I spose not."

"Are we not losing our freedoms with an over-reaching government that has chosen to meddle in the affairs of private business?" Oswald concluded.

Bailey felt no need to reply.

Oswald went on. "I mean, if the government can tell us how much we can charge, it won't be long before they start telling us how much we have to pay our workers, then what?"

"What does all this have to do with me?" Bailey asked.

"First, let's be clear about something. Do we agree that what's good for business is good for the country?"

"Get to the point," Bailey replied with a hint of impatience.

"We are satisfied that we have made every attempt to persuade President Roosevelt to be reasonable about his anti-trust crusade, but he is determined to remain inflexible. Resolutely inflexible."

"Did you want me to speak to him?" Bailey asked incredulously.

"No. More talk is pointless. Some of my associates and myself agree that you could be of assistance in another way," Oswald explained.

"What did you have in mind?" Bailey asked, thinking finally we are getting to the crux of this bizarre dance.

"We need you to kill President Roosevelt," Oswald said calmly. The room was heavy with silence for a few moments.

"You need what?" Bailey could not have been more dumbfounded if Oswald had asked him to fly to the moon.

"I believe you heard me."

"You do know what I do for a living," Bailey inquired.

"Yes, of course. You work for the Secret Service."

"Doesn't that make your request seem just the slightest bit preposterous?" Bailey explained.

"Actually, it strikes us as perfect."

"Really? Because I get paid to protect the President," Bailey reminded Oswald of the obvious.

"Yes and how well has that gone? You lost Garfield in '81 and McKinley in '01. Oh, maybe not you personally, but you shared the blame, and it's dogged you ever since."

"How do you know so much about me?" Bailey demanded.

"You've been overlooked for promotions, given menial jobs, disrespected. Disregarded. Disdained," Oswald noted. "At your age you should have been made station chief a long time ago."

Hearing those words stung Bailey's pride to the core and stirred up old feelings of deep resentment. Oswald continued.

"How many good years do you have left? Saved anything for retirement? No, I think not." Bailey was becoming agitated.

"What do you make in a year? $5,000?" Oswald guessed.

Bailey declined to answer.

"We are prepared to offer you $200,000. That's 40 year's worth of wages to you. That should salve your conscience."

"That's a pretty safe offer considering I'll never live to spend it," Bailey sneered. "Presidential assassins don't have much of a life expectancy."

"Please, Mr. Garrett, nobody expects you to walk up with a pistol and shoot him. I am sure a man with your imagination has learned more ingenious ways to dispose of someone without leaving a trail that leads back to you." Bailey let the notion percolate in his brain.

"Think about it tonight. Let me know your decision in the morning. My driver will take you back to the city at 8:00 am. In the meantime enjoy your accommodations tonight," Oswald said.

They both rose and nodded their heads farewell. Oswald left the room, leaving Bailey to search his soul.

CHAPTER 29

Men of conscience would like to believe that their integrity is not for sale. But men of weak character know that just about anything can be bought for the right price. Bailey walked to the bathroom in his suite at the Oswald estate that night and looked himself in the mirror. What he saw turned his stomach. He actually let a man believe he was not morally outraged at the request to murder someone for money. He could remember the day he took his secret service oath. Back then he would have thrown Oswald through the window at such an offer. He examined the age lines in his face, and muttered, "How did I come to this?"

In a sudden fit of righteous indignation, Bailey stormed out of his room and marched down the hall to tell his host to go to hell. At the end of the hallway, he couldn't remember whether to turn left or right. Rather than enduring the humiliation of a housemaid leading him around, he returned to his room to simmer down.

I gotta think this through, Bailey thought. It's not like I've never killed a man before. Certainly not for money. They all had it coming. He mused for a few moments. I can't fool myself into believing that the President has it coming. He may be unpopular in some circles, but I'm not sure he deserves to die. He sat in a chair and stared out the window. But what's 'deserve' got to do with anything? Did I deserve to be the scapegoat over Garfield's assassination? No. Did I deserve to get passed over time and again for promotions? No. What I do deserve is compensation and retribution for 20 years of smiling and saluting while less qualified men leap-frogged over me and took jobs that should have been mine." He was working himself into quite a state. For that matter, does anybody always get what they deserve in this life?

Bailey walked back over to the mirror to persuade the man in the reflection. "If you don't do this thing, they'll just find somebody else, and they'll get the money that YOU deserve. Is that what you want?"

Once he got past the question of should it be done, he began strategizing how it might be done. "Is it possible to kill the President in such a way that nobody would ever suspect me?" He let the wheels in his brain spin for a few minutes. "Yes," he concluded, "I think I could. In fact, I know I could."

He sat at the desk and took out a piece of paper and began jotting down the details of such a scheme. The hours flew by as he itemized every element of the master plan. By dawn he was ready to speak to Oswald again.

The two sat in Oswald's office for Bailey's reply.

"I have given this considerable thought," Bailey began. "And I have decided to accept your offer to do this deed." Oswald sighed with relief.

"Excellent," he said.

"I have conditions," Bailey went on.

"Let's hear them," Oswald nodded.

"First, I'm not going to be pushed into a deadline. I will do this thing when I am ready and not a day sooner. There is much to prepare."

"Well, there's no point in waiting till he's out of office," Oswald countered. "So, I expect it will be done sometime during his first term."

"Agreed," Bailey nodded. "Condition two; I will need ten percent up front to cover the expenses I will incur to set this up. People. Materials." Oswald nodded.

"If you get other people involved, it cannot come back to me. It's all on you. Do you understand?"

"Absolutely," Bailey agreed. He went on. "Condition three – I want the balance of the fee to be placed in an escrow account at the bank of my choosing with written instructions that it is to be released to me the day Roosevelt is pronounced dead. Not on your say so. I don't want you to suddenly forget to pay me. You will not be allowed to withdraw that money once it is in escrow, and I will not be able to collect it until the terms are met. Do we understand each other?" Bailey said. Oswald did not like that condition.

"That's going to seem rather fishy, don't you think, that a bank will be instructed to pay you this large sum the day Roosevelt dies?"

"Not at all. We'll make it clear that I am a reckless gambler who likes the thrill of betting on uncontrollable events. We will establish that in a fit of impulsive risk, I wagered you with 100-to-one odds that Roosevelt will die in office. If he does not die before his term ends in 1904, I pay you $2,000. If he does die, you owe me $200,000." Oswald felt that was a workable cover story.

"I'll agree to that," he said. "Anything else?"

"Just one last thing. If I should die for any reason between today and 20 years from now, I will leave instructions with a trusted and reliable associate to kill you. And believe me, you are easy to find. It doesn't matter if I die of pneumonia or get run over by a freight wagon, you die."

"I'm not sure I like that. There are a lot of ways that you could die that are totally out of my control," Oswald urged.

"That's your problem. I'm taking all the risk. You need to share some risk. I don't want you to think you can cover your tracks by eliminating me. You better make damn sure I stay healthy." Oswald remained silent.

"You don't have any say-so over that last condition. I'm just advising you that I will look after myself. So, do we have a deal?"

Oswald had thought he would find a dupe who would be easily bought off and could be easily disposed of. He didn't expect a man as cautious as Bailey Garrett. This would not be a risk-free arrangement. But leaving Roosevelt alive to continue in his trust-busting crusade was even more unthinkable. He now understood the old saying that when you dance with the Devil there is a price to pay. Too late to back out. No time for second thoughts. He knew he didn't get rich by playing it safe. Oswald extended his hand.

"It's a deal."

The Showdown at Yellowstone

CHAPTER 30

"All right, everyone take a seat and let's get this meeting started," bellowed John Wilkie, Director of the Secret Service. It was February 1, 1903 and the regular first of the month meeting of all the agents assigned to the President was called to order.

Bailey Garrett sat among the gathering, waiting for his marching orders.

"The White House has given us the President's travel plans for the month of March and April and it's going to be rather hectic."

Wilkie moved to the chalk board behind the podium to go over the agenda.

"The President has arranged a grueling eight-week speaking tour around the county starting the first of March. He is scheduled to travel 14,000 miles through 25 states, visiting 150 cities, and giving about 200 speeches."

The agents in the room groaned.

"That's outrageous. How are we supposed to protect him with that kind of schedule?" asked one of the agents.

"It gets worse," Wilkie went on. "At the end of this whirlwind tour Roosevelt intends to take a two-week holiday into the wilds of Yellowstone National Park. He's calling it his fortnight's rest."

Bailey's ears perked up at the mention of Yellowstone.

"Beggin' your pardon," said another agent. "But that park is over three thousand square miles. You have got to be kiddin' me."

"This isn't the first time he's visited a National Park," reminded Wilkie. "If you'll recall, he's camped at Grand Canyon and Yosemite in the past."

The grumbling continued.

"I don't want to hear it," Wilkie raised his hand. "This whole trip has been long in the planning and carefully calculated," Wilkie silenced the crowd. "You'll each have your individual assignments, and I expect you to carry them out in a professional and coordinated manner. I'll be talking to each of you one at a time to give you your assignment. If you have any objections you can talk to me then."

Bailey saw this as the perfect opportunity to carry out his deeds. While the President was in the Nation's Capital, he was too carefully guarded to pull off the scheme he had in mind. But out west in the wide open spaces of Wyoming and Montana, the President would be far more vulnerable, providing the best conditions for foul play to occur.

In the days to follow, Wilkie systematically made the rounds to each agent to brief them. He sat down with Bailey in his office.

"Garrett, you will be part of the Kansas City detail, working with Reynolds and Anderson," Wilkie began. "The President will be speaking in Kansas City on March 27 and 28, then you'll follow him over to Topeka and up to Omaha. The Omaha team will take over from there."

"If you don't mind," Bailey said, "I'd like to be part of the Yellowstone team instead. I think I can be more help there."

"Why?" asked Wilkie.

"I know Yellowstone very well," he lied. "My parents made a trip out there when I was young and I feel quite at home there."

None of this was the truth. He had never been to Yellowstone in his life, but there was no way that Wilkie could verify or dispute that.

"Besides, I'm good on a horse and I've spent a fair amount of time roughing it in the back country."

Wilkie agreed those were good points and he made the switch on the spot. "Okay. I'll make you part of the advance team that's leaving tomorrow to meet with the detachment at Fort Yellowstone," said Wilkie. "The train leaves in the morning at 7:00. Be there."

From Washington D.C. the team of five agents, including Bailey, took the Pennsylvania line west to Chicago, where they transferred to the Chicago Great Western rail up to Minneapolis. At Minneapolis they boarded the Northern Pacific, which took them all the way past Billings to Livingston, Montana. At Livingston they boarded a special train used to carry passengers on the branch line, built in 1883 to make travel to the National Park easier. The line ran south 50 miles to the terminating point at the town of Gardiner, Montana, the northern gateway to Yellowstone National Park. The trip took the better part of a week, and gave the team ample time to devise various scenarios for protecting the President.

"One thing is in our favor," said John Hawkins, the team leader, "Yellowstone Park is not open to the public until June. So all access points will be under constant surveillance by soldiers and scouts. The President should have Yellowstone completely to himself."

As the train made its way along the spur line from Livingston to Gardiner, Bailey sat by the window to observe the terrain. The railroad line followed the Yellowstone River, which flowed north from Yellowstone Lake, deep inside the Park. The geography was mostly flat bottom land framed by the Gallatin Mountain Range to the west and Absaroka Range to the east. The passage narrowed to a gorge, as the train approached Gardiner, through Yankee Jim Canyon. From the mouth of the canyon to Gardiner the railroad line crossed the river in three places: the Yellowstone Bridge, the Yankee Canyon Bridge, and the Crittenden Bridge. Bailey made a special note of these three trestles.

The train made a brief stop at the town of Cinnabar, a few miles north of Gardiner. It was originally the last stop of the branch line to Yellowstone Park, where the Northern Pacific had established a depot while the final depot at Gardiner was being completed. They took on a few more passengers and continued to Gardiner.

Major John Pitcher, the commanding officer at Fort

Yellowstone, met the advance team at the terminus, along with several soldiers from C Troop of the Third Cavalry, stationed at the fort in Mammoth Hot Springs. He shook hands with John Hawkins.

"So glad you could make it," he said. "I hope the trip was to your liking." John smiled.

"Who did you have to bribe to be stationed out here? This is breathtaking," he joked.

The elevation was 5300 feet above sea level, and the February air was crisp and bracing. The surrounding mountains were capped with snow, and the lodge pole pines cradled a light dusting of snow. It was a picture.

"I'm not only the Fort Commander, I'm the Superintendent of the Park, so I'll be your contact person to help make sure the President's visit is safe and secure," Pitcher added.

In Pitcher's office, the planning continued.

"The approaches to the Park are all guarded by soldiers and pickets," Pitcher said, pointing to a large map of Yellowstone Park on the wall. "So, it will be absolutely impossible for anyone to enter Wonderland while the President is here."

Hawkins liked the sound of that. Bailey, on the other hand, did not.

"Troop B will be scheduled to accompany the President on his vacation and will always be available in its full strength," he added.

"What about guides?" asked John.

"Billy Hofer is the Park's leading woodsman. He will be joined by six other park scouts to accompany the President."

"Fine," Hawkins nodded.

"Will the President wish to participate in a mountain lion hunt inside the Park?" asked Pitcher. "We do authorize such hunts to control the species."

"Definitely not," Hawkins said. "The White House wants to avoid anything that might be perceived by the public as special privilege afforded to a powerful politician."

"Even outside the Park?" Pitcher offered.

"Not on this trip," John insisted.

"That's fine, then," Pitcher nodded. "One last thing…we will need a detailed list of everyone who intends to join the President on this vacation. We need names and matching photographs."

"Understood. We are preparing that list now. You'll have it in the next two weeks," Hawkins assured. Bailey was becoming more frustrated by the minute, realizing that Roosevelt was going to be much more tightly watched than he had anticipated. His diabolical options were dwindling.

For the next two days the Park Superintendent and the Secret Service team rode horseback over all the back country in the Park that Roosevelt intended to explore, noting every possible access point from outsiders. Every vulnerable point was flagged for extra security. The Secret Service was determined that Roosevelt would have a quiet and uneventful vacation in his precious Wonderland.

On the train ride back to Washington, Bailey could see that he only had one option to exterminate Roosevelt, a scheme so flawless in concept and unexpected by his fellow agents that he already began making plans for how he intended to spend his $200,000.

The Showdown at Yellowstone

CHAPTER 31

Thorn sat on the front porch of his ranch home watching the wranglers breaking in new horses in the corral. He remembered the days when he wrangled. They were hot, dusty, exhausting days with meager pay, but he could not recall a time that brought him more joy. At the end of a day of grueling chores, he would flop down in the mess house for evening chow, laugh with his fellow buckaroos and eat a hot meal. Now, there seemed nothing to look forward to, no adventures to embark upon, no reason to climb into the saddle.

Hank, Thorn's foreman, rode through the front gate and up to the porch. He had just been in town for the day's mail and had a telegram for Thorn.

"Tommy said it's from Washington. Thought it might be urgent," Hank said as he reached out from his saddle to present the telegram. Thorn slowly rose and walked over to Hank and took it.

"Thanks, Hank," he said softly. Hank nodded then tugged on the reins of his horse and eased on over to the corral to check on his wranglers. Thorn sat for a moment examining the sealed telegram.

"From Washington," he thought. "Wonder what's up." He slowly tore the envelope open and began to read.

Mason sat at his desk reading the newspaper while his deputy, Sebastian Huntley, worked to organize the filing system of the office. The task was daunting. After twelve years of paper work, the office shelves were stacked with letters, notices, court orders, invoices, receipts, wanted posters, and assorted correspondence organized in a system that defied understanding.

"Where is the Huntington file?" Sebastian asked. Mason looked up and pointed.

"It's halfway through that stack on the left side of that middle shelf."

Sebastian shook his head and muttered as he grabbed the entire stack and began leafing through it.

"Whoa! What are you doin'?" Mason asked.

"I'm trying to get this office organized. I can't find anything. It's a hopeless mess," Sebastian replied.

"I got a system," Mason said. "I know where everything is… just ask me. But don't start shuffling things around."

Mason knew what Sebastian was up to. He was determined to modernize the sheriff's office, starting with the filing system and finishing with Mason himself. But Mason was not about to be tinkered with.

"How do I find anything when you're not here?" Sebastian countered. Mason was about to offer a reply when the door opened and Thorn walked in.

"Well, look what the wind blew in," Mason said. Thorn's face showed a glow and his eyes had a sparkle that Mason had not seen since Sadie died. Thorn gave a nod to Huntley then turned to Mason.

"What's up?" Mason asked.

"I just got a telegram from the White House," Thorn said, holding up the message.

"You mean The White House?" Mason asked. Thorn nodded excitedly.

"Yep," Thorn replied.

"Well, what's it say?" Mason prodded. Thorn opened the paper and read it out loud.

To Thorn Hickum. Stop. You are invited to join President Roosevelt and a select group of guests on a two-week back country vacation in Yellowstone National Park. Stop. Be at Fort Yellowstone on April 8. Stop. Horse and supplies will be provided. Stop. Send a recent photo of yourself to Major

John Pitcher at Fort Yellowstone in advance of your arrival. Stop. Please reply to the director of the Secret Service that you received and accepted this invitation. Stop."

Then he looked up at Mason, all smiles.

"Whaddaya think about that?" he said.

"That sounds like just what the doctor ordered if you ask me," Mason replied. "I ain't seen you this full of fire and dash since you kissed your sweetheart for the first time." Mason glanced over at the calendar hanging on the wall. "You got about two months to get your picture made and get yourself ready."

"Damn," Thorn smiled. "I wonder why he asked me?"

"You obviously made an impression, and what the heck, he knows you live out here. That counts for a lot with him," Mason conjectured. Thorn turned to Huntley.

"Well, whaddaya you think?" he asked Huntley.

"Two weeks in the back country isn't exactly my cup of tea, but anytime you can have the President's ear uninterrupted, you can go a long way towards feathering your pillow," Huntley offered.

"Feathering my pillow?" Thorn asked.

"You have any idea how long people stand in line for a meeting with the President?" Huntley said.

"Actually, I do," Thorn replied.

"Well, then you know what I'm talking about. You'll have him for two weeks. I wouldn't squander it," Sebastian said. Mason intervened.

"Never mind about Huntley. He's on a different track. Just get your picture made and get your gear ready," said Mason.

The Showdown at Yellowstone

CHAPTER 32

The tinkling bell at the top of the door jamb told the butcher that a customer just entered his questionable establishment. In the 'Tenderloin' district of New York City you always needed to know when someone was entering your shop. This unsavory neighborhood earned its odd nickname from Captain Alexander Williams back in 1876, shortly after he transferred from a quieter precinct. He knew he was about to become rich from the bribes he stood to receive by ignoring all the crimes happening in front of him.

He said, "I've had nothing but chuck steak for a long time, and now I'm going to get a little of the tenderloin."

By 1903 this corrupt side of town had not changed much. The Tenderloin was notorious as a haven for prostitutes, criminals on the lam, hoodlums and anyone looking to disappear. A heavy set butcher pulled a curtain back and stepped behind the deli counter to see Bailey Garrett eyeing the hanging cured meats. The shop specialized in meats prepared in the tradition of Eastern Europe. The entire room smelled of vinegar from the sauerkraut.

"I'm looking for Emil Varga," Bailey said. The butcher just stared back.

"I don't know any such name," he muttered back in a thick Slovak accent. Bailey had no patience for this shell game. He pulled out an envelope heavy with hundred dollar bills from his inside coat pocket and tossed it to the butcher.

"Give him that and tell him I want five minutes. If he doesn't like what I have to say, he can toss me out and keep the money."

The butcher opened the envelope and fanned the stack of bills. It looked to be easily over $5,000. He gave Bailey one last look and disappeared behind the curtain. In a couple of minutes he returned and turned the 'OPEN' sign hanging in the door to read 'CLOSED'.

"Come with me," he said.

The two passed through the curtain and down a long dark hallway to a door. The butcher turned to face Bailey.

"Hands up," he instructed, pointing to the ceiling with his thumbs. Bailey knew he was in for a pat-down, and pulled out his .38 pistol and offered it to the butcher butt end first. He took the gun and signaled for his customer to turn around anyway. Bailey complied and the butcher checked him for additional weapons. When he was satisfied, he opened the door and the two walked in. Once Bailey entered, the butcher closed the door and stood in front of it to prevent anyone from leaving. It looked like a supply room with sacks of potatoes and baskets of cabbage stacked neatly in rows. In the center sat a round table with three wooden chairs and a dim overhead light.

"Sit down," the butcher said. Bailey obeyed. Two dark haired gentlemen entered the room, both well groomed. One was small and lean, wearing a snug suit and a scowl, which Bailey figured was intended to make him look more imposing. The other wore slacks and a dress shirt with a three-day stubble and wire rim glasses that gave him a studious air. Neither of them sat down. The man in the dress shirt took charge. He adjusted his wire rims and cleared his throat.

"My name is Emil Varga," he began. He spoke with a strong Slovak accent, rolling his R's and exchanging V's for W's.

"This is my associate, Andre Sturnavent. Vee avoid strangers for our own safety, but you made a compelling offer," he said, as he tossed the money-filled envelope on the table. "So you have one minute. Vot can vee do for you?"

"I said five minutes," Bailey countered.

"You may need five…I only need one. So, don't vaste it arguing."

Bailey opened both hands to show they were empty, then slowly reached into his coat for another thick envelope. He eased it out and tossed it on the table beside the first envelope.

"My name is Bailey Garrett. I work for the United States Secret Service."

The two gentlemen gave each other a quick glance then turned back to Bailey. Andre slowly eased one hand around his back where a pistol was tucked under his belt, just in case. Garrett pointed to the envelope he had just placed on the table.

"That contains the complete travel schedule for President Roosevelt for the next two months." Emil gave it a quick glance, unimpressed.

"And vot makes you tink such tings might be of interest to us?" Emil asked.

"I know who you are, Emil Varga. You write for the radical Free Society newspaper. You are a leader in the American anarchist movement. You went pretty much underground after the assassination of McKinley, because as a matter of principle you advocate the overthrow of the government, starting with the President. But after he died, the police tried to put you out of business. That's why your current office arrangements are, shall we say, rather sketchy."

Emil offered no reaction. Bailey wasn't even sure he was listening.

"Shall I go on?"

"It's your minute," Emil nodded. Bailey turned to Andre.

"Then there's you, Andre Sturnavent. Expert with small arms and specialist with explosives, thought to have been responsible for the bombing of the 35th Police Precinct last year."

Andre could barely contain his agitation at the recitation of his resume.

"I think I've heard enough," Andre blustered. He pulled his pistol and aimed it at Bailey. "Let's take him out back and shoot him, then dump his body in the river." Emil remained icy. He inched a little closer to Bailey.

"Did you come here to arrest us?"

"No," Bailey calmly replied. Emil pressed further.

"Are they vaiting for you outside, vaiting for your signal?"

"I came alone," Bailey urged. Emil looked at the butcher.

"Go take a look," he said. The butcher left the room. Andre eased closer to Bailey and placed the barrel of his pistol to Bailey's forehead.

"You'd better hope for your sake you're not lying," Emil cautioned.

"Listen, hear me out. I could go to jail for just giving you those travel schedules, that should earn me a little trust."

"Vee shall see," Emil shrugged. "Those papers could be anything. They could be the Grand Central departure schedules. You see, vee have outlived many of our comrades because vee are very suspicious by nature."

The butcher suddenly returned and shook his head no. Andre slowly removed the pistol from Bailey's head, and sat down.

"So," Emil looked at his pocket watch. "I give you one more minute."

"I need your help," Bailey said.

"And vy should vee help you do anything, mister secret service man?" Andre sneered.

"For reasons too complicated to explain, trust me when I say that at this moment your interests and my interests are identical," Bailey began.

"And vot interests vould those be?" Andre interjected. Bailey stared them both in the eye like the angel of death.

"We both want the President of the United States dead." Both Slovaks rose to their feet.

"You are one crazy man to vok in here and suggest such a thing," Emil said angrily. "I do not know you. But I know that you and I have nothing in common." Emil pulled his pistol out and aimed it at Bailey.

"And now you've had your five minutes. Say good bye." But Bailey didn't say "good bye." He had a far different message in mind.

"Čoho sa kto bojí, o tom sa mu najskôr sníva," Bailey replied in fluent Slovak.

Emil was stunned. Hearing Bailey speak flawless Slovak threw him into utter confusion. Slovak was not exactly one of the cornerstone languages of the world. He never heard it spoken by anyone outside Slovakian heritage. He slowly set the trigger hammer back in place and sat back down.

"How do you know this saying?" He asked.

"It's what my Slovakian mother always used to tell me. 'The thing we fear, we soon dream about.'"

"Your mother was Slovakian?" Andre asked.

"She came to America from Bratislava. Taught me the language 'cause she loved to hear it." Emil looked at Andre, who just shook his head.

"Put the gun away," Andre said. Emil took Andre aside.

"Vot shall vee do with him?' Emil asked.

"You might vant to hear vot he has to say," Andre said. Emil turned to Bailey.

"Just vot is your game?" Emil asked.

"We have a saying in our country, 'the enemy of my enemy is my friend'. We need each other right now to accomplish a goal we both desire. You can provide the skills and the manpower, and I can open doors for you that you cannot open yourself." Emil and Andre knew that much was true.

"Vy do you vant this to happen?" Emil asked, still incredulous.

"Does it matter?" Bailey replied. Emil had to agree. He merely shrugged his shoulders.

"This is not a suicide mission," Bailey went on. "The travel schedule I gave you has a complete set of plans for the extermination of President Roosevelt in a way that no one will ever know who did it," Bailey explained. Then he straightened his suit and turned to the butcher. "My gun, please." Emil nodded his OK and the butcher gave Bailey back his pistol.

"You go. This story of yours...these plans. I vill investigate to see," Emil said.

"I'll be staying at the Huntington Hotel tonight," Bailey said. "Keep the money and the travel plans. Pay close attention to the President's trip to Yellowstone in two months." He began to leave the room then he turned back.

"There's another three envelopes waiting for you if you're in," he said.

———————

Four hours later there was a knock on Bailey's hotel door. He opened it to see Emil Varga.

"How can vee get hold of you?" Emil asked.

CHAPTER 33

The *Prairie Queen* steamboat slowly angled toward the Coulson dock, loaded with supplies for Fort Grant. The *Prairie Queen* was a handsome two-decker sternwheeler that routinely delivered civilian and military shipments up and down the Yellowstone River. The Coulson dock was the closest drop off for supplies headed for Fort Grant about 20 miles west of town. After Coulson, the next riverboat dock was at Big Timber about 70 miles further upriver.

In the 1870s the fort originally served as a military outpost assigned to protect miners and settlers from hostile Indians. After the subjugation of the Sioux and Cheyenne, the fort was decommissioned and refitted to function as a trading post for trappers, hunters, and merchants, as well as a way station for travelers between Bozeman and Coulson.

The Coulson dock bustled with activity. Although the railroads now handled most of the passenger traffic, steamboats were still vital in ferrying supplies and today the *Prairie Queen* was laden with wooden crates marked 'canned goods'. A convoy of four supply wagons lined the dock, waiting for the cargo to be off-loaded. The captain of the steamboat eased the ship into place from the wheelhouse, as the crew on the main deck threw lines to the dock workers to tie her off.

The captain noticed the supply wagons were under the command of an army Colonel, which struck him as odd. A high ranking officer was not usually assigned to such a menial task. When the boarding plank was lowered the captain approached the Colonel.

"What's a army Colonel doin' wet nursing a shipment of canned goods?" he asked.

"The last shipment got plundered by a gang of road agents half way to the fort. That ain't gonna happen again," the Colonel smoothly replied.

The steamboat captain eyed the Colonel's side arm, a .38 caliber Colt revolver, another detail that seemed amiss. Pointing to the Colonel's holster, he observed, "I see you're packing a .38. I thought the army changed over to .45's two years ago."

The Colonel slowly gave the captain a withering glare as he handed him the requisition order for the goods.

"We got goods to haul...fifty crates, if you don't mind," he said. Then turning to his men, he shouted, "These crates ain't gonna load themselves." The pine crates were each one foot tall, one foot wide, and two feet long with dovetail joints and the words stenciled on the sides – "MILITARY – CANNED GOODS."

Four privates jumped into action as the steamboat captain scanned the paperwork, hoping it might reveal what exactly these crates contained. Then he noticed the requisition wasn't actually signed by anyone. The back of his neck started to itch at all the irregularities that were piling up.

"Hold up a minute," the captain said, pointing to the privates, who were halfway down the boarding plank with an armload of crates. "This paperwork's out of order." The Colonel was becoming annoyed at this nosey captain, who was becoming a genuine nuisance.

"What the hell are you talkin' about," growled the Colonel.

"Excuse me, but what's your name, Colonel?" the captain asked. The Colonel slowly let his right hand rest on the holster of his .38.

"Handley. Colonel Handley," he answered, studying the captain to gauge his reaction. The captain handed the requisition back to the Colonel.

"Well, Colonel Handley, these crates ain't goin' anywheres except to the warehouse across the street until you produce the proper signatures for me to release them to you."

"What?" the Colonel demanded.

"You wouldn't want all these canned goods fallin' into the wrong hands, now would you?" the captain explained. "I don't know who you are, septin' you're wearing a Colonel's uniform claiming these crates belong to you."

The Colonel sized up the situation as he lightly fingered the smooth texture of his holster. He scanned the levee. Too many people standing around for him to take these crates by force. His privates stood motionless waiting for his next order.

"Okay, captain," he said. "We'll play it your way." Then turning to his men he ordered, "You heard the captain. Take these crates over to the warehouse."

Then looking the captain in the eye, he said, "I'll be back tomorrow, and these crates better be here, every last one, or you're gonna find yourself in a crate, a big wooden one." He gave a quick glance to the wheelhouse where the name of the ship was painted 'Mr. Prairie Queen Captain'. Then he grabbed the requisition papers from the captain's hands, mounted his horse and rode off.

The Colonel's stooges were left to do as they were told, and for the next hour they moved the fifty crates over to the warehouse and stacked them neatly in the corner. When they were gone, the captain's curiosity got the best of him, and he took a crow bar to the lid of one of the crates and pushed back the packing straw to reveal a box full of highly explosive dynamite sticks, all stacked in rows and columns and insulated with straw to keep them from overheating.

"Holy shit!" the captain muttered. "There must be over a hundred sticks of dynamite in this box alone." Then he scanned the stacks and stacks of crates in front of him. His jaw dropped. "Canned goods my ass," he mumbled. "Why would the military try to sneak this shipment in under false pretense?" he mused. In his day, he had shipped numerous military ordnance clearly marked to avoid any confusion or mishandling.

Suddenly every instinct in his being told him something was very wrong. He covered the crates under a heavy tarp and locked the warehouse door.

Mason was opening the mail at his desk when the *Prairie Queen* Captain opened the door.

"You the sheriff?" the captain asked. Mason stood up.

"Yes, sir," Mason said, "C.J. Mason. What can I do for you?" The captain walked over and extended his hand.

"I'm Captain Buchanan." They shook hands. "I pilot the *Prairie Queen* steamboat. We just pulled into dock and off-loaded supplies."

"Well, there's no need to clear anything with me," Mason said.

"Well, I wouldn't be so sure," Buchanan replied. "I've been running these waters for ten years now, but I ain't seen anything like I did today. Something's awful fishy and I didn't know who to tell. So, I figured they'd be no harm in telling you."

"Well, have a seat," Mason offered.

"Well, first let me ask you this…you know any of the officers out at Fort Grant?" Buchanan began.

"Pretty much everyone, but you know, they come and go. Why?"

"You know a Colonel name 'a Handley? Big feller. Dark hair. Mustache?" Buchanan asked. Mason thought for a moment.

"I'd have to say no. Why?" Mason asked.

"He was at the dock today to pick up fifty crates marked canned goods. But his paperwork was out of order, so I wouldn't release them. We got 'em stored in the warehouse for now. I reckon he'll be back tomorrow to fetch 'em," Buchanan explained.

"Sounds like you did the right thing," Mason concluded.

"I ain't got to the good part yet," the captain continued. "After they left I opened one of the crates. It's full of dynamite. Those fifty crates marked 'canned goods' are all full of explosives. That seem odd to you?"

Mason thought a bit then shrugged his shoulders. "I spose they didn't want any undue attention over such a large shipment of ordnance."

"But that's crazy. If you think a crate is just full of canned peaches, you might not be too careful with how you toss it about. You could get yourself killed."

"I know what you mean. That stuff will send you to Saint Peter faster than a lizard can lick his eye."

"Well, I just thought you should know," Buchanan pronounced as he stood to leave.

"Duly noted," Mason said, as he opened the door to send the captain on his way. For a moment he scratched his three-day stubble in thought then returned to opening his mail.

Around 3:00 am a small band of eight goons eased their way to the back side of the Coulson Shipping Warehouse. After a brief survey of the perimeter, they gathered in a tight cluster for their final orders. Handley, still in disguise as a Colonel, took charge.

"We don't want to draw any attention or wake anybody up. If we do this nice and quiet, we'll be long gone before anyone knows what happened," he said. "You all know your jobs. Let's go get those crates."

While four dark figures moved the four supply wagons into position, two others began drilling large holes in the massive double doors of the warehouse. The few gas street lamps along the street provided adequate light to see what they were doing.

Handley stood around, checking the side streets for any sign of people. The workers traded off taking turns with the large hand drill until the holes were complete. Chains were brought up and bolts were slid through the last link of each chain then passed through the hole in the door. The chains were pulled tight and each bolt, now sideways, anchored themselves to the inside of the door.

Two horses were brought up to the door and the chains were fastened to a harness around them, and the horses played tug-of-war with the chains until the door latch gave way. The first wagon was moved into place and the loading process began.

"Easy, boys," whispered Handley. "Set'em in gentle."

One of the gang was clearly not a back alley bruiser. He was dressed in a dapper suit and carried a satchel. It was Andre Sturnavent, one of the two anarchists who originally met with Bailey Garrett. He ordered the first crate to be opened so he could inspect the contents. One of the workers pried open a crate and the dandy slid out one of the sticks of dynamite. He checked its weight, felt it for moisture, smelled it to be sure it contained the right proportion of diatomaceous earth to absorb the nitroglycerin for stability. He nodded to Handley that he was satisfied, and the stick was returned to the crate and re-sealed.

The first wagon was filled and a canvas tarp was thrown over the crates and cinched down. With a hand signal to the driver, Handley sent the wagon on its way. As the second wagon was being loaded, Handley noticed an old deck hand staggering back to his ship to sleep off the night's frivolities. The deck hand stopped and stared at the vigorous activity at the warehouse, and ambled over for a closer look. Handley saw him and cut him off.

"Whas goin' on?" he stuttered, as he squinted to control his double vision.

"Rats," Handley replied. "You have to stay back. They are moving some crates to exterminate the colony." The deck hand nodded with complete understanding.

"When you are done, you should come to our steamboat. They are everywhere," he confided.

"Excellent idea. I will speak to your captain in the morning," Handley said. "Now you better keep moving. When we're finished, this area is not going to be fit for man or beast." The deck hand winked and continued on his way.

Soon wagon number two was full and disappeared into the night. Handley checked his pocket watch, 4:00 am. In another twenty minutes the third wagon was full and quietly followed the first two wagons. The fourth and final wagon was halfway loaded when Handley heard voices approaching. He turned and saw the station clerk for the Northern Pacific and his security guard cutting through the warehouse district to get to the depot to start the day's business. This was not expected and could prove disastrous. Handley waved to his team to stop moving. They all crouched behind the wagon hoping that the two would pass on by.

No such luck. The clerk noticed the warehouse door

open and stopped. Pointing at the door he asked the security guard, "Why's that door open?"

"Somebody's getting lazy," the security guard surmised. "I'll shut it," the clerk said, as he crossed over to the warehouse. Handley waved for his people to crawl back into the shadows. By the time the clerk reached the door, the half-loaded wagon sat abandoned. He turned to the security guard.

"Can you believe somebody just left this wagon here with a bunch of canned goods still on board?" he called out. The security guard decided to come over and see for himself. As he approached, the clerk's mouth dropped open and his knees buckled. The security guard watched as the clerk dropped to the ground face first, with a knife in his back. As he dropped, the figure of Handley appeared from behind the fallen clerk with his revolver drawn. The security guard suddenly realized his own peril and tried to run, but caught a bullet in his back, and he too collapsed.

Andre Sturnavent ran out and began yelling at Handley, "There wasn't supposed to be any killing!" He grabbed Handley from behind to stop him from any further bloodshed, but Handley spun around and shoved him away.

"Let's get out of here," Handley growled.

"But we're not full yet," Andre yelled. Handley was already climbing into the supply wagon with the remaining crew.

"Let's go," he shouted to the wagon driver. The wagon driver slapped the horses with his reins and the rig began to move. Andre was trying to catch up to the departing wagon when the wounded security guard rolled over, drew his pistol, and fired a desperate shot at the wagon.

The explosion was staggering. The blast concussion threw Andre back twenty feet, where he landed in the middle of the street in a crumpled heap. The wagon was blown to bits, along with the driver, Handley, two hoodlums, and the front half of the warehouse. The blast woke up the neighbors, who started to descend on the warehouse to investigate. Finally, the drunk deck hand staggered back to the scene and muttered, "Now that's how you get rid of rats!"

The Showdown at Yellowstone

CHAPTER 34

By the time Mason and Deputy Huntley arrived on the scene, the city fire department was busy putting out the blaze. Thank goodness the warehouse was constructed of brick, rather than pine boards, or the entire neighborhood might be up in flames. While Coulson's fire-fighting equipment wasn't the most modern, it was a sight better than the bucket brigades used in the Great Coulson fire of 1892. Coulson was now using a horse-drawn fire engine. But fire fighters still had to run to the fire on foot. So, while the fire pump arrived quickly, it just sat there until the fire crew could arrive and catch their breath.

"What the hell happened?" Mason asked one of the firemen.

"Some kind of explosion," the fireman answered. Suddenly Mason remembered the conversation he had with the steamboat captain about the crates of dynamite.

"Anyone hurt?" Mason asked. The fireman pointed over to the far side of the street, where the security guard was being attended to. Mason turned to Huntley.

"I'll see what I can find out from that fella. You see if there were any other survivors we can talk to." Huntley nodded and took a closer look at the damage. He approached one of the firemen.

"Anybody die?" Huntley asked.

"Yeah," the fireman said, as he continued to pour water on the flames.

"How many?" Huntley asked.

"Hard to tell. We're piling up body parts as we find them.

Maybe you could help us sort 'em out."

"Body parts?" Huntley grimaced. The fireman pointed to the far side of the warehouse where a canvas tarp lie spread out on the ground.

"They're over there. We've found two legs, but the shoes don't match, a severed arm, something that looked like part of a head." Huntley raised his hands.

"OK, I get the idea," he said. Huntley walked over to the pile of body parts. The gruesome sight turned his stomach and he puked his guts out.

Mason walked over to the guard, who was on a stretcher with a doctor working on his bullet wound by lantern light.

"What the hell happened here?" Mason asked.

"This fella took a bullet in the back," said the doctor.

"Somebody shot him?"

"That would be my professional opinion," the doctor replied.

"Can I talk to him?" Mason asked.

"Make it quick, he's in bad shape," the doctor replied. The doctor stepped back to give Mason room. Mason eased up to the guard.

"I'm the sheriff here," he said. "Can you hear me?" The guard slowly turned his head around and looked at Mason.

"Yeah," he muttered.

"Can you tell me what happened here?" Mason asked. The guard closed his eyes for a moment to gather his wits. Then with his eyes still closed, he whispered, "I got shot by an army officer," he recalled. Then he faded into semi-consciousness.

"Do you remember anything else?" Mason gently continued the interview. "Sir, can you talk?" The doctor tried to intervene.

"He's really in no shape to talk right now. Maybe later," the doctor said. Mason raised his finger for permission to ask one last question. The doctor nodded.

"Sir, is there anyone else alive?" he asked. The guard slowly turned his head and opened his eyes and scanned the scene. He lifted one arm and pointed to Andre, who had been blown across the street by the blast concussion and was also receiving medical attention under a tree. His strength faded and he dropped his arm. The doctor stepped in.

"I'm sorry, but that's all you're going to get right now." Mason nodded and walked over to the tree where Andre was stretched out. He was bandaged around the head, as a nurse was trying to make him comfortable. Mason turned to the nurse.

"I was told this fella was here when the explosion happened," he said.

"The firemen were the first on the scene. They found him unconscious over there," the nurse said, pointing in the general direction of the warehouse.

"Is he okay?" Mason asked.

"He probably has a few broken ribs, and some lacerations from flying debris and he's a little disoriented right now," she explained.

Huntley found Mason and brought over the drunk deck hand, who had spoken to the army Colonel earlier.

"Mason," Huntley said. "I found a guy who says he actually spoke to the people who were here earlier." Mason looked at the deck hand who was semi-sober and ready to talk.

"What did you see?" asked Mason.

"It was a couple of hours ago," the deck hand began, "I was walking back to my ship when I saw this wagon in front of the warehouse loading crates."

"Did you talk to anybody?" Mason asked.

"Well, some officer told me that they were exterminating rats and had to remove some of the crates to reach the colony."

"How many were there?" Huntley asked.

"Maybe five or six," he answered. Then he saw Andre on the ground. "And this fella here, he was one of them." Mason quickly turned to see Andre try to get up to leave, as the nurse tried to get him to lie still. Mason turned to Huntley.

"Check this man for weapons, take him over to the jail and put him in a holding cell," Mason ordered. "We've got some questions to ask him." He noticed that Andre had a satchel hanging from his neck with a leather strap. Mason took the satchel from him, and the three marched over to the jail.

It was getting along dawn when Andre found himself in a cell. Mason and Huntley examined the contents of the satchel. It contained various topographical maps and photos of a railroad bridge.

Andre was finally alert enough to talk. "You have no right to go through my valise," he stammered, pointing his finger through the bars at Mason.

"Shut up and sit down," Mason barked back. The prisoner complied. "For starters, what's your name?"

Andre stood up again. "My name is John Vilkie. I am the Director of the Secret Service, and I demand to be released immediately." Mason and Huntley suddenly looked up in surprise.

"Secret Service? As in the United States Secret Service?" Mason asked incredulously. Mason studied this fella with a new interest. He dressed sharp enough to maybe be a government official, but he had some kind of a foreign accent that Mason could not place. Since he had never met the Director of the Secret Service, Mason was in no position to confirm or deny his assertion.

"I have papers in that valise that vill prove who I am," Andre stammered. Mason flipped through the papers in the valise and came across some blank official stationery from the U.S. Secret Service.

"Dat stationery is from my office," he declared. Mason turned to Huntley. "You ever met the Secret Service Director?" Huntly shook his head.

"No." Andre was becoming impatient.

"Go ahead and vire Vashington. They'll confirm I am who I say I am," he demanded.

"You just hang on a second," Mason countered. "First you tell me what you were doing in the warehouse."

Andre suddenly assumed a very serious demeanor. "I vas on assignment for national security, and I cannot divulge the details." Mason was not impressed.

"Vire Vashington," Andre repeated.

"I'll do you one better," Mason replied, as he grabbed his hat and walked to the door. Turning to Huntley he said, "Keep an eye on this guy. I'll be right back."

CHAPTER 35

Mason went in search of Thorn, who used to work for John Wilkie. If anybody could identify him, Thorn could. But where to look first? It was 6:00 a.m., but given Thorn's recent state of mind, Mason decided to check the Crystal Palace Saloon. Sure enough, there was Thorn sitting at a corner table staring at a half empty bottle of whiskey. Mason sat down beside him.

"You just getting started or just finishing up?" he asked.

"I got woke up a couple hours ago. Sounded like an explosion. I was coming over to see what it was and I got kinda sidetracked here," Thorn explained.

"Yeah, it was a pretty big explosion. They're still putting the fire out," Mason said.

"Was there something you needed?" Thorn asked.

"Oh, I just thought you'd like to say hello to an old friend of yours."

"And who would that be?" Thorn muttered.

"I've got John Wilkie, the Director of the Secret Service, locked up in my holding cell." Mason suddenly had Thorn's attention.

"You said what?"

The two started walking over to the jail.

"He actually said he was John Wilkie?" Thorn asked to make sure he heard Mason right.

"Yes, sir. He made a big deal about it. Told me to wire Washington if I needed proof. Pretty safe request, considering the time of day. Besides, I figure you're all the proof I need."

"What did you tell him about me?" asks Thorn.

"Nothing," says Mason.

The two entered the jail where Huntley was examining the stationery from the valise, and Mason pointed to the man in the cell. "I'd like you to meet John Wilkie," Mason said. Thorn stared at the man for a moment.

"You're John Wilkie?" The man tentatively nodded his head "Yes," like he wasn't sure if he was or not.

Thorn slowly approached him, extended his hand through the bars and gave him a friendly hand shake.

"Welcome to Coulson, Mr. Wilkie." Then he turned to Mason and Huntley.

"Can I talk to you two outside?" The three stepped onto the boardwalk just outside the jail.

"That man is NOT John Wilkie. I know John Wilkie."

"Son of a bitch," Mason muttered. "I knew something was fishy."

"He's obviously relying on the fact that nobody this far from Washington would know what the Secret Service Director looks like."

"I sure as hell wouldn't," Huntley agreed.

"The question is, how does he know that name, and why would he feel safe to use that cover," Mason asked.

"And how did he get his hands on that stationery?" Huntley added.

"Let's ask him," said Thorn. They all walked back inside and found their prisoner dead on the floor in his cell. Mason opened the cell door and checked the man for cause of death. Thorn noticed a small empty vile on the floor and smelled it.

"Poison," he concluded. "Sewn into the collar of his coat," Thorn pointed out.

"Why would he kill himself?" said Huntley.

"He must have known the jig was up when Mason brought me in to identify him," said Thorn.

"What the hell is going on?" Mason asked.

"Did he have anything else with him?" Thorn asked.

"Just this valise," Mason pointed to the satchel on the desk. Thorn opened the satchel to look for anything that might shed light on this character. He pulled out several photos of a tall railroad bridge from various angles. He studied it.

"You recognize this bridge?" he asked Mason.

"No. Never seen it," says Mason. "And I've been over every railroad bridge from Miles City to Bozeman."

"What about you?" he asked Huntley. Huntley gave it a look.

"No."

"Where do you suppose it's from?" asked Thorn.

Mason was stumped. He pondered for a moment then decided to put his observation skills to work, just like Sherlock Holmes would do. He studied every detail of the dead man from head to toe. Then he got an idea.

"Show me that guy's fingers," Mason said.

"His what?" asked Thorn.

"I want to see his fingertips, see if they're stained." Thorn lifted up one hand of the dead man and Mason could see plainly that they were not stained.

"Whoever this guy is, he didn't take those pictures. Somebody else did," Mason deduced.

"How do you know?" Huntley asked.

"Look at his fingers, every photographer ends up with brown stains on their fingers from the development chemicals," Mason explained. "This guy's fingers are clean. He had somebody else shoot these pictures."

"Well, that could be anybody," Huntley said.

"There's only two professional photographers in the region who can shoot this kind of picture,' said Mason. "Here in town, Osborn Photography." Mason turned and gave Thorn a brief look.

"You remember them," Mason said. He saw Thorn try to hide a small shot of pain that ran from his head to his gut. Mason continued.

"And then there's an outfit in Bozeman. Let's start with Osborn."

Mason and Thorn grabbed their hats to leave. Mason turned to Huntley.

"You get a hold of Sam Stokes. Tell him he's got a new customer."

Mason and Thorn walked over to the Osborn Studio where Thomas Osborn had just arrived to get to work on developing some shots of the town.

"Thomas," Mason greeted him. "How's business?"

"I figure there's enough to keep me busy," Thomas said. He suddenly recognized Thorn. "I heard about your wife. I'm so sorry for your loss." Thorn nodded.

" 'preciate it," he said. Thomas turned back to Mason.

"But you know I don't just do wedding portraits. Photography is all the new art form now, you know," he said.

"Is that right?" Mason said.

"Oh, yes. Nobody paints landscapes anymore. We take pictures of landscapes."

"Well, funny you should say that," Mason said, as he laid out the photos of the mystery bridge on the table.

"I got some photos of a bridge right here. Take a look." Thomas examined the photos and quickly turned to Mason.

"Why, I took those photos myself a couple of weeks ago. How do you like them? And how did you get them?"

"Did somebody pay you to take these pictures?" asked Thorn.

"Yes, a Mr. Sturnavent. Why?" Thomas asked.

"Where were these pictures taken?" Mason asked.

"They're taken a few miles north of Yellowstone, the Crittenden Bridge," he said.

"Did he say why he wanted you to take these pictures?" Thorn asked.

"Said he was an engineer collecting photos of bridges for study. He paid plenty for the three days we spent getting the shots he wanted," Thomas recalled.

"Well, Mr. Sturnavent, or whatever your name is, what the hell were you up to?" Mason muttered under his breath.

CHAPTER 36

Mason knew one thing for sure, dynamite and bridges do not belong together. Anyone with a keen interest in both was likely up to no good.

"Thorn, you were in the army. Is there any reason a trading post like Fort Grant would need fifty crates of dynamite?" Mason asked.

"Fifty crates? Hell, no. Not even fifty sticks," Thorn snorted. "But I'll find out. Let me take a ride out there and talk to the post commander."

"I'd sure appreciate it, if you feel up to it," Mason said. "That don't make you a deputy though."

"I'd prefer it that way," Thorn said. "What are you gonna do?"

"I'm going to have a little talk with the steamboat captain who brought that shipment in. See if I can track down who sent it," Mason said.

The ride out to Fort Grant took about four hours. By noon Thorn was in the office of Colonel Stevens.

"I understand you were a Rough Rider under Teddy Roosevelt," the Colonel said. "What was that like?"

"If you've been in combat, you already know. At first you think you're fighting for glory, but in the end you're really just fighting for the fella beside you," Thorn reminisced.

"That's about right," Stevens nodded. Thorn sighed over the painful memories of comrades lost.

"What about yourself?" Thorn asked.

"Oh, I've had a very distinguished career," he began in a tone dripping with sarcasm. "Thirteen years ago I was a major with the 7th Cavalry in South Dakota under Colonel Forsyth. We were ordered to disarm a camp of Lakota Indians at Wounded Knee. Only they didn't want to be disarmed… felt they needed their rifles for hunting. One thing led to another, and pretty soon shots were fired, then all hell broke loose. By the time it was all over twenty-five soldiers were dead along with a hundred and fifty men, women, and children of the Lakota tribe," Stevens recalled.

"Yeah, I heard about it," Thorn said.

"Everyone did," Stevens muttered. "During the inquiry, I was asked for my account of the events, and I guess I didn't tow the army's version, 'cause I got re-assigned to this dead-end post."

"Sorry to hear that," Thorn offered.

"So, I'm finishing up my illustrious military career overseeing mountain men, fur traders, trappers, hunters, herders, wagon trains, and local Indians. We have a few cannons here but mostly just for looks. We mostly just keep the peace, settle disputes. Not exactly what I signed up for." Stevens fell silent and sighed as he looked out the window.

"Anyway, enough about me. What brings you out here?" Colonel Stevens asked.

"A couple things…first, do you know a Colonel Handley?" Thorn said. Stevens thought for a moment.

"No, can't say as I do. Why?"

"A fella answering to that name wearing a Colonel's uniform was at the Coulson dock yesterday to pick up a shipment of fifty crates of dynamite for Fort Grant." Colonel Stevens was stunned.

"For here? Are you kidding me?"

"No. And I take it from your response that you didn't order all that ordnance," Thorn said.

"What the hell would I do with fifty crates of dynamite out here? This is a backwater trading post. Nobody needs dynamite here. We get trappers once in a while who need to bust up a beaver dam, but that's about it," Stevens said.

"Well, whoever picked up that shipment obviously ain't hauling it out here, but if you hear anything, let me know," Thorn said.

———————

Mason boarded the *Prairie Queen* steamboat about 9:00 a.m., which was still in dock, and found Captain Buchanan supervising the crew loading cargo.

"Captain," Mason greeted Buchanan with a hand shake.

"Sheriff Mason," Buchanan smiled. "What can I do for you?"

"I suppose you heard about the explosion last night," Mason said, pointing to the gaping hole in the warehouse across the street. The captain shook his head in grief.

"I told you that whole business was trouble. I heard people died."

"That's what I came to talk to you about," Mason said.

"I hope you don't blame me for all this?" Buchanan said. "I was just shipping cargo." Mason tried to put the captain at ease.

"Don't worry none of this is your fault. But I could sure use your help in trying to get to the bottom of it."

"Just tell me what you need," the captain offered.

"I need to track where that shipment came from. Where did you pick up those crates? Who presented them to you?" Mason asked.

The captain thought back for a moment. "They were loaded when we docked in Bismarck. They came from the armory at Fort Lincoln."

"How does that work exactly?" Mason asked.

"Fort Lincoln is pretty much the supply center for military equipment for the whole region. If a fort needs restocking, they put in a request to Fort Lincoln. We pick up the load and deliver it to the nearest dock."

"Where does Fort Lincoln get its stocks?" Mason asked.

"Probably St. Louis," the captain speculated. "Big shipping center there for the US Quartermaster Department."

"Who keeps records of all this transfer of equipment?" Mason asked.

"You'd have to check with St. Louis," the captain said. "I just haul cargo."

"Got it," Mason nodded. "Did you keep the shipping manifest for your trip here?"

"Of course," the captain said. The two went to his office on the cabin deck and he sifted through his files.

"Here it is." He handed it to Mason and pointed to the line reading "Canned Goods…fifty crates."

"That's it right there."

Mason took the information off the manifest and marched over to the telegraph office. Tommy was busy transcribing an incoming message when he saw Mason walk in. He nodded at Mason to acknowledge him then continued to take the telegraph feed off the wire until the message was complete. He turned to Mason.

"Yes, Mr. Mason, what can I do for you?"

"I need you to send a telegraph to the St. Louis office of the US Quartermaster Department. I need the original order for a requisition of 50 crates of dynamite. The requisition number is ND-082052."

"Got it," said Tommy as he wrote it all down. "You want to wait for a reply?"

"No, just come find me when it comes in," Mason said, and he turned to go back to his office.

At dinner that night, Mason met up with Thorn, who had just returned from Fort Grant. Thorn gave his account of the meeting with Colonel Stevens. As they were finishing the pot roast special, Tommy found Mason and brought the reply.

"Sorry, it took me awhile to track you down," Tommy apologized, handing Mason the incoming telegram.

"Thank you, Tommy," said Mason. "Whatever they're paying you is not enough." When Tommy excused himself, Mason opened the telegram and read it out loud for Thorn to hear-

Apologies for the delay. Stop. Tracking down this irregular order proved difficult. Stop. Order originated from the US Treasury Office, Secret Service Department. Stop. No explanation for the mislabeling. Stop.

Mason folded the telegram up and looked over at Thorn

for a reaction.

"Well, I was only with the Secret Service for a short time, but I can tell you that there is no legitimate reason for that department to order fifty crates of dynamite to be shipped anywhere," Thorn said.

"Okay, what do we got?" Mason tried to put the pieces together. "We got fifty crates of dynamite ordered by the Secret Service and labeled 'canned goods' but nobody knows why. The order is filled in St. Louis and shipped to Bismarck, transferred and shipped to Coulson, to be picked up and delivered to Fort Grant overland."

"Right," Thorn agreed, "Only Fort Grant never ordered it."

"It's picked up at the Coulson dock by someone representing himself to be Colonel Handley," Mason continued. "A bogus name. He is blown into a million pieces, leaving an Andre Sturnavent to answer questions. Once incarcerated, he declares himself to be none other than the director of the Secret Service, and produces papers to that effect then kills himself once he is exposed as an imposter. In his possession are numerous photographs of the Crittenden Bridge, the very railroad bridge over which President Roosevelt will soon travel to reach Yellowstone Park."

He paused to catch his breath.

"I may not be Sherlock Holmes, but this is what it looks like to me. Roosevelt appears to be the target of an assassination attempt by blowing up the Crittenden Bridge. The plot appears to be organized with the coordination of people who know Roosevelt's travel schedule, making this an inside job."

He looked Thorn in the eye and concluded, "We can't take this to the authorities. We don't know who's in on it and who we can trust." He stopped and looked around to be sure no one was eavesdropping. Then he leaned in closer to Thorn.

"If we talk to the wrong person, they'll just shut down the whole operation and cook up a new scheme somewhere else."

"Yep," said Thorn. "And we'll never know when, where, and how."

Mason heaved a sigh. "It's up to us to save the President."

The Showdown at Yellowstone

CHAPTER 37

The Presidential speaking tour was nearing completion, with only two stops left; Coulson and Livingston, Montana. Eight weeks, fourteen thousand miles, twenty-five states, a hundred and fifty towns and two hundred speeches; one of the most ambitious cross-country ventures ever attempted by a President.

Roosevelt's consolation was the luxury by which he traveled. His special train, dubbed 'The Elysian' was the most uniquely outfitted and self-contained home on wheels ever to ride the rails. It consisted of a locomotive, coal car, and six special use railway cars.

The first car, closest to the locomotive, was the baggage car, where all the luggage and supplies for the entire entourage were stored. The second car was called 'The Atlantic', a club car designed with wood and leather interiors, used for relaxation, drinks, and casual conversation. It was even equipped with a fully functioning barber shop chair.

The third car was named the 'Gilsey Diner', an elegant dining car, stocked with champagne and cigars, serving meals to all the reporters, dignitaries, and security who followed the President in his travels. The fourth car in line was called 'The Senegal', a lounge car carrying reporters, photographers, telegraphers, and secret service agents in comfort.

The fifth car was called 'The Texas', a compartmental sleeping car for any White House staff and guest onboard. The last car in the line was the largest of them all. Named 'The Elysian', this seventy-foot long railroad car was dubbed the 'rolling White House'. It was detailed in solid mahogany, plush velvet, and deep soft furniture. It included two sleeping chambers with brass bed frames, two tiled bathrooms, and a private kitchen staffed with the Pennsylvania Railroad's top chef. This car also boasted a private dining room, a stateroom with picture windows, and an airy rear platform for whistle stop speeches.

The Elysian pulled into the Coulson train depot on April 4, 1903 amidst the jubilant welcome of the local population. Colorful banners draped the depot station and American flags waved from improvised flagpoles. Sam Stokes, Mason and Thorn stood among the masses waiting for a glimpse of the President.

"I'll say this for him, he knows how to travel," Mason said.

"Don't let all this fool you," Thorn replied. "He's as back country as the Elkhorn Mountains."

"A man in his position is entitled to certain comforts," Sam noted. "After all, he is our commander-in-chief."

A band struck up a lively tune, as if to tease Roosevelt to come out and listen. Finally the door to the back car opened wide and out stepped the President onto the rear platform, flanked by two secret service agents. The crowd cheered as he leaned over the railing and waved to everyone with his broad signature smile. He surveyed the throng as if looking for someone, waving to all while his eyes darted from side to side. Finally he spotted Thorn, and their eyes met. Roosevelt pointed at Thorn and nodded. Thorn returned the nod.

For the next few minutes the nation's President spoke of America's greatness, the need for conservation, and the importance of family. He ended with his usual rousing anthem:

"Thrice happy is the nation that has a glorious history. Far better is it to dare mighty things, to win glorious triumphs, even though checkered by failure, than to take rank with those poor spirits who neither enjoy much nor suffer much, because they live in the gray twilight that knows neither victory nor defeat."

Larry Richardson & Tom Richardson

With a final wave of both outstretched arms, Roosevelt retreated back into The Elysian. The band struck up 'Hail Columbia', photographers captured the moment, and reporters cornered the Mayor of Coulson for his comments on this momentous occasion. Mason turned to Thorn.

"I always thought he was taller," said Mason.

"He looked robust," Sam observed. "Perhaps even stout."

"He's put on a pound or two since I seen him," Thorn replied. "I expect a few weeks in the back country should thin him out a bit."

"Gentlemen, I will see you back in town," Sam said as he strolled down the street, both thumbs tucked in his vest pockets.

From the rear of the train Bailey Garrett slipped away from the crowd, down an alley and into town. He looked over his shoulder to be sure he wasn't being followed, then darted into the Harrison Hotel, a sad looking establishment that served those who couldn't afford better.

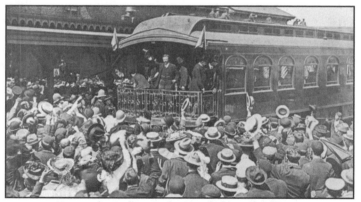

Roosevelt speaking to the crowds from The Elysian

Back at the railroad station, a secret service agent carved his way through the crowd to reach Thorn with a message. When he got within a few feet he called out.

"Thorn Hickum!"

Thorn and Mason turned around to see who was calling. The agent caught up to them and handed Thorn a note.

"The President has invited you onboard The Elysian for the remainder of the ride to Yellowstone." Turning to Mason he added, "Of course, you are welcome to join as well, Mr. Mason. We leave in the morning." He tipped his hat and returned to the train.

"Now, how'd he know my name?" Mason pondered. Thorn just looked at Mason and laughed. They returned to town and gathered up all they thought they might need for the next few weeks. Mason had a few words for his deputy, Sebastian Huntley.

"Now, don't touch anything till I get back," he warned. "I may not be easy to reach for the next few weeks, but you can wire any messages to Fort Yellowstone. That's likely where I'll be staying."

"Don't worry, I'll take charge, and maybe I'll have this place organized by the time you get back," Huntley assured. Mason thought that promise sounded ominous, but he dismissed it to focus on his travel essentials. He began gathering his Sharps and Winchester rifles, ammunition pouch, change of clothes, a coat for the high country, and a bag of elk jerky.

In a small room at the end of the hall at the Harrison Hotel a heated discussion continued.

"I'm sorry about Andre's death," said Bailey Garrett, "but he was aware of the dangers. Now we have to continue, even without him." Emil Varga and three other Slovak conspirators had ideas of their own.

"Vee just vant to finish this now," Varga argued. "No more vaiting, no more loading and unloading explosives." The other Slovaks muttered their approvals.

They were all in their 30s, wearing work pants, shirt, unbuttoned vest, and fisherman's cap. They spoke almost no English, but mumbled Slovak to each other, which annoyed Bailey to no end.

"Just shut up," Bailey hissed. "We are not changing the plan."

"Vy not?" Emil demanded. "He is right here. Vee can set the charges under his train tonight and blow him up while he is sleeping."

"Are you kidding? You'll never get near that train. It's so heavily guarded a rat couldn't get onboard," Bailey countered.

"Except a rat like you," Emil joked.

"Just stick to the plan," Bailey said.

"Then I say vee blow the bridge as he is arriving in Yellowstone, two days from now, not vait until he is leaving to go back home in two veeks," Emil insisted.

Bailey was about ready to shoot the four of them dead and just finish the job himself. He took a deep breath.

"I'm going to explain this one more time," he said through his grinding teeth. "The train will be overflowing with passengers on the return leg. If we blow the bridge then, they'll be so many bodies and so much chaos it'll take weeks to sort it all out, and by then, we will all be long gone." They grudgingly agreed.

"I'm going on ahead tomorrow in the train. You follow behind. I'll meet you at the bridge in two weeks," Bailey concluded.

———————

When he finished packing, a thought occurred to Mason. He rounded up Thorn and the two walked over to the telegraph office.

"What are we doin' here?" asked Thorn.

"You know, one of us might as well say what's on both our minds," Mason began.

"Go ahead," Thorn replied.

"If someone actually intends to blow up a bridge underneath the President's train, do we really want to be on that train when it happens?"

"I spose not," Thorn had to agree.

"I know someone at Fort Yellowstone, Captain Kellerman. I competed against him a few years back at a marksmanship competition. I'm going to wire him to check out the Crittenden Bridge for explosives, then station sentries along the bridge until the President's train arrives."

"How we gonna know he got the message in time?" Thorn asked.

"We're headed for Livingston in the morning. I'll have him wire Livingston with an 'all clear'. If we don't get a telegram, We're not gonna let that train get near Yellowstone," Mason vowed. Thorn exhaled slowly.

"I'd like to see you try to stop it," Thorn sighed.

In the morning Mason met up with Thorn at the depot and the two climbed on board. The Elysian blew a farewell whistle to Coulson and continued west to Livingston.

"I never in my days seen a train like this," Mason marveled. Thorn had to agree.

"Yeah, it's pretty well stocked. I been on it a few times."

"I spose there has to be some reason for a fella to run for office," Mason muttered. "Livin' on this train's a mighty fine temptation."

They dropped their things in the "Texas" car and sauntered up to the "Atlantic" – the club car.

"Let's just see how well stocked they are," said Thorn, as he eased up to the liquor bar. He waved the attendant over.

"My good man, you happen to carry Old Bushmills Whiskey?" he asked.

"Yes, indeed," the attendant smiled.

"I'll have two, one for me and one for my partner," Thorn said. With drinks in hand, Thorn realized there's nothin' better in life than your pard' by your side and two fingers of whiskey in your glass. They joined the other secret service agents, some of whom remembered Thorn from his days back in Washington.

"So, you boys drew the short straw on this assignment," Thorn laughed. The other agents joined in.

"You mean there ain't no electric trolley cars up there in Yellowstone?" one of them chimed in.

"Nope, and I hope you brought your woolies," Thorn added, "or you're gonna freeze off your little peckerwoods." The laughs continued.

Just then the door at the rear of the club car opened

and in walked Bailey Garrett. Thorn saw him and the smile evaporated from his face. He just stared at Garrett while the conversation retreated into another realm far from his attention.

"S'cuse me a second," he said, as he handed Mason his glass and approached Garrett. Mason followed him over. Suddenly Garrett noticed Thorn and the look on his face turned sick, like a man who just saw his ex-wife, mistress, and girlfriend all talking to each other.

"What the hell are you doin' here?" Thorn asked.

"I could ask you the same question," Garrett replied.

"Invitation by Roosevelt," Thorn answered, holding up TR's personal note with a smile. Garrett turned his eye to Mason.

"You must be the legendary Mason," Garrett said. Mason nodded.

"And you, I take it, are the infamous Bailey Garrett," Mason replied, sipping his whiskey.

"You two ever travel apart?" Bailey jabbed.

"No, didn't you hear? We got married," Mason dished it right back.

"Hey, wait," said Thorn, "That's not funny."

"No, it's not," agreed Bailey. "Speaking of which, I heard about your wife. So sorry. How long were you married? Two days?"

The mood turned icy as the pain of Thorn's loss was suddenly compounded by Bailey's callous remark. Mason saw Thorn's expression turned very dark.

"Thorn, weren't you gonna show me the famous Elysian railroad car?" Mason side-stepped with Thorn before things got worse. Bailey stopped them.

"Sorry, off limits. President, family, and Secret Service only. And last time I checked, you don't work for the President." And without waiting for a retort, he turned and exited the club car.

"What the hell was that?" Mason asked. "You used to work with that guy?" One of the nearby agents overheard Bailey's crass comments and came over.

"Don't pay any attention to Garrett," he said. ""He's been

a shit ass ever since he announced his retirement."

"He's quitting?" asked Thorn.

"Yep. Packing it in after this assignment. He said something about moving to Europe."

"Can't happen soon enough," Thorn muttered.

CHAPTER 38

The Elysian rolled into Livingston and the last speech of Roosevelt's grueling eight week whistle stop tour of the country. From his perch on the back porch of his Elysian car, the President waved at the crowd and delivered a heart-felt tribute to the grandeur and beauty of the American West:

"Nothing could be more beautiful than the view at nightfall across the prairies to these magnificent hills,
when the sky is painted with a red after-glow that fills the horizon at sunset.
There are no words that can tell the hidden spirit of the wilderness, that can reveal its mystery, its melancholy,
and its charm."

When the audience finally dispersed, Mason and Thorn told the engineer to hold the train until they got an 'all clear' telegram.

"I don't take orders from you," the crusty old engineer growled. Thorn jumped in.

"We got reports of possible sabotage up ahead, so you'll hold this train or we'll have you arrested for accessory to a conspiracy," Thorn thundered. The engineer stared him down for a few seconds then acquiesced.

"All right, but I ain't gonna take the blame for throwing us off schedule," the engineer insisted. Thorn pointed to Mason.

"This here's Sheriff Mason. He's got it all under control," Thorn pronounced, then turned away from the engineer and gave Mason a wink.

"We're headed over to the telegraph office right now for the 'all clear' message," Mason told the engineer. Then the two turned and walked away.

"What are you gonna do if there ain't no telegram?" Thorn asked.

"If it comes to it, we'll just have to spill the beans to the President and let the chips fall where they may."

It was nearing 3:00 in the afternoon when the two marched into the Livingston Telegraph Office. The office was full of reporters trying to file their news reports with their newspapers around the country. Their descriptions of the events of the day were burning up the wires. Mason and Thorn carved their way through the press of people to reach the counter.

"Any incoming telegrams from Fort Yellowstone?" Mason called out.

"Yeah, we got one for a C.J. Mason from a Captain Kellerman," the office manager said.

"That'd be me," Mason replied. The manager gave him the telegram and Mason opened it on the spot.

"What's it say?" Thorn squeezed in for a look. Mason read it out loud.

"Mason. Stop. All clear. Stop. Sentries are posted. Stop."

Mason and Thorn looked at each other and heaved a sigh of relief, then wedged their way through the crowd and left the office.

The Elysian train was transferred to a fifty-mile spur line created by the Northern Pacific to provide rail service directly to the northern entrance of Yellowstone.

Roosevelt busted out of his presidential garb and into his back country camping clothes. He could feel the vitality of his youth coursing through his veins again. He was home , back home in his precious Yellowstone.

The Elysian pulled into the Cinnabar station to pick up more passengers then continued on. Halfway between Cinnabar and Gardiner they crossed over the Crittenden Bridge, and Mason looked out his window to see military sentries posted on both sides of the gorge. In a few miles the train finally arrived in Gardiner on April 8, 1903. He was met by C Troop from Fort Yellowstone, and given a royal welcome to the Park.

Roosevelt Arriving at Gardiner with Major Pitcher at his side.

Thorn and Mason watched the joyous commotion from a distance. They had plans of their own.

"You'll keep an eye on the President in the back country," Mason said, "while I stay here and keep an eye on the Crittenden Bridge."

Just then Captain Kellerman stepped up.

"Sheriff Mason," he said with a handshake.

"Captain, you saved our bacon today," Mason confided.

"Yeah, I'd like a little explanation, if you don't mind," Kellerman answered. "What the hell was that all about?"

"I'll fill you in later. First, I want you to meet my pardner, Lt. Thorn Hickum, retired U.S. Army. Thorn, this is Captain

Joshua Kellerman." The two shook hands.

"Pleasure," Kellerman said. Mason continued.

"Captain Kellerman here gave me a devil's time at the sharpshooting competition two years back. Nearly kicked my ass," Mason said.

"I'm impressed," Thorn offered. "Mason's a crack shot drunk or sober."

"I wouldn't want to put that to the test," Kellerman replied. He turned to Mason.

"You gonna be in the competition this year?" Mason scratched his cheek.

"I doubt it. I ain't kept up with practice. I'm afraid you'd put me to shame."

"Well, heck fire. You haven't taken up the rockin' chair, have you?" Kellerman chided. Mason smiled.

"It gets more invitin' every year."

A ruckus was brewing in the Fort Yellowstone dining hall. The list of people who expected to join Roosevelt on his wilderness adventure had become ridiculously large. Troops from the fort, Secret Service, newspaperman, park rangers, cooks, guides, Roosevelt's personal doctor, his secretary, assorted naturalists, devoted followers, friends, and admirers.

Roosevelt began to feel like Moses about to lead the Children of Israel into the wilderness. This was not his idea of freedom and solitude. He craved to be alone with nature, the way it was before his life in politics. By thunder, he decided to put a stop to this circus. In the dining hall he assembled everyone together for an announcement.

"I have chosen only a select few to join me. The following will be instructed to remain behind in Gardiner; newspapermen, my physician and private secretary, the general public, well-meaning nature lovers, and yes, even the Secret Service men are not welcome on this vacation."

There was a sudden audible gasp in the hall as over a hundred expectant participants were turned away.

The Secret Service was outraged.

"How are we supposed to protect the President if we won't even let us get near him?" they blustered. In a hurried strategy session, the Secret Service designed a way to widen his ring of security to extend beyond his line of sight.

Thorn was among the favored few invited to join the vacation party, which consisted of Major John Pitcher, the Park Superintendent, John Burroughs, the renowned naturalist and dear friend, Billy Hofer, the official Park Guide, various camp laborers and orderlies to pitch the large Sibley tents and set up camp, and Thorn.

Thorn could not help but gloat as he passed Bailey Garrett on his way out the door.

"Oh, so will you be joining us? No, I guess not. You work for the Secret Service."

When the meeting adjourned, the newly defined camping party gathered their supplies, mounted up and tramped over the ridge and into the heart of Yellowstone.

The Showdown at Yellowstone

CHAPTER 39

The first member of the National Park system, Yellowstone National Park was dedicated in 1872 by an act of Congress and signed into law by President Grant. The dedication of the park described it as a place to be preserved 'for the benefit and enjoyment of the people'. However, its remote location and limited access points left the Park largely untouched by man. When the Northern Pacific Railroad ran a spur line south from Livingston, Montana, to Gardiner, the northern entrance to the Park became the primary access point for the general public.

However, the Park administrators agreed that this most important entrance lacked sufficient visual fanfare to serve as the gateway to the grandeur of America's first and most famous national park. Ideas to dress up the park entrance were bandied about. The winning idea was a grand triumphant arch, reminiscent of Roman architecture and similar in concept to the Arc de Triomphe in Paris, France. To honor the one person who was the strongest advocate of the National Park system, Teddy Roosevelt, they determined to name the arch the 'Roosevelt Arch'.

The arch tower was to rise to a height of fifty-two feet with an arch opening twenty-five feet wide. Native stones were quarried from the surrounding area, and construction began in March of 1903. The local press took notice, and soon the entire nation heard of the news of 'The Great Arch'.

By the time Roosevelt arrived for his two-week vacation, the foundation was complete and the cornerstone ready to be set in place. The timing seemed perfect for a cornerstone dedication ceremony, with President Roosevelt himself as the honored guest speaker. The invitation was made, and Roosevelt heartily accepted.

"After I complete my vacation, we should hold the event," he insisted.

That was not a problem. It gave the organizers time to make announcements, invite essential dignitaries and politicians, inform the public, prepare a band, construct grandstands, orchestrate transportation and housing for the visiting public, and allow the Secret Service time to establish the needed security to protect the President from any harm.

For the next two weeks the town of Gardiner was all a flurry. American flags were hung from the second story banisters of every building along Main Street. Extra food was shipped in to feed the expected crowds. Water tankers were wheeled in to provide drinking water for the public.

'Roosevelt's Arch' under construction.

"Looks like I'll be tied up for the next two weeks," Captain Kellerman warned Mason. "Troops B and C will be making a mounted entrance ahead of the President, and I've been asked to lead the parade, so we'll be rehearsing quite a bit."

"That's all right. I can find my way around," said Mason. Kellerman pointed to the frontage road."

"That's the road to the Crittenden Bridge, if you've a mind to. Otherwise, I'll catch up to you at mealtimes."

" 'Preciate it," Mason tipped his hat. He took his horse, on loan from the military stables, and made a ride out to the Crittenden Bridge. It was only a few miles north of Gardiner, and spanned the Yellowstone River. The bridge was a wood trestle design, with a span of about five hundred feet and a drop of about seventy-five feet. Along the side of the railroad tracks was a pedestrian walkway wide enough for foot traffic and wagons.

Mason took note of the sentries posted at both ends of the bridge.

"Seems safe enough," he thought.

He rode on ahead to the town of Cinnabar, a few miles north of the bridge. The train depot was getting ready to receive the arrival of its twice daily commuter train from Livingston. The sound of the train whistle in the distance told him it was pulling in. He tied off his horse and took a seat on the platform bench. The train pulled ten cars full of passengers. Most were continuing on to Gardiner, but took advantage of the stop to get out and stretch their legs. Mason walked over to the porter.

"You seen anything unusual lately?" he vaguely asked. The porter didn't know quite how to take his meaning.

"Mister, after doin' this for ten years, I wouldn't recognize unusual if it stepped up and offered me a drink," he replied. Mason nodded. He spotted a diner nearby and decided it was time for lunch.

Sure be nice if Sam was here to join me, he thought. Sam Stokes was always a welcome dinner companion, easy company and full of uncomplicated conversation. He took a seat and ordered a bowl of chili. He liked chili, maybe his favorite meal – he measured a restaurant's standing by the quality of its chili. When the waiter brought over his food, Mason slid an extra dollar toward the waiter.

"You notice anything lately that seemed unusual to you, anything out of the ordinary?" he asked as he pushed the dollar closer to the waiter. The waiter eyed the dollar and gave it a thoughtful moment.

"I seen a dwarf and a man with a twelve-inch mustache about a month ago, is that what you mean?" Mason shook his head no.

"What about any foreigners in the last week or so?" Mason clarified. The waiter thought again and then snapped his fingers.

"I'll tell you I did have some customers a few days ago that didn't speak no English, like they came from Europe or something. There was a white gent with 'em who spoke for them, seemed to know their language," he explained.

"Where'd they go?" Mason asked.

"Don't know. You could ask over at the hotel," the waiter offered. Mason threw him another dollar and finished his chili. It was pretty good. He sauntered over to the hotel and stepped up to the registration desk. The clerk was reading the paper when he saw Mason standing there.

"You looking for a room?" he asked.

"No, lookin' for some men. C.J. Mason, sheriff up in Coulson," he said by way of introduction.

"Well, ain't you a bit out of your jurisdiction?" The clerk asked.

"Ain't arresting nobody, just had a few questions for 'em. They'd be foreigners, maybe European with an English speaking interpreter," Mason said.

"Yeah, they stayed here a few nights ago. But they're gone now," the clerk replied.

"They give a name?" Mason asked.

"Nope, and even if they did, they'd probably be fake. Folks who stay here like their privacy, if you know what I mean," the clerk explained.

"Could you describe 'em?"

"They were three of 'em, looked to be in their 30s, dark hair, seemed nervous."

"Why do you say that?" Mason probed.

"They didn't look me in the eye, always looking at the ground."

"What direction they go?' Mason asked.

"don' know."

" 'Preciate your help," Mason tipped his hat and walked out. It was getting late in the day, so he turned back to Fort Yellowstone. At dinner in the dining hall he shared with Captain Kellerman his findings from the day.

"I'm pretty busy gettin' ready for the parade and the dedication ceremony, but if I see anything odd, I'll give you a holler," Kellerman offered.

The Showdown at Yellowstone

CHAPTER 40

For two weeks Roosevelt tramped, rode, and skied his way through some of Yellowstone's most beautiful country. At Norris Geyser Basin he listened to a perfect chorus of bird music from robins, western purple finches, juncos and mountain bluebirds. In the woods he closed his eyes and meditated to the sounds of the mountain chickadees and pygmy nuthatches, together with an occasional woodpecker. While the geysers and boiling mineral springs quickly bored the President, he felt awestruck with the scenery and the wildlife. John Burroughs could see that respite was the gift this wonderland offered to his friend Roosevelt.

Although there was respite, there was no rest. Roosevelt and company followed a jam-packed schedule, camping throughout the Park, and traveling the geyser basins through the snow by sleigh. Roosevelt and Burroughs even found time to go skiing one morning. Roosevelt spotted some low hills separated by gentle valleys and challenged Burroughs to a race to the bottom.

"I'm not sure I have the energy for a race," Burroughs said.

"Nonsense," Roosevelt assured him. "All we have to do is stand up straight, and let gravity do the work." Burroughs reluctantly agreed to the adventure. Major Pitcher gave the call to "GO" and the two leaned forward and began their run. Within seconds they picked up speed and soon appeared out of control. The group at the top of the hill looked on in horror as the snow gave way beneath Roosevelt and he sprawled head first into the white powder and disappeared from sight.

Thorn panicked for a moment, thinking Roosevelt had killed himself. How was he going to explain this to Mason and everyone else? Major Pitcher and Billy Hofer frantically plowed down the hill to rescue the President, when he suddenly popped to the surface, shaking off the snow and laughing like a school boy. The spirit of the boy was clearly in the air and the biggest boy of them all was Roosevelt.

On another day they ventured to the Grand Canyon of Yellowstone to witness the majesty of the Lower Falls. A stout rope knotted every eighteen inches and secured to a massive lodge pole pine tree served as their life line down the hill to an observation landing where they could get a close view of the colossal falls, the deep gorge, and the colorful soil striations along the canyon walls. Hand over hand they eased themselves down the rope, using the knots as grasping points. Thorn marveled at Roosevelt's gripping strength for a man his age and relative inactivity. Once at the landing, they stood quietly and let the roar of the falls and the mist rising up wash over them. No words were needed. An occasional bald headed eagle sailed across the gorge, using the updraft to propel him. The sun's rays, shining through the mist, created a stunning rainbow. It was a moment that no camera could adequately capture.

The camp always had a big fire at night in the open near the tents. After dinner the group gathered around it on logs and campstools to listen to Roosevelt talk. He filled the nights with anecdotes, history, science, politics, adventure, literature, bits of his experience as a rancher, Rough Rider days, police commissioner, governor, and president. Before this intimate group of friends and colleagues he shared the frankest confessions, the most telling criticisms, and delicious secrets of prominent political leaders and foreign rulers. The group drank it in, astonished by his candor, amazed at his memory, and charmed by his humor.

One night after the group turned in for bed, Roosevelt took Thorn aside.

"Let's go look at the stars," he suggested. The two went for a short walk away from the campfire, where the dark night sky revealed the dazzling dance of the constellations.

Leaning against a couple of boulders, the two talked.

"I've thought about you often," Roosevelt began. "San Juan Heights...what a day. Your steady solid work ethic, your dedication and commitment." Thorn wanted to reply, but Roosevelt waved him to stay silent.

"I want to say again how sorry I am about your wife's passing. When my wife died, I died with her, so I know your pain." Thorn's thoughts suddenly flew to Sadie and her sweet smile. Roosevelt continued.

"I know in my soul you were not to blame for McKinley's death and your treatment at the bureau was undeserved. But I also know that your heart was not in the political world. Your world is here in God's country. I released you from my service for your own good and if I had the guts I'd toss this crazy life of mine away and join you."

They sat quietly and watched Orion the Hunter as it pushed Taurus the Bull back across the heavens. Little did Roosevelt know but this would be the very last time he would ever return to his precious Yellowstone. Again Roosevelt broke the silence.

"Tell me about your home in Coulson."

"What can I say...it's the west. It's a small growing town with a big city attitude. But we got a long way to go. We don't even have a fire truck to be proud of...not like Washington."

Roosevelt in camp with Burroughs and others at Yellowstone 1903.

Roosevelt sighed. He felt the vacation speeding to its conclusion too quickly.

Roosevelt drank in every moment and etched them in his memory, knowing that in future nights back in Washington while gazing into his marble hearth's bright glow, he would see this campfire instead, and when sipping his deep red wine from a stately goblet, he would imagine the crisp mountain water from a Yellowstone stream. And he would smile.

Back at Fort Yellowstone, Captain Kellerman noticed that one of the Secret Service agents mounted a horse every morning and rode north along the wagon trail that followed the railroad line. At first, he thought nothing of it, figured the agent was just getting the lay of the land or sight-seeing some of the scenic landscape. But after five straight days of disappearing into the woods in the morning and returning near dark, this behavior seemed odd.

What's this feller doing? Kellerman thought to himself. He's not sight-seeing 'cause he takes off in the same direction every day.

Rather than report this behavior to Mason, he had some free time and decided he would follow him if he lit out again. Sure enough, the next morning the agent mounted up quiet like and rode north. Kellerman waited till the agent rounded the bend, then he saddled up and followed. He stayed a good distance back so as not to draw attention. In fact, at times he thought he must have lost him, 'cause he rode past Gardiner, past the Crittenden Bridge, and even rode past the tiny town of Cinnabar with no sign of the agent. "Where in thunder did this fella go?" He muttered.

A few miles north of Cinnabar he came to the Yankee Canyon Bridge when he heard the sound of men working and talking. He dismounted and tied off his horse, then eased over to the edge of the deep gorge to see what was going on. At the base of the gorge he could see a few men chopping wood and digging into the soil around the base of the trestle towers. The Yankee Canyon Bridge was a quarter mile long and spanned a gorge 200 feet deep where the Yellowstone River flowed. Kellerman instantly realized that this might be the sabotage Mason and Thorn expected. He crawled back to his horse and grabbed his binoculars, then eased back over to the edge of the gorge for a better look.

Through his binoculars, he saw men down below stacking crates of dynamite around the base of four trestle towers, while one of them looked to be wiring up a detonator box. He scanned the area for the whereabouts of the Secret Service agent, but he was nowhere to be seen. Kellerman's heart started pounding. He knew he had to do something. His mind raced. "Could that Secret Service agent be part of this deadly scheme, or is he just like me, stumbled onto this band of bastards and trying to figure a way to stop them? In any case, I gotta get back and bring help."

The last thing Captain Kellerman heard was the cock of a pistol from behind. He spun around to see Bailey Garrett leveling his .45 revolver at him. He desperately reached for his own pistol when Bailey fired his weapon. The impact of the bullet sent Kellerman over the edge and down the gorge. His body rolled for fifty yards until it slammed into a boulder. Bailey looked over the rim and shook his head.

"Now I got a body to bury and a horse to get rid of."

The Showdown at Yellowstone

CHAPTER 41

"Have you seen Captain Kellerman?" Major Woods asked Mason at dinner in the Fort Yellowstone dining hall. The Major was a no-nonsense career military man with thinning hair and well-groomed beard. He was used to barking orders to lower ranked cavalrymen, but since Mason was a civilian, he did his best to rein in his brusque manner.

"No, I thought he was with you getting ready for the dedication ceremony," Mason replied.

"We thought he was with you, and we've got a lot of loose ends that he needs to get to work on, so we wanted you to know that we need him back," Woods explained.

"Are you telling me he's gone missing? For how long?" Mason demanded. Major Woods suddenly felt foolish.

"It's been four days since anyone's seen him, and his horse is missing too, so we thought you might have sent him on some special assignment."

"That's crazy," Mason snapped back. "If he's gone without notice for that long, he's either absent without leave or he's dead."

Major Woods lowered his voice to avert any rumor mill chatter among the men.

"Given his service record, there is zero possibility that he's gone AWOL," Woods said. Mason just shook his head then pointed his finger at the Major.

"This is not good," Mason muttered.

"We know that you wired him from Coulson to check

out some possible sabotage along the Crittenden Bridge. He reported that he posted sentries along the bridge. Could his disappearance have anything to do with that?" Woods asked. Mason stood up, no longer interested in his meal.

"Anything is possible. The dedication ceremony is in two days. I suggest we mount a search immediately," Mason said. "If there's been foul play with Kellerman, I guarantee the President's in danger."

Major Woods dispatched troops to make a discreet ten-mile sweep around Fort Yellowstone with no success. The next morning Mason made a ride out to the Crittenden Bridge. The sentries on duty were not the same ones stationed on the bridge four days earlier, so they could only confirm whether or not Kellerman had passed by them in the last three days. "Where the hell are you?" Mason thought to himself.

By mid-morning the Roosevelt camping party arrived, full of stories and covered in trail dust. Mason took Thorn aside.

"How'd it go?" he asked.

"Couldn't have been better," Thorn replied.

"Well, it couldn't have been worse here," Mason shot back. "Kellerman's missing, probably dead."

"What the hell?" Thorn shot back. "What's goin' on?"

"I don't know, but I don't like it. I don't know who to tell. I don't know who to trust. But I can tell you one thing, Roosevelt's going to be standing on a big fat platform tomorrow, and that's going to make him about as big a target as you could ask."

Thorn grit his teeth.

"I am not going to let him die tomorrow. I don't care what we have to do." Mason could see by the look in Thorn's eye that to reach Roosevelt the Grim Reaper would have to pass by Thorn first. And good luck with that.

On the morning of April 24, 1903 crowds began pouring into Gardiner. The Northern Pacific Railroad had engaged 40 stagecoaches at Livingston to take overflow passengers who couldn't fit on the train, and carry them down the fifty-mile road in time for the event. The town of Gardiner was festooned with flowers, American flags, and red, white, and blue bunting along the store fronts. Over 4,000 spectators surrounded the speaker's platform, with dignitaries from Billings, Red Lodge, Big Timber, Bozeman, and Miles City. Three regional newspapers sent reporters, and professional photographers from Coulson, Billings, and Bozeman captured every moment on film.

Security was everywhere. Guards were posted all around the base of the platform and at every vantage point on the closely surrounding hillsides. The roped pathway to the speaker's stand was lined with cavalrymen, and over a hundred special deputy sheriffs were scattered all over the grounds. Thorn joined the speakers on the platform at Roosevelt's request, and Mason, with his Sharp's rifle in hand, stood atop the base of the arch scanning the horizon for possible sharpshooter snipers.

A second train rolled into the Gardiner depot at 2:30 with as many people as the earlier train, leaving Gardiner simply overwhelmed. Many would have gone hungry had not ample provisions been delivered in advance. The Livingston Volunteer Fire Department band played lively tunes to entertain the restless throngs.

Finally, at 3:30 the march of the dignitaries began. Troops B and C of the Third Cavalry, under the command of Captain Johnson, trotted through town and lined up on the road to the south to await President Roosevelt. The Masonic Grand Master and his following marched down the street with a marching band, and climbed onto the platform.

Finally, the President's entourage arrived. The eager eyes of the crowd recognized him on horseback from a half mile away, and gave a mighty cheer. The flashing swords of the officers, the martial music of the band, and the lusty cheering of the multitude gave the scene an aspect that would inspire patriotism in the breast of even the coldest cynic.

Roosevelt rode down the street, along with the Mayor of Gardiner and Major Pitcher. As he dismounted and ascended the stairs to the platform, the cavalry presented sabers in a salute to the President. Roosevelt walked quickly with hat raised in acknowledgement of the salute.

Thorn and Mason were trained not to look at the President, but to study the crowds for any threatening or provocative movement. Their eyes darted from left to right, and right to left. Every Secret Service agent, save one, was on high alert with their eyes on the crowd, and one hand on their pistol grip. Bailey Garrett stood far back at the outer fringe of the assembly, watching the time and reviewing his carefully laid plans over and over in his mind.

Roosevelt speaking at the Yellowstone Arch dedication ceremony.

Welcomes were made to the attendees, preliminary speeches were offered, and the ceremonial cornerstone to the arch was set in place with a crane and the guiding hand of Roosevelt himself. Finally Roosevelt spoke. He expressed his gratitude for the overflowing hospitality of the locals, his commitment to preservation of the forests and the management of Yellowstone National Park. He concluded by saying:

"Let me thank you again for your greeting. It has been to me the most genuine pleasure again to see this great western country. I like the country, but above all I like the men and women."

With that, the ceremony ended. Roosevelt descended the platform and mounted his horse. He rode through the crowd, acknowledging the cheers from the people. At the depot, he prepared to board when a rough-looking man approached him.

Not knowing who he was, an alert agent quickly grabbed him by the neck and shoved him back ten feet. Seeing that the man meant no harm, Roosevelt reached out his hand. The man took it and grinned, flattered that he had been mistaken for a dangerous person.

Mason and Thorn breathed a sigh of relief when they heard the train whistle blow in the distance, signaling its departure.

"I guess that's all," Mason said. "I feel kinda foolish now, whipping ourselves into such a froth about plots and saboteurs."

They started walking back to town when Mason noticed Thomas Osborn, owner of the Osborn Photo Studio in Coulson, putting away his camera equipment.

"Thomas!" Mason called out. Thomas looked up and waved.

"Did you get some good photos today?" Thorn asked.

"We'll see when I get them back to the studio and develop them."

"I'm happy to report that those photos of the Crittenden Bridge were nothing to worry about," Mason admitted.

"Worry? About what?" Thomas asked.

"We thought they might be part of a plot to blow that bridge up to kill the President," Mason explained. "But obviously we were wrong."

Suddenly Thomas' face turned pale. Mason noticed it right away.

"What's the matter?" Mason asked.

"That wasn't the only bridge I photographed," Thomas explained.

"What are you talking about?" Thorn asked.

"They had me photograph the Yankee Canyon Bridge too, and they said they liked it better," he replied. "I didn't ask what they meant, but I assumed they just thought the picture was prettier."

Suddenly Mason and Thorn panicked.

"Why didn't you say something?" Mason demanded.

"You didn't ask," Thomas defended himself. But he wasn't sure they even heard him, because they were already running as fast as they could to catch the train.

CHAPTER 42

The train had just pulled out of the station.

"Can you stop that train?" Mason hollered to the depot agent standing on the platform.

"Certainly not," the agent replied. Thorn was almost too winded to speak, but he gulped some air and blurted out, "This is an emergency. Can you get a message to the train?"

The agent sensed the grave nature of these inquiries, and tried to be helpful.

"No, but it's stopping at the Cinnabar depot in a few miles to pick up more passengers. If you try, you might be able to catch up to it. I mean, not on foot, but if you have a fast horse, maybe."

Mason scanned the depot quickly in search of a couple of likely mounts. He spotted a few cavalry horses tied off at the end of the platform. Their owners were nowhere to be seen.

"Let's go," Mason shouted to Thorn, pointing to the horses. They ran to the end of the platform and leaped on the two closest mounts. Mason shoved his Sharps rifle into the saddle's empty scabbard, grabbed the reins, and put a boot to the horse's hind quarters. Within seconds they were in full gallop. They looked like a couple of Kentucky Derby jockeys, hunched over their steeds, flailing their horses wildly with their reins.

For the next two miles not a word was spoken between the two of them. Every ounce of concentration was applied to pushing their horse to maximum speed. Folks walking the same road had to dive out of the way to avoid a collision with these frantic riders. When they rounded the bend, they could see the waiting train in the distance.

"Please just stay put for a few more seconds," Mason prayed to the panting locomotive. Too late. A shrill whistle from the engine gave the signal that the train was pulling away. Thorn and Mason knew they couldn't reach the train in time to board. Mason shouted to Thorn as they galloped ahead.

"You get on that train and get to the locomotive. Try to get the engineer to stop it." Thorn nodded.

"What are you gonna do?" he shouted back.

"I'm gonna ride on ahead. Maybe I can stop the detonation before the train gets there." Again Thorn nodded. Their assignments were clear. One or the other of them had to succeed.

"Not today," Thorn whispered. "The President is not going to die today."

As the train eased away from the Cinnabar station, Thorn could see that it groaned from the overcrowded passenger load. There were so many people on board it was taking extra-long for the train to pick up any speed. That gave him time to catch up to the rear car. Two Secret Service agents stood guard on the outside rear platform. They could see Thorn galloping towards them, and thought at first the rider might be up to no good. As Thorn drew closer, they recognized him and helped to grab him as he made the transfer from his saddle to the train platform.

"What the hell are you doin', Thorn? Are you crazy?" Asked one of the agents.

"I gotta get inside. The president's in danger. I gotta stop this train," he hollered over the noise of the grinding wheels.

"You can't get in. The door's locked from the inside," the agent hollered back.

"How do you get in?" Thorn demanded.

"Shift change every hour. They open the door from the inside."

Thorn had no time for that protocol. He leaped to the side of the car and grabbed the ladder before the agents could stop him, and scrambled to the top of the car. If he couldn't get to the locomotive from the inside, he was just going to have to get there from the outside, running the roof of each car all the way to the front of the train. The Elysian was slowly picking up speed, but still moving slow enough to allow him to make the dash. He had to run the tops of six cars on a train swaying from side to side and lurching from time to time as it continued to accelerate. He could not make one single mistake. Falling off the train might not kill him, but it would surely mean the death of the President.

Mason continued to press his horse for every ounce of energy it possessed. He passed the train, but he needed enough lead time to reach the Yankee Canyon Bridge and put a stop to the detonation in case Thorn failed to bring the train to a halt.

"C'mon, boy," he urged his horse. "Go, go, go!"

On the train top Thorn had to duck a few low lying tree branches. He was halfway to the coal car as the train continued to gain speed. A sudden jolt of the cars upended his balance, and he fell to the roof. He started sliding off the side when he grabbed an air vent pipe and held on until he could regain his footing.

Mason rounded the bend where the Yankee Canyon Bridge came into full view. He ran his steed to the edge of the gorge and jumped off the horse, grabbing the butt of his rifle as his feet hit the ground. He stopped suddenly to listen for the train. He could hear it approaching. In a minute or less it would be crossing the bridge. Seconds mattered. He ran to the rim and dropped to the ground. Looking across the span he spotted four men hunkered halfway down the gorge. He took his Sharps rifle and set it into position. The distance looked to be 800 yards. He could shoot that far in his sleep. He won the competition with a shot at 850 yards. He loaded the cartridge and took aim. The shadows in the canyon were rising as the sun dropped lower and lower in the sky. He needed to be able to see his targets if he was to have any chance of hitting them. He paused and rubbed his eyes.

Inside the train Bailey Garrett lay quietly in his sleeping

berth in the Senegal, car number four. He knew that in a few seconds he would need to jump from the train before it reached the bridge. The catastrophic train disaster would take weeks for rescuers to sift through in search of victims and survivors. Many passengers might never be identifiable. It would be assumed that his body was among the horrific wreckage, and an empty casket funeral would be held in his honor. Just another minute or two...

Thorn scrambled back to his feet and managed to clamber to the top of the baggage car, just behind the coal car. He leaped to the coal car and climbed down to the locomotive where the engineers held the train on course.

"Stop the train," he shouted. "The bridge is out! Stop the train!" Without questioning this mystery messenger, they pulled the brakes and the train's wheels started squealing and grinding.

Mason exhaled for a moment and pulled the trigger. The bullet found its target a split second before the sound of the shot could be heard. Emil Varga, with his hand still on the plunger, jerked back from the impact of the bullet, and slumped to the side of the hill. His three cohorts could not make sense of what they just saw. As one of them lifted up the lifeless corpse of Emil to examine, a second shot rang through the gorge and he slumped over the dead Emil.

The remaining two men crouched and reached for their pistols, pathetically useless at 800 yards, and searched for the location of their attacker. One of the saboteurs decided he'd had enough, and stood to climb out of the gorge and escape. The moment he stood, the sound of a third shot resounded, and he dropped to the ground. The last man looked at the plunger nearby, still primed and ready, and determined that he would die in glory by finishing the job himself. With new resolve, he crawled to the detonator box. Mason spotted him by his movement in the growing shadows. He set his sights, adjusted for windage, and pulled the trigger. If this had been the sharpshooting competition, he would have won another trophy - four bull's eyes at 800 yards in under one minute. He stood up just in time to see the cowcatcher of the Elysian coast to a stop at the edge of the Yankee Canyon Bridge.

Bailey knew that something was wrong. The train was not supposed to stop here. It was supposed to sail over the Yankee Jim Canyon and into the abyss below. He had an alternate plan ready but never expected to actually need it. He pulled out a large suitcase from under his berth and opened the lid, it was a time bomb similar to the one he had demonstrated to Thorn years ago.

Only the mechanisms were more advanced and reliable now. He checked his pocket watch, it was 5:45. He set the timer to go off at 6:00 pm. That would give him 15 minutes to find the car that Roosevelt was in, drop off the suitcase behind a piece of furniture, and escape before anyone would suspect. The explosion would be untraceable and he would flee the scene before anyone would be the wiser.

He turned and went to the back of the train, expecting Roosevelt to be resting in his private car. As he passed through the 'Texas' sleeper car, with his suitcase in hand, he asked one of the White house staff if the President was resting.

"No, he's having drinks with some congressman in the club car." The club car? That was all the way back in the other direction. He angrily turned on his heels and marched back where he came from, passing through the Senegal and Gilsey car.

Thorn was not satisfied that the danger was over. He thanked the engineers and made his way through the baggage car to the club car in search of Roosevelt. His timing couldn't be more perfect. Just as he opened the front door of the club car, Bailey opened the back door of the same car. They both laid eyes on Roosevelt at the same time, standing at the bar with a drink in hand talking to Montana Congressman Dixon. Two Secret Service agents stood nearby and nodded at Bailey as he entered.

Bailey did not hesitate for one second. He pulled out his pistol and shot both agents dead, and was about to shoot Roosevelt when Thorn pulled his gun and leaped in front of TR as a shield.

For a moment Bailey and Thorn were locked in a stalemate, both pausing to assess and react as needed.

"So, it was you? You're behind this whole damn thing?" Thorn uttered in amazement.

"Just step aside," Bailey said. "You can't stop this." But Thorn remained resolute.

"It's over," Thorn said. "The dynamite, the bridge. You lost. Just put the gun down."

"Get out of the way or I'll kill you right now," Bailey insisted. Thorn immediately noticed that Bailey's girth was a bit wider than he had remembered. He might be wearing a bullet-proof vest, he decided. That would eliminate several larger and easier targets. He couldn't take the chance of aiming for the chest. He would have to aim for the head or the pistol arm, both of which were low percentage shots.

"Last chance," Bailey offered. The two stood twenty feet apart, pistols drawn and at their side. Thorn's free arm was wrapped around Roosevelt, who stood behind him. Thorn knew not to look at the opponent's eyes in a draw down. They will tell you nothing. Look at the shoulders…they tell you everything.

The instant Thorn saw Bailey's shoulder flinch; he snapped off a shot so fast he even surprised himself. The bullet hit Bailey in the right shoulder, only an inch or two away from the bullet-proof vest. The shot knocked Bailey to the floor and for a few seconds everyone in the cabin froze.

Thorn walked over to Bailey to examine the wound. Bailey's shoulder was shattered, which might heal in time, but he was bleeding out. The bullet severed the brachial artery and he had only moments to live.

"Why?" Thorn asked, not really expecting an answer. Bailey slowly smiled.

"I didn't lose. You lost. Tick tock." His eyes slowly closed and his body turned limp.

"What did he mean by that…tick tock?" Thorn pondered. Suddenly his eyes darted around the cabin in search of an object. There it was, a suitcase tucked behind a stuffed chair in the back of the car.

"BOMB!" Thorn shouted.

He ran to the back of the car, grabbed the suitcase then leaped from the train. He ran to the trestle bridge with seconds remaining, and threw the suitcase into the air over the side of the bridge. It sailed down about a hundred feet until it exploded harmlessly in flight, leaving small bits of debris to splash into the Yellowstone River. The President, the train, the bridge and nearly a hundred passengers were saved.

A tight lid was put over the entire Yellowstone incident. The two agents shot on the train, and the missing Captain Kellerman were given heroic cover stories to explain their death, all in the line of duty, complete with honorable burials. Families received generous death benefits to assure that their lives would not suffer unduly. The Slovak saboteurs were quietly laid to rest with no notification in the press or otherwise.

As for Mason and Thorn, a discreet ceremony was held in the basement of the Fort Yellowstone administration building to thank them for saving the President. They were both awarded the Medal of Valor, which was then taken back for safe keeping, with the strictest instruction that they never divulge to anyone the events that transpired and the disaster barely averted.

The future of the Secret Service and the confidence of the nation depended on the reputation of the agency as the bulwark of safety and security for the President. Mason and Thorn swore an oath of silence that the showdown at Yellowstone would go with them to the grave.

———

The usual gathering of business elites just concluded at The Union Club, in New York, and Henry Oswald collected his overcoat, with a generous tip for the coat girl. He donned his top hat and exited the building, where cars and drivers were waiting for their pampered boss. Oswald's car rolled up to the door and the driver stepped out and opened the back seat door. His cap was pushed down over his eyes more than usual, but Oswald thought nothing of it.

"Thank you, Steven," Oswald said as he climbed into the back seat. "Just take me straight home." The car sped away as Oswald helped himself to a late evening libation from the small liquor bar in the back seat. He glanced out the window just in time to see the driver making a wrong turn.

"You idiot, you missed our turn," Oswald growled. The driver glanced over his shoulder to inform Oswald of the change of plans.

"We won't be going home just yet," he said. Suddenly Oswald realized that this wasn't his usual driver Steven. In fact he didn't recognize him at all.

"Wait a minute. Who the hell are you? Where's Steven?" Oswald demanded.

"Steven's resting now from a nasty blow to the back of his head," the driver calmly reported. "You and I have some unfinished business." A wave of fear swept over Oswald.

"What do you mean?" he asked. "I don't even know you."

"I'm an associate of Bailey Garrett and unfortunately his recent unexpected passing requires that I settle accounts with you and Mr. Garrett over a certain contract you drew up together."

"Now wait just a minute, we never put anything in writing," Oswald explained in a panic.

"Mr. Garrett was very specific that a verbal contract with you was binding," the driver said. Oswald knew that at his age he was no match for the strength of this husky driver, who looked like he could easily go the distance with Jim Corbett in the ring. Fear gripped him like never before.

"You can't do this," he pleaded. "I had nothing to do with his death. Now you stop this car. You hear me! Let me out." But the car sped on. Oswald resorted to the only thing he knew that motivated people…money.

"What are they paying you? I'll pay you double." No reaction from the driver.

"Triple!" Still no reaction.

"Name your price, damn you!" Oswald shouted. Despite his protestations and monetary offers, the limousine disappeared into the night.

CHAPTER 43

Three months after the showdown at Yellowstone, the city of Coulson was all abuzz.

"I call this meeting to order," the Mayor shouted, pounding his gavel on the podium. The chatter of conversation in the Coulson Town Hall was as noisy as a duck farm. Mason and Thorn made their way over. Thorn was sporting his campaign hat from his days as a Rough Rider.

"I see you've got a new look," Mason noted, pointing to the hat.

"Since I can't wear a medal for what we did, I thought I'd wear this hat instead. Nobody will ever know what it means, but I will," Thorn said.

Mason nodded his approval. They stepped into the town hall just as the meeting got started.

"We are here to announce some very important changes that will affect us all. Everyone please settle down," the mayor declared. The audience quieted themselves and the mayor continued.

"As this city continues to grow, we must grow with it. I am proud to say that we have already benefited from several improvements. Streets are paved. You can actually walk across Minnesota Avenue and never get your boots muddy or step in a horse pie." The audience chuckled and nodded in agreement.

"Our swelling civic pride demands new ways of administering the population. So today we are announcing the end of the sheriff's department under its current structure and the creation of a formal police department."

Most of the congregation seemed intrigued with the notion. They wanted to hear more.

"Now, this is nothing new and we've been studying it for some time. There are many benefits to this new system, and dozens of cities have already successfully converted over to a police department."

"What's wrong with what we got now?" asked one citizen.

"With no disrespect to Sheriff Mason, the sheriff system just doesn't make a strong enough statement to the public. Under the new system, we are going to have nine policemen and a chief of police. And you're going to like the way they look, because everyone will be wearing a police uniform."

Up until then, Mason and his deputies simply showed up to work in their own civilian clothes and the duds for the day usually amounted to the outfit that needed washing the least.

"Take a look for yourself," said the mayor as one of the city councilmen walked on the platform modeling the new uniforms. It was a natty navy blue serge uniform with brass buttons, white gloves, and a derby style hat with a police star affixed to the crown.

"They make a man look authoritative and dignified, and it standardizes police wear," the mayor added. Mason and Thorn, standing in the back of the hall, winced at the sight.

"Now we would like to introduce the new Chief of Police for Coulson," the mayor beamed. He paused for dramatic effect before announcing the name. Several members of the audience turned to look at Mason, the obvious choice.

The man we have chosen is Sebastian Huntley," announced the mayor. An audible gasp could be heard in the hall.

Most everyone assumed Mason would be named the chief of police. After all, he had been the man in charge for the past 12 years, cleaning up the streets and making the city safe. Sebastian Huntley was the current deputy and had only served in that position for barely a year. He wasn't even a local. He had relocated from Denver to become deputy, and now the real purpose of that move became obvious…he was being groomed for this very moment.

The mayor ignored the dissenting mumblings and primed the audience to applaud by clapping his hands as Huntley stepped onto the platform.

Sam Stokes stood up. "What's going to happen to Mason?"

"He's been offered a position with the new police department, which he's accepted. He is being awarded the rank of sergeant."

Thorn turned to Mason. "You can count me out," he whispered. "Let's go get a drink." Mason stayed motionless. He wasn't quite ready to slip out.

"Was the chief position offered to Mason?" asked another concerned citizen. The audience turned suddenly silent to hear the answer. Mason definitely wanted to hear what the mayor had to say about that.

The mayor cleared his throat.

"Well, actually, no. We wanted to use Mason's skills --" but he was cut off by Sebastian Huntley, who stepped up and took control of the podium.

"If I may," he said out of the side of his mouth. Then he turned to the audience. "There are a lot of responsibilities that this new police department will assume. They will include, of course, pursuing and apprehending individuals who break the law." The audience nodded their heads in agreement.

"But they will be widened to include directing traffic on some of our busy streets, handing out citations or warnings to those guilty of minor infractions, writing reports and maintaining records."

"Which ones will Mason be doin?" asked Howard Wilkins, the local barber.

"Mason will be patrolling your streets, keeping you safe," Huntley replied. Rockwell Stevenson, the owner of the dry goods store, raised his hand.

"Mason's been sheriff here for twelve years. Is that the best use of his skills?"

"I'd say definitely yes." Huntley replied. "You see, we want a familiar face patrolling the streets, someone you know and trust. We think that's Mason." Huntley looked around the room for a sense of the crowd's feelings, and decided that answer was not sitting well.

"Also, the job of Chief of Police is mostly paperwork and meetings, hearings and such, not the kind of thing Mason is trained for or would even enjoy." The crowd seemed to like that explanation a little better.

Mason turned to Thorn and whispered, "You know, he probably did me a favor."

"You know what…I know just how you feel," Thorn said. "Let's get out of here. These damn politicians could twist the Devil's cursings 'til it sounds like an angels' choir. I can't take it anymore, at least not when I'm sober."

They slipped out the back door and headed over to the Crystal Palace Saloon for a drink or two, or more.

"What do you figure they'd all do if they knew you had a hand in saving the President's life?" Thorn asked.

"I don't know," Mason shrugged.

"I do. You'd have the keys to the city and a statue of you in the park, I'd wager," Thorn said. Mason smiled.

"And what about you? It would have to be a statue of both of us on horseback," Mason added.

"Yeah, with swords drawn and everything," Thorn pronounced with a laugh. They let that thought play out in their imaginations for a few seconds.

"Unfortunately, that's not a story we can tell," Mason said.

They walked down the street and turned onto Minnesota Avenue.

"This town ain't gonna be the same," Thorn sighed.

"I know," Mason agreed. "The whole country's changing. I just read that a couple of bicycle builders from Ohio are going to try to get a gas-powered motor airplane off the ground. I swear I don't know what's next."

"Mr. Mason," called out one of the city councilmen. "Mr. Mason!" Mason and Thorn turned to see who was calling.

"You need to come see this," urged the councilman.

"See what?" asked Thorn.

"Just come see," replied the councilman with a broad smile. "It's in front of the town hall."

The three turned and walked back to the town hall, where the entire congregation had flooded out of the building and into the street. Mason and Thorn pressed through the crowd until they broke through the circle of humanity that was gawking at the delivery of three brand new self-propelled steam-powered motorized fire trucks, complete with running boards and back steps. These were so modern and expensive that only big cities like New York and Chicago had them. They gleamed with shiny brass fixtures and bright red paint. The name "Coulson Fire Department" was already painted on the side doors.

Mason and Thorn were as dumfounded as everyone else.

"Where did these come from?" asked Mason. The mayor stepped close to Mason to reply.

"You left a little too soon. We were saving this special treat for the end of the meeting. They were shipped here by train from New York," the mayor beamed. "A representative from Mack Trucks followed them out here."

"When did you buy these?" Mason asked.

"We didn't. They were a gift," the mayor replied.

"From who?" Thorn asked.

"From our friends in Washington," said the mayor.

"What are you talking about?" Mason asked. The mayor waved the Mack Truck representative closer.

"Read the letter out loud again for Mason," he said to the representative. The Mack Truck spokesman produced a letter, cleared his throat, and read at the top of his lungs.

"To the city of Coulson, Montana, courtesy of the United States Congress at the insistence of the President of the United States. In recognition of the importance of our citizens living on the western frontier." The mayor beamed. He pointed at the letter and said, "It's signed by President Roosevelt himself."

Thorn's eyes welled up and his heart swelled. He hadn't felt this good about life for a long time. He turned quickly before anyone noticed.

"You okay?" Mason whispered.

"Yeah," Thorn replied. "Just something in my eye." He cleared the glint in his eye with his sleeve and heaved a sigh. Then his gaze turned to the sky as the twilight stars began to twinkle. He put his hand on Mason's shoulder.

"Ain't it good to be alive," he said, soft as a prayer.

"It sure is, pard," Mason nodded.

The mayor continued playing to the crowd.

"What have I been saying all these years…if we stick to our knitting, the nation will take notice. I'm telling you, Coulson's day is just now dawning. If you all continue to trust me as your mayor, this town will become the San Francisco of the Northern Plains." The crowd cheered. Many shook the mayor's hand and congratulated him for a job well done.

Mason and Thorn worked their way through the crowd to get shed of the street party. As they stood at a distance they turned and looked at everyone surrounding the mayor in this high moment of jubilation.

"Can you believe that?" Thorn said. "That pompous ass thinks those fire trucks were for him. I've a mind to go down there and straighten them all out."

"But you know you ain't goin' to," Mason said. "You got your redemption. You saved the president's life and you don't need a slap on the back from a stranger to give you self-respect."

They walked through the saloon door and over to the bar, where Jake gave them a warm welcome and a couple of drinks on the house.

What the future held for Thorn and Mason was unclear to them both. But they knew one thing for sure, with your pard' by your side and two fingers of whiskey in your glass, the future was as welcome as a pat straight flush.

THE END

Get ready for more adventures with Mason and Thorn—

BOOK 2
"THE BIG HORN"

In the wake of General Custer's tragic massacre at the Little Big Horn, a celebrated steamboat captain who rescued the tragic survivors of the 7th Calvary, is forced to bury a fated gold shipment along the banks of the Little Big Horn to make room for the wounded.

Thirty years later, while trying to solve a murder, Mason and Thorn stumble upon a clue that might not only solve the crime, but possibly lead to the whereabouts of the lost gold, a discovery that puts them on a collision course with those determined to stop them."

BOOK 3
"THE TREASURE
OF
BITTER CREEK"

Mason and Thorn discover an illegal mining operation on Cheyenne Indian Reservation, and determine to shut it down. Unknown to them, the company responsible is in possession of the mother of all copper fissure veins, and will stop at nothing to extract all of its riches no matter the cost, including the elimination of these two Montana lawmen. *(Coming in 2018)*